CW01239620

# THE PANOPTICON

**Vernon Muller**

Published by New Generation Publishing in 2021

Copyright © Vernon Muller 2021

First Edition

The author asserts the moral right under the Copyright, Designs and Patents Act 1988 to be identified as the author of this work.

All Rights reserved. No part of this publication may be reproduced, stored in a retrieval system or transmitted, in any form or by any means without the prior consent of the author, nor be otherwise circulated in any form of binding or cover other than that which it is published and without a similar condition being imposed on the subsequent purchaser.

ISBN
- Paperback    978-1-80369-996-7
- Hardback    978-1-80369-995-0
- Ebook    978-1-80369-994-3

**www.newgeneration-publishing.com**

New Generation Publishing

To Frances

*Give thanks for the courage of others in this fear-ridden land*

(Alan Paton, as quoted by Randolph Vigne in *Liberals Against Apartheid.*)

# Introduction

This story is set in South Africa and starts in 1964. At that time it was commonplace amongst white South Africans to use highly offensive language like 'kaffirs' when referring to black people. In the interests of authenticity, I have retained those terms in dialogue although they were then and still are rightly regarded as obnoxious and insulting. All the characters are fictional, although there are references to actual people in keeping with the historical setting of the story. The locations of Pemberton, Hopedale, KwaBophela and KwaThemba are all my creation. I have, however, tried to recreate accurately a white liberal perspective of how opponents to the Apartheid regime were terrorised and, although this is a work of fiction, many of the events described, actually happened.

# Prologue

(June 1964)

The *Windsor Castle* steamship was nearing Cape Town. On board were a white Anglican priest and his wife, returning to their homeland. They had spent a year on placement in a London parish. Being in England they had relished the sense of freedom they experienced in sixties' England. They had been to see the West End satirical show 'Beyond the Fringe' and never missed an episode of 'That Was the Week That Was' on television. It was a relaxed, anything goes, atmosphere.

On the morning of their arrival the couple had got up at dawn. They wanted to see the wonderful sight of Table Mountain as though it was rising out of the sea while the liner steamed towards Table Bay. It appeared every passenger on board had the same idea as the decks were crowded. The silhouette of the mountain under the vast blue sky brought to mind the start of creation and the garden of Eden. It was a romantic moment filled with emotion.

The couple were still leaning on the deck rail enjoying the sights as the ship nosed into the harbour. But then it felt as though a cloud came over them, although the sun was still shining. From their exalted position high on deck, they looked down on the perspiring black dock labourers looking like slaves hauling in the heavy ropes that tethered the vessel to its berth. These men had never experienced the freedoms those privileged white passengers on the ship enjoyed. The Wordsworth line 'shades of the prison-house begin to close', came to the mind of the priest and a chill ran down his back. Those feelings were quickly relegated in the hustle and bustle of going through immigration and customs. Once through the barriers, he did feel some relief as their baggage had not been searched which could have revealed that he was smuggling into the country some politically-banned reading. Not that that had worried him too much. He always comforted himself in that whilst he opposed the apartheid government, his opposition was very low key. He was no Trevor Huddleston or Canon John Collins and thought that he was extremely unlikely to come to the attention of the feared Special Branch police. How wrong he was…

# Part 1 RICHARD and SIMON

# Chapter 1

(July 1967)

The Reverend Richard Atwell is feeling a bit queasy and looking paler than usual. He does not like heights, and he is hundreds of feet above street level in the half light of the observation deck of the Post Office Tower in Johannesburg. The reason for him being there has to do with one of the quirks of apartheid. He is currently attending a national inter-church clergy conference that includes some black ministers. Tonight, is a free evening in the conference programme. Being a mixed racial group there are no public places, under apartheid, where they may spend an evening out together. However, one of the local delegates has mentioned that the tower will admit black people on one evening of the week and this is it. It is certainly not the sort of place Richard would have chosen to visit, but he wants to show solidarity with the other delegates and so he had agreed to join them.

Despite the magnificent view, Richard is standing with his back against the lift shaft as far away from the observation glass as he can get. Although he is a short slight man, the floor is raked so he can see over the shoulders of the people in front. He peers through thick-rimmed owl-like spectacles to take in the sea of distant twinkling lights and flashing neon signs of the city, but he has no wish to venture forward to look down at the more immediate scene.

While standing there he is approached by a tall, slim, lanky, black man – the Reverend Simon Ndlovu.

'Hey, you don't look very happy man. What's the trouble?'

'Ag, I can't cope with heights. I'll be glad when my feet are back on terra firma.'

'Well, I feel for you, but I can tell you I'm enjoying it.' He starts swaying from side to side. 'Don't you like the way the tower sways up here?'

'Oh, don't say that, I'll be sick.'

Simon laughs, patting Richard's shoulder.

'No, I'm just teasing you.'

Richard has been impressed by the relaxed and irrepressible attitude Simon exudes, so unlike most other ministers he has known. Amongst conference delegates Simon has been immensely popular and his laugh has been infectious. However, meeting him at the conference proved to be an awkward event for Richard, because although Simon has been the minister at the KwaBophela Methodist mission in the adjoining district to Richard's Anglican parish for some time, they had never met. An American observer at the conference had remarked with disbelief:

'You mean the two of you are neighbours and you don't know each other?'

Richard found this all very embarrassing. Although brought up with typical white South African racist attitudes, this had all changed for him on leaving school. He had been fortunate to go to a liberal university where his racist attitude was challenged, and he soon realised how limited his outlook had been. Although working in a white church within the confines of apartheid, he now opposes racism and wants to meet and mix socially with black people however difficult that might be. So it is that Richard is determined to get to know Simon and has offered him a lift so that they may travel home together.

When they set off on the long journey, Simon sits back, rolls his window down and with his elbow on the sill starts singing Zulu songs. He has a lovely baritone voice and Richard enjoys the entertainment. When not singing, Simon's curiosity takes over and he is persistently questioning Richard.

'Hey man, you must be a very highly-educated bloke. At the conference you mentioned the theology of, was it… Bulman? I didn't know what you were talking about, but it all sounded very clever. I have never heard about this chap Bulman – who is he?'

'Actually, it's Bultmann. He's a German theologian, but I wouldn't worry about not knowing anything about him.'

'You see, I've not had much education. I managed to get my Junior Certificate, but we didn't have the money for me to get my matric. So, I got a job as a porter on the railway; and in my spare time, which wasn't much, I helped at the church and managed to get my local preacher's certificate. Then after a few years,' and he chuckles, 'they foolishly decided to ordain me, and I became a full-time minister. Anyhow, one thing led to another and now I am at KwaBophela. But you see, I've no education to speak of. But what about your training?'

'Well you have clearly done well for yourself. Ja, I was lucky. My parents had the money to send me to university and I got on very well and got a scholarship to do research in Classics. Perhaps the best thing for me about university was that it was there that I met my wife Noelene.'

'*Yebo*,' Simon exclaims. 'There is nothing like a good woman. My wife Florence, she keeps me in order. But didn't you say you were overseas as well?'

'Again, I was incredibly lucky. Just after we got married, we went on an exchange to a parish in the East End of London.'

'In London! Wow, what was that like?'

'It was quite an eye-opener I can tell you. My first surprise was the large number of black people living in London and many of them, just like here, seemed to be working as cleaners and in menial jobs.'

'Really! But I thought there was no apartheid in England?'

'That was my second surprise. Many of the white people in the parish where I was working were as racially prejudiced as whites here.'

'Never!'

'Ja, they would grumble about black people coming over to England and taking their jobs, and many landlords refused to have black tenants. But I don't want to give you the wrong idea. There, discrimination is not the law as it is here. Black and white people travelled together on the buses and trains. There was no Group Areas Act, and in fact, Noelene and I had a black Trinidadian family living next to us. Actually,' and Richard smiles at the recollection, 'One day the little boy from next door asked me why *I* wasn't black because I came from Africa.'

Simon laughs, playfully nudging Richard.

'You see, even overseas kids know Africa is for the Africans and you whites are intruders. What has happened here in South Africa is that the whites have taken over and we blacks are made to feel like foreigners in our own land. Of course, I don't blame you personally.' For a moment Simon is quiet. Then he continues, 'But man, I would love to go to England. Perhaps one day – you never know.'

At midday they arrive in Ladysmith where Richard would normally stop at a filling station restaurant to have a meal and use the toilets. With Simon he cannot do so. Instead he buys take-aways, and on the outskirts of the town they stop at a road-side picnic site to have their lunch. It is a lovely cool spot next to a dam bordered by willows under which are concrete picnic tables and benches. One of the tables is already occupied by a white family, so Richard parks at the far end of the site.

Having started their lunch they soon become aware that their presence is causing some stares and head-shaking from the white family. After a while, the father of the family saunters over to them with his thumbs in the pockets of his khaki shorts and speaks to Richard:

'Excuse me, but I don't think natives[1] are allowed to use this picnic place.'

Before Richard can say anything, Simon jumps up and throws his shoulders back with his hands clasped on his stomach.

---

[1] <u>Native</u>: A term used by white people referring to black people. In the 1940s it became a derogatory term.

'Oh, and what makes you think that?' Then looking around and with a chuckle adds, 'I don't see any *WHITES ONLY* signs growing like apples from the trees.'

The man becomes red in the face and, turning quickly, strides away. Having rejoined his family, Richard and Simon can overhear him saying in a loud voice:

'If there is one thing I can't stand, it's a cheeky kaffir.'

By now Simon is sitting down again and in a low voice, imitating the man's accent, comments to Richard, 'If there is one thing *I* can't stand, it is a whitey who thinks he owns the world.'

Although in awe at Simon's reaction, Richard can't help giggling into a cupped hand, which is noticed by the white family who promptly pack up their picnic and with hateful glares and a shout of 'Bloody Communists', they drive away in their big expensive car.

Laughing, Simon comments, 'These ignorant people with their illogical fear of communism.'

Frowning, Richard counters, 'Actually, I think communism is a great danger.'

In a more serious tone Simon replies, 'Well, I must tell you; many of our people don't see it that way. They see communists as being concerned about the suffering of black people and want to help. They see communists like the Good Samaritan. He was a foreigner, but he wanted to help where there was a need and Jesus commended him. Those who passed by the injured man are like the whites here, and to justify themselves they paint the one who helps as the very devil, and they ban people who call themselves communists.'

'But wait a moment. Communism has some good points; but basically it's anti-Christian, regarding religion as the opium of the masses and all that.'

'Hey man, don't get me wrong. I have an uphill battle trying to show my people the Christian way when they point to our so-called Christian government, whose leaders are in church on Sunday, but on Monday they pass laws that oppress black people. And what about those people who were here just now. Did you see their car had a Free State registration? Calling that province, the Free State is hypocritical because the vast majority of people there are black, and they are certainly not free.'

The irony of the name of that province had never occurred to Richard. Being with Simon he feels a whole new world is being revealed to him.

Late that afternoon as they are nearing the Natal-Cape border and the little town of Pemberton, which is Richard's parish, they turn off the main road towards the black township of KwaBophela. As the car rattles over the corrugations of the dirt road, Simon mentions that Richard should drop him off at the entrance to the township.

'Why do you say that? Why can't I take you right to your home?'

'Well you see they have this stupid law that whites need a permit to come here, and as it's after five o'clock the Bantu Affairs office will now be closed, so you won't be able to get a permit.'

'Will anyone know if I take you all the way? I mean there are all these buses and taxis on the road; do they check each one going through the gates?'

'Ja, but these are all black people. No, there is no gate, but there are big signs on the boundary warning whites that you are not allowed there and if you don't have a permit you will be breaking the law and I don't want to get you into trouble.'

Now, Richard is quite a timid man who normally obeys rules. He was brought up by strict parents and the memory of getting the belt from his father is painfully seared into his mind from the few occasions when he transgressed. However, being with Simon he is feeling quite brave and wants to show his new friend he will not be put off by petty apartheid regulations and says blithely:

'Well I don't care. I'm going to take you to your Manse, and in any case, I want to know where you live so I can come and visit you again.'

'Ja, okay man, but don't say I didn't warn you. It can be quite dangerous for whites to mix with us blacks.'

They drive on and pass the township entrance where Richard begins to feel some collywobbles in his stomach when he sees the red warning sign, under which is printed in big black letters UNAUTHORISED PERSONS ARE FORBIDDEN TO LEAVE THE ROAD OR TO STOP IN THIS AREA. He begins to have second thoughts about his rashness; but nonetheless they continue, and he drives up a long steep hill. Near the top Simon asks him to stop.

'Well this is where you must leave me,' says Simon. 'There is no road to the church so this is the nearest you can get by car.' Looking down the side of the hill he points out his church – a large, whitewashed building with a cross on the apex of an asbestos roof. Next to it is a small cottage that is the Manse. Covering the hillside are wattle and daub huts with conical thatched roofs interspersed by some wood and iron shacks. There are a few trees; the only other vegetation being some small gardens, and here and there patches of rather limp-looking mealies. Chickens can be seen around some of the huts scratching in the earth, and some nomadic goats are tugging on the little greenery to be found on a few scraggy bushes.

'Thanks very much for the lift. My family will be surprised to see me as they were expecting me on the train tomorrow. Give my best wishes to your wife and tell her I'm looking forward to meeting her. So, go well my friend.'

'Right, and will I be correct if I say *sala kahle*[2]?'

Richard's attempt at a little Zulu brings a huge grin to Simon's face. 'That's right my friend,' and laughing he calls back, '*Yebo. Hamba kahle*[3] *Mfundisi*[4].'

Richard waves and, despite his nervousness, feels a sense of achievement as he turns the car around and heads

---

[2] Sala kahle and

[3] Hambe kahle: Zulu – Farewell. Literally 'stay well' and 'go well'

[4] Mfundisi: Zulu – Pastor or minister

back towards the main road. He becomes aware that he has not seen any electricity or telephone lines and wonders if Simon and his people have any public utilities. At least he had noticed a few standpipes, so assumes they do have something of a water supply. These thoughts are interrupted because on leaving the township he spots a police van at the side of the road and simultaneously sees a white policeman step into the road with his hand up. At first Richard thinks it is a speed trap, but a glance at his speedometer shows he is well within the limits. He slows down and stops opposite the officer who politely addresses him.

'Excuse me, Sir. Have you just come from KwaBophela?'

Richard regrets not travelling in his clerical collar, as that would have identified him as someone with authority. Instead he answers nervously, with a crack in his voice, 'Yes.'

'May I see your permit please?'

Feeling like a schoolboy who has been caught in some naughtiness he explains, 'I'm sorry, I don't have a permit. You see the office was closed when I arrived. I am a minister and what I was doing was taking the Methodist minister back to his Manse. I promise you I turned around and came straight out.'

'I'm sorry Reverend, but that is no excuse,' the policeman says, shaking his head. 'You should have applied earlier for a permit when the office was open or applied to the Bantu Affairs Department. You see, there is a lot of crime here and it is extremely dangerous for a white man to enter a Bantu area, so we need to know when and where people are going. Now, as you are a reverend, I believe you when you say you only made a quick visit, so I'll take no further action on this offence today. But I must make a note of your name, address and car registration for future reference.'

With relief, Richard thanks the officer and assures him he will get a permit in future.

When the officer has completed his notes he stresses:

'I must warn you, if you come here again you must get a permit. It is for your own protection. Okay; you may go.' The officer strolls back to his van and, feeling chastened, Richard drives away.

Although preoccupied with thoughts about his new friendship and the dangers that may involve, as he has just experienced, he is very much looking forward to getting back to Noelene. Richard is someone who hates being away from his wife and their home. Turning into the driveway and seeing the familiar long-whitewashed bungalow with its red-railed veranda that is his Rectory, gives him a good feeling.

As soon as he is indoors, he and Noelene are seated at the kitchen table drinking coffee. Noelene is a self-confident, rather plain small woman with short auburn hair greying rather prematurely at the temples. It is her deep confidence that attracted Richard to her and from which he draws strength. Their rather cluttered kitchen is where Richard and Noelene spend much of their time when at home together.

Richard is talking with passion. Whilst he wants to hear the parish news, he cannot wait to tell her about meeting Simon and what an exceptional person he is. He dismissively mentions his encounter with the police at which Noelene raises her eyebrows but makes no comment. He excitedly suggests they invite Simon and his wife to dinner one day and Noelene immediately agrees.

'Oh, that will take me back to my youth. As you know my mum and dad were always inviting black people for meals in our house. It was the sort of thing Liberal Party members did.'

'Of course, that would never have happened in my home. Anyhow, I'll call on Simon next week to arrange a visit.'

So it is that one Sunday, after his morning service, Richard drives out to KwaBophela to fetch their guests. This time Richard has previously obtained the necessary permit. When he returns with Florence, Simon and their children,

Noelene is on the veranda to greet them. She and Richard have changed into informal clothes, but Simon is still in his clericals. Florence is in a long dark-blue dress with a bright blue and yellow headscarf and the two boys are clearly in their Sunday best.

'Welcome to our little house,' says Noelene. 'I'm so glad to meet you.' She gives Florence a hug, but when she wants to shake Simon's hand, he has none of it and envelopes her in a great embrace. The children shyly hang back, but Simon introduces them.

'This is Amos and the little one is Moses.'

Moses is whispering something to his mother who gives him a slight reprimand, 'You must not whisper in company. Tell the lady what you said.'

But he clings more closely to her and hides his face in her skirt. However, Amos volunteers, 'Madam, I think he said; why did you say this is a *little* house when it is *so big*?'

Simon's laugh eases the slight awkwardness.

'You see Noelene, I'm afraid he is right. Your house looks about four times the size of our house and while the rectory might be small for Pemberton, it is certainly far bigger than anything in KwaBophela.'

Noelene goes down on her haunches to be at the same height as the children.

'Thank you, Amos.' Then she turns to Moses. 'Do you know, I am a teacher? But today, *you* have taught me something important. You are right and I am wrong. This is a *very* big house and I hope you will enjoy playing in it.' She stands up. 'Now, let us all go into this big house.'

Later, after lunch, while the boys are exploring the garden and the adults are sitting in the lounge drinking coffee, Simon wants to tell Richard and Noelene all about the children.

'Children are funny you know. Our two boys are so different—' He has just started speaking when interrupted by the strident ringing of the Rectory phone.

'Damn the phone!' Richard says as he gets up, 'Please excuse me for a minute. I'll be back as quickly as possible.'

He walks through to the study to take the call, which is from his neighbour Charles.

'Hi Richard, I thought I'd just let you know. There are two little picanins in your garden. I saw them eyeing your naartjies[5], so I guess that's what they're after, the little skelms[6].'

For a moment Richard does not know how to respond. However, he quickly decides to be honest about the boys.

'No, Charles,' he says, chuckling nervously. 'They are not skelms. An African minister is visiting us, and he brought along his two sons, that's who they are.'

'Oh!' There is a moment of silence. 'Oh well, I suppose that's okay then. If you know about them that's all right. Sorry to have troubled you.'

'No, that's okay. Thanks for letting me know anyway.' He rings off and goes back to the lounge.

Simon, who has overheard the call, says, 'Have our boys done something wrong? That would be unlike them you know.'

'No,' says Richard. 'That was just our nosy neighbour. By the way would you like some naartjies? We have a tree full of them. We can get the boys to pick them before you go.'

Florence says, 'Thank you very much. That will be kind of you.'

'*Yebo*. That will be nice. It's a long time since I had a nice naartjie. But as I was saying about our boys, Amos is the confident tough guy. He is extremely popular with his friends as a champion stick fighter. And if they were getting up to any mischief in your garden, then I'm sure he would be the one instigating it. Moses on the other hand is very quiet and wants to be a minister like me. Of course, he's still only a little boy, but you should hear him say his prayers at

---

[5] Naartjies: A citrus fruit similar to mandarins.
[6] Skelms: Afrikaans – rascals.

night. Then in the afternoons I sometimes see him playing church. He puts a white cloth round his neck for a collar and then preaches to his friends. Only I am glad they are not my congregation, because they don't listen for very long before they run away,' and Simon's loud laughter rings out again as he slaps his thigh.

Florence, who is quite reserved, taps her husband on the wrist and suggests, 'Simon, you talk so much you don't give others a chance. All the time you talk talk talk.'

'Oh yes, I'm sorry. I don't mean to monopolise the conversation.' Then in his very direct way he adds, 'So, what about you two? You have this lovely *big* house and a big garden. When are *you* going to have some children?'

Richard and Noelene look at each other, clearly in some discomfort. When in company they have always avoided this subject. But now there is something about Simon's innocent plain-speaking that leads Noelene to drop her head and say quietly:

'Well, sadly we can't.'

'What do you mean, can't?'

Florence glares at him and gives a warning cough.

Richard fidgets in his chair and looks around the room avoiding Simon's puzzled gaze and says, 'It's very personal and I'm not sure we want to talk about it.'

'Hey man, I'm sorry. I didn't realise it was a sensitive matter. I hope I haven't offended you. Please, Noelene and Richard, please forgive me.'

Florence says, 'I'm sorry, my husband has a big mouth, and he is always—'

But Noelene interrupts her, 'No, no please don't apologise. We have come this far it will only be fair to tell you. Go on Richard, you tell them.'

'Well, okay. You see, Noelene was born with a hole in the heart and has been advised by doctors not to have children.' He pauses for the gasps from Simon and Florence and his voice becomes thick with emotion. 'There is a risk that giving birth could... could kill her.'

Simon exclaims, '*Hau*!' and Florence gives him another restraining look, but Richard continues:

'She told me about this before we were engaged and... and as much as both of us would like to have children, I for one, wouldn't want to take the risk.' He sighs. 'So, we have just had to be reconciled to that.'

'*Hau*!' Simon exclaims again, 'I didn't know. What a terrible thing! Noelene, you look so healthy you would never know there was anything wrong with you.' He gets another glare and a nudge from Florence. 'I'm sorry, I didn't say that right, but you know what I mean.' He then adds with a frown, 'So there is no way you can have any children?'

Richard has now regained his composure.

'We have talked about adoption, but the children who really need adopting in this country are black and of course we are not allowed to do that. And there are very few white children being offered for adoption. We have often hummed and hahed about it but got no further than that.'

Noelene adds, 'You wouldn't believe it, but it is actually incredibly difficult to adopt a child. So, we just accept it as God's will. At least I'm lucky to be alive.'

'Hey man, I'm really sorry for you,' says Simon with sympathetic nods from Florence.

Richard says, 'Would you please regard this as confidential?'

Noelene chips in, 'I think the parishioners suspect something is wrong, but we haven't told them. I don't want them feeling sorry for me. In any case, I think it's our private business and, being a minister's wife – as you must know, Florence – it is very difficult to keep anything private.'

'Oh yes, they always want to know everything, especially the grannies. But my heart is very sore for you and thank you for telling us. It is not an easy thing.'

Simon assures them, 'Of course, we won't say anything. But you know at times like this I always take it to God. I'm sure you won't mind if I say a prayer.'

Richard and Noelene are not used to having guests in their home take the initiative in prayer but they both, together with Florence, bow their heads while Simon stands up clasping his hands under his chin. He prays with some intensity that God may comfort Richard and Noelene and keep them from harm. He switches over to Zulu and continues praying. Richard and Noelene are unable to follow the Zulu, but the beautiful cadences of the words are like a soothing balm washing over them.

Finally, Simon says, 'Aaamen' and sits down. He looks at his watch. '*Hau*! If you don't mind, it's time we were going home.' He stands up again and goes to the door. 'I'll go and find those two rascals and then we must go.'

'Okay and I'll fetch a basket to get the naartjies,' says Noelene.

Before they leave, Florence invites Richard and Noelene to Sunday lunch with them in KwaBophela and a date is readily agreed upon.

## Chapter 2

(August and September 1967)

One afternoon Richard is working in his study when there is a knock on the back door of the Rectory. On answering it he is confronted by the huge beaming smile of Simon who is wearing a dark suit that, although clean and neat, shows signs of wear. His clerical collar is slightly frayed, but his black shoes shine like glass. He greets Richard in his cheery, loud, and husky voice:

'*Sawubona*[7] my friend, and how are you?'

'Hey, welcome! It's lovely to see you. But you don't need to come to the back door you know.'

Simon playfully bows his head and with his hands together says, '*Hau baas*, I know my place.'

Richard, laughing, ushers him in and says, 'Oh, come in, come in.' He closes the door and then gives his friend a big hug. After the usual enquiries about their respective wives and Simon's children, Simon says:

'Hey, have you got a spare hour? I want to show you something.'

'I was just doing some reading that can certainly wait and, in any case, you have now got me intrigued.'

'Okay. It isn't far, but can we go in your car?'

They drive out to the southern edge of Pemberton where Simon directs Richard to turn onto a track leading across the veld towards the railway line. After bumping slowly along for a short distance, Richard notices a settlement of shacks alongside the railway with a pall of smoke hanging over them.

'You can stop here,' says Simon. 'I want to introduce you to the settlement of Twenty-One and Three. You see over there,' and he points to a railway mileage marker. 'You

---

[7] Sawubona: Zulu – Greeting.

see, that says Twenty-One and the three ones under the line means three quarters. That is the distance to the next station which is of course Hopedale. So, the people have christened this place Twenty-One and Three. Many of the people living here work in Pemberton, but they can't live there because it's a white area and they have nowhere else to go. But I bet there are very few whites who know of this place.'

'I'm one of them,' replies Richard. 'I've been in Pemberton for over two years and I didn't know this settlement existed.'

'Well, let's have a look around,' says Simon, getting out the car.

Emerging from the car, Richard is hit by the pungent smell of smoke from several cooking fires dotted about between the shacks. As they walk around, he can see that the ramshackle dwellings are constructed from scavenged building materials, rusting corrugated iron sheets nailed to ill-fitting wooden beams. There are some slightly more substantial mud-daub huts roofed with tin, the latter held down by wire or weighed down by stones or old car tyres. Windows are simply a hole in the wall with makeshift wooden shutters or a curtain of sacking. He notices a circular thatch screen that he assumes is a toilet. A few women can be seen tending cooking pots on the fires or sweeping the bare earth around the shacks. A rag-tag group of curious barefoot children, who seem to know Simon, begin to follow them around. At one of the dwellings Simon stops and after greeting the lady of the house, she invites them in. She is a big stout woman, barefoot, an apron tied around her loose-fitting grey dress and a floral doek on her head.

Richard is amazed at the order and neatness he discovers inside the gloom of this one-room slum shack. The hard earth floor has been carefully swept, an old cupboard and some cardboard boxes appear to contain their few belongings, a mattress is rolled up in the corner, and the only furniture is a table with two chairs and some crates to sit on. The table is covered with a spotless white embroidered cloth, and in an empty jam jar is an arrangement of wildflowers.

Simon introduces Mrs Mazibuko to Richard saying, 'She says she's going to make us some tea. Have we got the time, or do you need to get back?'

'I'm quite overwhelmed by all this, so time doesn't matter. Please tell Mrs Mazibuko, I will really appreciate a cup of tea.'

While waiting for the tea, Simon explains to Richard that there are no taps and that the people must walk up the valley to a stream to get water. He says their hostess has three children, two of whom were amongst the group following them and the third and eldest, a daughter, is now boiling water on a fire outside for their tea. Her husband is away working on the mines in Johannesburg, but he hopes to be home for Christmas. Mrs Mazibuko works four mornings each week as a domestic cleaner for a white family in Pemberton. He adds that the mothers take it in turns to care for the young children so that as many of the women as possible can be out earning.

While their hostess is pouring the tea Richard says to Simon:

'Please ask Mrs Mazibuko, when it is her turn how many children does she have to look after?' Hearing her answer, Simon translates from the Zulu.

'She says about twenty to thirty.'

'Wow, that's quite a lot.'

Richard finds the tea rather oversweet as it has been made with condensed milk, making him aware that fresh milk could not be kept here in the heat. He comments to Simon:

'It must be really difficult living here with no running water or electricity. So, what's the biggest problem the people face here?'

Mrs Mazibuko understands enough English to have understood what Richard was asking.

'*Hau*!' she exclaims. 'Government bulldozers come one day and push us all away. Then we must build again somewhere, I don't know where.'

Simon adds, 'So, you see they don't know how long they can stay here.'

'But that's dreadful. Surely if the government moves them, they have to provide a place for them?'

Simon cocks his head to one side and smiles indulgently at Richard.

'Hey man, we are talking about black people here. The government doesn't think we have any rights. At the best they may provide some God-forsaken place five, ten miles away where they will dump the people and their possessions.'

That evening Richard tells Noelene about the settlement. Hearing this she has an idea:

'Hey, what about, nearer Christmas time, we give those children a Christmas party. Twenty to thirty would be a nice number for a children's party.'

Richard is feeling so helpless about the situation at Twenty-One and Three that his response is cautious:

'Well that's a thought, but are you thinking of having them here?'

'Of course! Where else? You could borrow Bill's kombi and in two or three trips bring them all over here. Perhaps some members of the congregation might like to help with the catering.'

'Some might. But there are also others who will think it's breaking the law.'

'Oh, come on Richard,' she says with some exasperation. 'Stop making excuses. I shouldn't think those children get very much if anything for Christmas, so think of it as being in the spirit of St Nicholas. You know, one of the things I miss, not having our own children – I never get the chance to play with little ones. It will be fantastic fun playing ring-a-ring-a-roses and that other game, what's it... where you run around the circle singing...?' She pauses,

'Ah, yes, I remember. It's "I wrote a letter to my love and on the way I dropped it…" and so on.'

'Gosh, I'd forgotten all those games we used to play at children's parties. But do you think these children will know those games?'

'Well I can teach them. Look I'm not ashamed to admit this is going to be fun for me as well as hopefully for them.'

By now Richard is being swayed by Noelene's enthusiasm. 'Okay. I think it might work. Perhaps I could lay out a treasure hunt in the garden where each child can find a little Christmas present.'

'That's another good idea. We will just have to make sure every child gets a present. So, let's strike while the iron is hot and fix a possible date, because you know how the diary fills up at Christmas time. When you see Simon, you can confirm it with him and ask if he will make the necessary arrangements with their mothers.'

'I'm sure Simon will want to be here as well. Actually, once the word gets around there may be more than thirty, so it will be safest to cater for about forty. Later this week I must go to KwaBophela to get the permits for our lunch visit to Simon and Florence next Sunday, so I'll mention the party to him then.'

Richard also wants to discuss with Simon a talk he is to give to the Christian students at Hopedale University. Being aware of the privileged life of white students he wants to tell them about his experience at Twenty-One and Three and about Simon's work at KwaBophela.

Of course, no permits were needed to go to Twenty-One and Three because it was not an official Bantu area. However, nowadays, whenever Richard goes to KwaBophela, he always stops at the Bantu Affairs office to get the required permit. The small grey forbidding-looking building is surrounded by high barbed wire security fencing. Inside, a bored-looking white official is leaning on the counter reading an Afrikaans newspaper. As Richard enters the official looks up:

'Ah, here's the reverend again wanting a permit.'

Richard explains that he wants permits dated for Sunday for himself and Noelene.

The shocked official cannot help uttering an Afrikaans expletive. He quickly apologises, 'Ag, sorry Reverend, please excuse my language.' Then assuming a solemn expression, he warns Richard, 'Man, you know, this is no place for a woman.'

Richard is getting used to these sorts of remarks and answers with a smile, 'But there are thousands of women living in KwaBophela.'

'Ja, but I meant a white woman.' He adds darkly, 'I know you are a minister so perhaps you don't think about these things, but when a Bantu man sees a white woman, his one thought is lust you know, and they will think nothing of killing you and raping your wife. I mean,' and the official warms to his subject, 'we get so many cases where they rape their own women, so you can just imagine what they are thinking if they see a beautiful white woman and particularly on a Sunday when most of the men are drunk or on dagga. You know, I would never come here on a Sunday, let alone bring my wife here. Actually, the only Europeans who come here on a Sunday are the police, and of course they come armed.'

'Well, we will be hosted by Reverend Ndlovu who, I am sure, will look after us.'

'Okay, if you insist,' he says, shaking his head. 'But I'm first going to phone my superintendent to make sure I'm allowed to do this.' He goes to an office at the back and closes the door. After about ten minutes he returns. 'My superintendent agrees with me that it is dangerous for you to bring your wife here, but he says there is nothing in the regulations to prohibit you coming, so I will have to issue the permits, but please do be careful and don't stop for anything until you get to the Mission.'

'Oh yes, I will be careful, as I am when I'm driving anywhere, and thank you for the permits.'

On the day, Richard and Noelene have a very pleasant visit with no trouble. In fact, it is quite the opposite and the people they meet walking the last short stretch to the Manse are most welcoming and friendly.

A deep friendship begins to grow between the two couples. Because of the need to get permits and the suspicion that arouses, Richard and Noelene do not go to KwaBophela as often as Simon and Florence visit them at the Rectory. In fact, Simon often needs to be in Pemberton on pastoral care visits and he makes a habit of calling in to see Richard and Noelene. On one occasion Richard invites him to preach at Sunday Evensong and to sleep over in the Rectory. By staying the night, Simon is breaking the law, because only black domestic servants, whose pass books are endorsed accordingly, can stay overnight in a white area, and then they would be living in the khaya[8] in the backyard. Although a little risky, this event is quite exciting, and Simon jokes that the police might raid the khaya for illegal occupants, while he is having a good night's sleep in the Rectory guest room.

One day when Richard is in the Bantu Affairs office, while the clerk is writing out the permit, the superintendent comes over and leaning on the counter causally enquires:

'You seem to visit this minister er… Ndlovu quite often, don't you?'

Richard is careful with his response, 'Yes; well you see my church is helping him with his work.'

'Um, yes,' he says, sucking through his teeth. Then with a frown and shaking his head he asks, 'But he is not of your church, is he?'

'Well I believe that all the churches should work together for God's glory.'

---

[8] Khaya: Zulu – Home. Most white South African dwellings had an outbuilding in the back yard to accommodate their black servants. These were basic, many without toilets or washing facilities other than an outside tap.

'Ja, if only that were so.' He straightens up and says to his clerk, 'It's okay. I'll finish this off.' Then speaking again to Richard, he asks, 'But what is this work you are helping him with?'

Richard hesitates as he wonders whether the man is simply making conversation or whether there is a sinister motive. He suspects the latter, but hopes it is the former and says:

'You see, I recently gave a talk to the Christian students at Hopedale University in which I mentioned KwaBophela, and the students have started a bursary fund to pay for a black child to be able to go through to matric. As I am sure you know, black parents must pay if their children go on to secondary school, and of course there are very few that can afford it. Don't you think education is very important?'

'Ja, well to be honest with you, I think education is important for people like you and me. But I worry about some of these Bantu getting educated. You know they begin to get ideas above themselves, and I worry that that Ndlovu chap is going in that direction. You see, I know the Bantu – after all, I've been working with them for over twenty years and take it from me, education is a waste of time with them.' As if to seal the matter he bangs his rubber stamp on the document and signs it. 'Anyhow, here is your permit and now I must get on with all this paperwork,' and he indicates a pile of papers on the counter which he gathers up and carries off to a back office.

# Chapter 3

(Thursday 14th September 1967)

Richard and Noelene are fast asleep when they are shaken out of their slumbers by loud banging on the Rectory front door and a harsh voice shouting:

'Open up, open up; police.'

Half asleep, they are confused as to what is happening. The thuds on the door continue and the shouts become more urgent.

'Open up, open up.'

Richard sits up, shaken and terrified. In a frightened voice Noelene whispers:

'My God, what's going on?'

'I don't know.'

There is a pause in the banging, but the shout is repeated, 'Come on, come on, quickly, open up.'

Richard sees a torch beam flit across the curtained bedroom window.

'I think it's the police.' At the best of times Richard does not feel very brave. He hates violence and would never dream of tackling any intruders. However, although terrified, he realises he must do something. He says, 'I'll have to go and see.'

Stumbling out of bed he gets tangled in the mosquito net that covers them. Flapping wildly at the netting he works himself free and feels in the dark for the bedside light switch. Normally he can locate it immediately, but now he fumbles around knocking the alarm clock which falls on the floor with a clatter. He finally finds the switch and turns the light on. He picks up the clock and sees it is only ten past three.

The shout comes again, 'Come on, hurry, open up.'

Richard shouts back, 'Okay, I'm coming.'

Grabbing his glasses he stumbles towards the bedroom door and into the passage. There he stops for a second, then quickly takes a few steps back to the bedroom to unhook his dressing gown from the back of the door.

Noelene says anxiously, 'Please be careful. Put the chain on before you open the door.'

'Okay, I'll do that.' He hurries down the corridor in his bare feet, while at the same time wrapping his dangling dressing gown around him. He switches on the hall light and then the veranda light. He sees that the chain is still on from when he locked up before they went to bed. Trembling he carefully turns back the Yale lock and opens the door a few inches. At the same time, the person outside puts his shoulder to the door giving it a mighty shove. The door flies open, the securing screws of the chain are pulled out of the splintering door frame, and Richard is knocked back against the wall. He tries to call out, but the words are strangled in his mouth as if in a nightmare. All he can do is to burble as though his mouth is too full of saliva. Two men push into the passageway. One of them has a truncheon which he probably used to bang on the door. He also has a torch and is commanded by the other man to immediately check all the rooms. As he disappears down the corridor, Richard finds his voice and exclaims with more bravado than he feels, 'Hey, what... what do you want?'

The man who is still with Richard pulls out from an inside jacket pocket a piece of paper which he unfolds and holds up for Richard to read.

'We have a warrant to search your house. I warn you, don't try to hide anything; and you must stay where I can see you.'

Richard is stunned. He glances over the formal language of the warrant. Just then Noelene, in dressing gown and hairnet, comes down the corridor. Her wide-eyed terror makes her look like a frightened old lady.

'Wh-What... what's going on?' she stutters nervously.

The first intruder who pushed the door in suddenly reappears from the spare bedroom and speaks to his colleague in Afrikaans.

Although he struggles with Afrikaans, Richard knows enough to understand that the man said that he had looked in all the rooms and there were only the two of them there. He is thankful this is not the night when Simon stayed with them.

The officer switches off his torch and clips it to his belt. He then officiously pushes past Richard and Noelene and, from the front door, tosses the truncheon to a black policeman standing guard at the bottom of the veranda steps.

The man with the warrant, who is clearly in charge, turns to Noelene and in a conciliatory tone says, 'I'm sorry, Madam, if we gave you a fright. But we have instructions to search this house.' Then gesturing to the other who is a giant of a man with crew-cut hair and a round, heavily pock-marked face, 'This is Sergeant Retief and I am Captain van Zyl.' Both are wearing blazers; Retief's looks as though it is a size too small for him. Van Zyl is smart with slicked black hair. The corner of a white handkerchief peeps out of his jacket pocket and he sports a striped tie. The point of a revolver holster extends below the hem of Retief's blazer and there is a slight bulge at the side of van Zyl's jacket that suggests he is also carrying a firearm. They do not say they are from the Security Police, but Richard assumes that is who they are.

Quivering with fear and anger, Richard, staring at the wide-open door with its chain hanging uselessly from a bent bracket, demands, 'I was opening the door. Why did you have to break it down?'

Van Zyl continues his attempt at being sympathetic. 'Don't worry about the door. We will see that it gets repaired. Now, what about going into the lounge where you can sit down while we start our search?'

Richard, while still terrified, is becoming more and more angry at his home being violated and at the officer's impudence at inviting him into his own lounge. Although he is much smaller than either of these two men, he feels he must regain some control. Looking up at van Zyl he says:

'By the way, you may have the power to invade our home, but I am still the host in this house.' Then, scratching his tousled fair hair as if searching for further inspiration, he lamely adds, 'Yes, I'll show you through to the lounge where we can talk and sort all this out.' Taking Noelene's hand, he leads the way, switching on the necessary lights as they go. Once in the lounge, Richard points distractedly at the chairs and says to the officers, 'Please sit down.'

Smiling confidently and with emphasis, van Zyl answers:

'No thanks. We won't sit down. I don't think you fully understand yet that we've got work to do. I showed you that I have a warrant to search this house and that warrant states clearly that, during the search, I am in charge.' Then with a hint of sarcasm, 'Now I suggest *you* sit down and allow us to get on with the search.' He looks around the room and his eyes light on a chest in the corner. Pointing to it he issues a command to Retief who is standing in the doorway. 'You look in there, while I have a look around to see what's here.'

Richard decides it is perhaps best if they do as van Zyl says. He sits down on the settee and is joined by Noelene. Van Zyl saunters around the room looking behind pictures and pulling back the curtains. He leaves a favourite picture, a reproduction of Utrillo's *Montmartre*, hanging slightly askew, which irritates Richard. In his nervous agitation he feels a need to regain some control and so gets up and goes to straighten it. Immediately both officers spin round and glare at him.

'It's okay,' says Richard. 'I'm just going to put the picture straight.'

Once he is seated again, his nerves cannot stand the silence, so he comments to Retief who is rummaging in the chest.

'You won't find anything in there.'

Van Zyl turns and, frowning, looks at the minister through lowered eyelids.

'Does that mean there is something we might find somewhere else?'

Richard now wishes he had kept his mouth shut. At least the banned books he owns are safely hidden with his aunt in Durban, but he knows that hidden between the pages of a Church History book in the study is a newspaper cutting from the London *Observer* of Nelson Mandela's speech at his treason trial. With butterflies in his stomach he answers cautiously:

'I mean, I don't think you will find anything anywhere in the house.' He fears that van Zyl has picked up the lack of conviction in his voice, so he adds more assertively, 'By the way, what are you looking for?'

'That I can't say, but I'll know if I find something,' says van Zyl with a meaningful look in Richard's direction. He then turns to a well-stocked bookcase, taking books down at random, flicking through a few before returning them, while also peering in to check whether there is anything hidden behind the books.

In his agitation Richard nervously runs a hand over the stubble on his chin, and looks down at his dressing gown, wrapping it tighter over his front to make sure the open fly of his pyjama trousers is not exposed. He looks at Noelene with her nightie protruding below her gown. She has her fluffy blue slippers on, but his feet are bare. Something about his bare feet makes him feel even more vulnerable. He addresses van Zyl:

'May we at least go and get dressed? It's not nice that we should have to sit here in your company in our pyjamas.'

'That's not necessary. You have to remain where I can see you.'

Despite feeling scared, Noelene notices van Zyl blowing dust off some of the books he is examining. She feels it reflects badly on her as the housewife, so she apologises, 'I'm sorry about the dust.'

Van Zyl responds, 'Ag, don't worry. The servants are hopeless these days. They never dust properly.' For a moment he has forgotten that in his briefing he had read that the Atwells do not have servants.

While this conversation has been going on, Retief has finished looking in the chest where playing-cards, board games and jigsaw puzzles are stored. Now he drops the lid closed.

'Captain, there's nothing but games here.' He goes over to the bookshelves to help his colleague. Suddenly he holds up a little book with a brown cover and exclaims in a dramatic whisper to van Zyl, 'Hey, look at this!'

Noelene breathes in sharply and her hands are quivering with tension. They are both sitting on the very edge of the settee and Richard nearly slides off as he leans forward to see what Retief has found. Van Zyl glances at the book.

'Ja, keep that.' Retief goes to the front door and speaks to the constable on guard. After a few moments he returns with a large transparent plastic bag into which he drops the book.

Craning his neck, Richard is just able to recognise the cover of the English translation of a book of Russian poetry. Sitting back, he thinks; *my God, now we are certain to be tarred as Communists.*

While the men are searching, the full import of what is happening begins to dawn on Richard. He wonders if this is a prelude to him or, worse still, both of them being arrested and imprisoned. He is terrified by the idea of going to jail. Up till then his opposition to apartheid has been largely without consequences. In response to a sermon in which he was critical of the government, two of his parishioners left the church, but nothing worse than that. This is his first contact with the Security Police, and he is very scared that he is now going to be punished.

After a while having found nothing further, van Zyl remarks to his colleague:

'I think we need to look in the office.' He turns to Richard and Noelene, 'You must stay here while we search your office.'

Noelene, hospitable as ever suggests, 'May I go to the kitchen to make you a cup of coffee or tea?'

Van Zyl is momentarily taken aback and, frowning, scratches his head. After a pause he relaxes and drops his arms to his sides:

'Ag, ja, why not? Let's all have a cup of coffee. We might as well be civilised about this. I'll just have a look in the kitchen while Sergeant Retief starts in the office and then it will be kind of you to make some coffee.' Getting the torch from Retief he follows Noelene down the corridor to the kitchen. Retief enters the study and on switching on the light exclaims, 'Gits, we have got a big job on here!'

He leaves the door ajar so Richard can see that after an initial glance round, Retief notices the tank of brightly coloured tropical fish in the corner. He feels some pride as he sees Retief, clearly fascinated, bend down to have a closer look with his nose almost touching the glass. Glancing over his shoulder, Retief calls out to Richard:

'*Jislaik*, but you've got some pretty fishies here.'

'Yes, they are rather nice.'

'Well, I must carry on,' and straightening up he goes to the filing cabinet and pulls a drawer out.

Richard gets up and goes to the door.

'Hey, where are you going?' demands Retief, his friendly tone of the moment before completely gone.

'Look – those files…' and Richard points to the filing cabinet, 'contain confidential information about my parishioners. I hope you will respect that.'

With a barely concealed sneer the officer replies in measured tones, 'We have authority to search wherever we like. So please go and sit down.'

'Well, as I say, I hope you will respect that information.' Richard feels embarrassed and very frightened at the thought of this stranger and others reading through his private papers. He returns to the settee. Almost immediately he hears Retief exclaim, 'Ah!'

Leaning forward from where he is sitting, Richard can see the cover of the file the officer has pulled out. Written in big black letters is KwaBophela. Richard silently swears at the Superintendent at the Bantu Affairs office and is now convinced the man was fishing for information to pass on to the police. He tries to remember what is in the file but there is so much whirling around in his mind that his memory doesn't function very well.

In the kitchen, van Zyl is making a cursory inspection while Noelene fills the kettle and starts putting cups out. Opening cupboard doors, he peers in and removes a few items to see what might be behind them. Using the torch and a mirror he has taken from his pocket he pays special attention to the area behind the pipes under the sink.

Noelene exclaims, 'Oh, it must be filthy back there.'

'Ag, never mind. But you understand I must make sure I do my job properly. Anyhow, I am finished here now and will really appreciate that cup of coffee. But please don't go anywhere else in the house without telling me.' He leaves her and goes to join Retief in the study. Entering the study, he gasps, 'Jeepers creepers!' He takes a few steps back to the lounge and says to Richard, 'Have you read all these books?'

'Many of them are reference works,' he answers curtly.

Van Zyl returns to the study and starts looking through some of the books, just as he had done in the lounge.

Richard meanwhile is silently praying that the book with the incriminating material will be overlooked. Strangely, although very frightened, he is also concerned that they put things back where they find them. He is compulsively particular that his books are always in their correct catalogued sequence. *If they get them muddled, I'll be bloody mad*, he says to himself.

After a while Noelene appears, carrying a tray with the cups of coffee and a plate of *Marie* biscuits. She takes them into the study. Van Zyl stops his work to take his coffee.

'This is really kind of you. Ja, I'll have sugar thank you.'

Retief also takes his coffee, ladling in three heaped spoons of sugar. After serving them Noelene goes through to the lounge with the rest of the coffee. When they are sitting on the settee, she whispers to Richard with a slight smile, 'They've taken your *Greek Testament*. They probably think it's Russian, possibly a work by Marx.' The two share a nervous giggle.

In the study the search continues while in the lounge, although fortified by the coffee, Richard and Noelene are becoming increasingly anxious as the time drags on. After what seems like ages, they suddenly hear Retief exclaim in subdued but shocked tones, 'Wow, look at this!'

A newspaper cutting has fallen on the floor from a book that van Zyl has been looking at. He has so far ignored the piece of paper, but a headline has caught Retief's eye and he picks it up.

'Look!' Retief says triumphantly and he points to the headline and reads aloud, "Assault Plans".'

Van Zyl eagerly takes the paper and reads it.

In the lounge Richard and Noelene anxiously look at each other. Richard is puzzled. He cannot recall any of his papers containing the phrase *Assault Plans*. In any case, he is essentially a pacifist. The thought that they might plant something on him increases the terror.

For a moment Noelene wonders if Richard is involved in something she knows nothing about.

Then comes joint relief as they hear an irritated van Zyl exclaim:

'Ag, you *dom kop*. This is about some French newspaper wars. It's got nothing to do with South Africa.' He hands the folded paper back to a crestfallen Retief and returns to the shelf of books. Retief stands there for a moment. In his disappointment he half-heartedly unfolds the paper and turns it around. His eyes nearly pop out of his head as he recognises a picture of Nelson Mandela. This time he does not immediately show it to his boss but, with a growing vindictive smile, he slowly starts to read.

Van Zyl glares at Retief.

'Come on, we haven't time to waste reading old newspapers.'

Retief responds, now looking as though he has just landed a huge fish off Durban pier. He is just able to stop himself saying, I told you so, as he hands the paper back to his boss.

'Perhaps *you* should read this.'

A quick glance at the paper is enough for van Zyl. He slaps his colleague on the back:

'Well done, *ou maat*. I could have missed that you know.' Then he whispers, 'You see, as we suspected, he is involved with the ANC[9] and this proves it.'

In the lounge Richard is shivering with nerves. When he sees van Zyl coming into the room bearing the yellowing page from the *Observer*, he nearly loses control of his bladder.

Van Zyl holds up the paper, 'Do you recognise this?'

Richard is not sure he can trust his voice so, swallowing, at first says nothing. He then pretends to look mystified and peers at the paper. However, he quickly realises it is pointless trying to deny anything and in a moment of inspiration attempts to feign surprise.

'Good heavens! I didn't know I still had that.'

Retief has also appeared, peering over his boss's shoulder with a barely concealed grin. Van Zyl taps the paper with his index finger:

'This is dated 1964, the year you returned to South Africa from overseas.' Then sarcastically, 'Do you mean to tell me you have had this for *three* years and not known it was here?'

---

[9] ANC: African National Congress. The political party most black people supported. It was banned in 1960 by the white government and regarded by most whites as a subversive force with links to communism.

Richard is taken aback that van Zyl appears to know so much about him, and he wonders what else he might know. He tries hard to keep his composure.

'Well, you know how things get overlooked. I was given that in England and when we packed up to come home it must have got packed in with all my books.'

'Now wait a bit. This is no accident. Look, you've obviously specially cut it out of a newspaper, kept it and then hidden it in the pages of a book. Why did you do that?'

'As I've said, it must have got put in that book by mistake.' He knows he is on the defensive and not sounding very convincing. Van Zyl certainly is not convinced.

'Well, that will be for others to decide.' Then in a severe tone, 'You know this is extremely dangerous material. People like Mandela are encouraging a Moscow-inspired conspiracy to overthrow our country. Is that what you want?'

'No. I'm not a communist, I'm a Christian.'

'Well then, what is this doing here?' He waves the paper.

Richard looks at the floor and is at a loss for words.

Van Zyl glares at him and then marches back to the study, carefully folding the page and dropping it into his plastic bag.

Richard's legs are twisted around each other, and he is sitting hunched forward with his arms tightly folded over his stomach. He looks as though he is studying the pattern of the carpet. Next to him Noelene is also very anxious but does not appear to be showing it. She reaches over to take his hand. They sit in silence, not knowing what to say. Eventually, barely holding back tears, he turns to Noelene:

'If they throw me or perhaps both of us in jail, I won't know what to do.'

'Oh, surely that won't happen.'

'Well, we don't know. They could do anything.'

'All they've found is a bit of banned material. They can't jail you for that.'

'Umm… Yes… I don't know. But remember some years ago when they made those mass arrests all over the country.

Some of those people were arrested simply for being members of the Liberal Party. And they were in jail for months without trial.'

'Well, we are not members of any party.'

They lapse back into silence, each preoccupied with their own fears.

After what seems like ages the two men come out of the study, Retief carrying the plastic bag with about half a dozen books and several papers. Van Zyl says, 'We have to search all the rooms, so I want both of you to come with us. We'll do the main bedroom next.'

Richard is so tense that when he stands up it feels as though the joints in his legs are going to lock. He walks stiffly, robotic-like, as he leads the way through to the bedroom with Noelene following. Entering the room, Noelene quickly pulls the sheets straight and tucks the mosquito net over the headboard. Van Zyl indicates that Noelene and Richard may sit on the bed. He opens Noelene's wardrobe. He pushes some of her dresses aside and rummages around her shoes on the floor of the cupboard. Retief is looking in Richard's wardrobe, even feeling through the pockets of jackets and trousers. He takes a diary out of the inside pocket of a jacket, opens it briefly and adds it to their other booty in the plastic bag. Richard cannot help expressing consternation:

'Do you have to take that? It's my diary with all my appointments. It has also got my contact addresses and telephone numbers. I won't be able to do my work without it.'

Van Zyl looks at him over his shoulder, 'Ah, your contacts! That's why we want it.'

Richard is feeling more and more impotent. It is as if his whole life is being laid bare. He also feels guilty that people whose names are in his diary may now be compromised.

When van Zyl goes over to the dressing table and opens Noelene's drawer where she keeps her sanitary towels, she cracks. Gripping Richard's hand like a vice and shuddering she utters in angry distress, 'I can't stand this!'

Her reaction actually helps Richard.

'Come on, love,' he says soothingly. 'We'll get through this. Remember, God is on our side.'

Van Zyl looks up, 'I'm sorry Madam, but to keep our country safe we have to do a lot of unpleasant things.' He quietly slides the drawer closed, evidently feeling too embarrassed to search there anymore, and turns his attention to taking down the suitcases from the top of her wardrobe. Although he must realise they are empty from how light they are, nonetheless he decides to open each one. Then he asks the couple to get off the bed so he may check underneath it.

Eventually they move on to the other bedrooms. Then it is the bathroom and even the toilet where the cistern cover is lifted and examined while Richard and Noelene stand waiting in the corridor. When finally, it seems as though they are finished, van Zyl asks, 'Where is the trap door to the loft?'

Richard points it out to him in the passage. Van Zyl tells Retief to fetch a step ladder, and turning to Noelene and Richard says:

'We have finished searching the house, so you don't have to stay here with me anymore. For the time being you are free to do as you wish, but you must remain in the house as we haven't yet done the garage and servant's quarters.'

Although still terrified, the time all this has taken has helped Richard to collect himself and to become a little more assertive. He asks van Zyl, 'May I phone a solicitor?' Personally, he has never needed a solicitor before, but once when trying to help a parishioner who had been found with some dagga[10], he had got in touch with a Mr Hall Green who had proved to be very helpful. He was thinking of contacting him now, feeling desperate for some help.

However, van Zyl is adamant, 'No, you can't. Not until I say you can.'

---

[10] Dagga: Cannabis

Outside, day is dawning and birds are beginning to sing. Noelene suggests they might as well get breakfast. Neither feels like having much to eat, but Noelene says they should eat, as doing something might help them to cope with the shock of what has happened.

After returning from the outbuildings and having sent Retief up into the loft, van Zyl interrupts their meal.

'I have to get your signature for the items we're taking away.'

Richard moves a cereal packet and makes a space for the officer at the table. Van Zyl hands Richard a list he has written out of books and papers. The *Observer* page heads the inventory on which is included the KwaBophela and Twenty-One and Three files. Glancing down the sheet Richard notices an item listed as, 'A foreign book with a black cover'.

'What's this?' he asks.

Van Zyl rummages around in the bag and draws out a *Greek Testament*. Richard immediately exclaims, 'Oh, that's a Bible.'

Van Zyl looks at him in surprise.

Feeling he has at last got one over the officer, Richard's confidence increases, and he asks, 'Why should you be surprised that a minister has got a Bible?'

'Ja, but why is it in a foreign language?'

'Because, you know, that is how it was originally written,' he says rather smugly.

Van Zyl still looks unconvinced, but with a grunt writes down in brackets next to his entry, 'Rev. Atwell says it is a Bible'. Richard signs the form and the officer begins to gather up his things to take his leave.

Richard asks again, 'May I now use my phone?'

'Ja, you can go ahead. You can also have the door fixed and you can send the cost of the repair to Hopedale police station. I see the *Yale* still works so you can lock the door in the meantime. Then you will be hearing from the court in due course.'

Richard heaves a sigh of relief that the police are leaving and at least he is not being arrested. From the front door he watches van Zyl, Retief and the uniformed police officer get into their vehicles at the bottom of the Rectory driveway. He returns to the breakfast table.

'I think we should phone that solicitor, Hall Green, as soon as possible.'

'But it has only just gone six thirty. He won't be in his office yet. You'll have to wait until later.'

They finish their breakfast and find it difficult to settle to anything. Richard prowls around the house examining all the places that have been searched and seeing if they put his books back in the correct order. He also checks his files. He can hear Noelene banging about in the kitchen and recognises the signs of her frustration and anger.

The moment eight o'clock strikes, Richard is at the phone with Hall Green's number at hand. He picks up the phone and then curses. There is no dialling tone.

'That bloody van Zyl has done this,' he mutters. 'I bet he had our phone cut off to ensure we wouldn't be able to phone anyone while they were searching.' He calls out to Noelene, 'The bloody phone is dead. I think it's probably the police who have cut it off. I'll pop over to Gwen's to see if I may use their phone.'

It is not too unusual for phones to break down and neighbours often help each other out in this way.

Richard takes a shortcut through a hole in the hedge that separates the two properties and hurries up the path. Gwen is home and her phone is working so Richard calls to report a fault on his line. He does not call the solicitor, not wanting Gwen to overhear about the search.

Once back home he says anxiously to Noelene, 'I think it is vitally important that we get some legal advice as soon as possible, so straight after my service I'll drive over to Hall Green's office and make an appointment in person.'

'Okay, but try to get a time when I can come as well. I'm also involved you know.'

Richard suddenly realises that in his anxiety he is forgetting that Noelene is equally upset and worried.

'I'm sorry love; I didn't mean to leave you out. It's just that we must find out where we stand as quickly as possible.'

'Yes, that's what I want as well, and in this crisis two heads are going to be better than one, so it's important I'm there too.'

Richard's Communion service is at nine thirty, so he starts getting ready for it while Noelene is preparing to go to work at the local school where she teaches English.

A few minutes before he is about to leave the phone rings.

'Thank God for that,' he calls out as he rushes to the phone, expecting it to be the telephone operator checking the service. However, when he answers, the caller identifies himself as a reporter from a Hopedale newspaper.

The reporter says, 'I understand you were visited last night by the Security Police. Please tell me what happened?'

'Look, I'm sorry, but I can't talk to you now. I have to take a church service.'

'Would you just tell me why you think they picked on you?'

'No. As I said I can't talk to you now.'

'Well could you speak to me after your service. I could meet you there. You see this is an important story as many people will want to know why they picked on you. Isn't this the first time the Security Police have investigated you?'

'I'm sorry. I must ring off now as I have to go.' Even while putting the phone down Richard can hear the reporter persisting with another question until the click of the receiver cuts him off. He has not much experience of the national press and feels extremely nervous about being in the press limelight. He also doesn't like having to cut the reporter off, as this paper has supported critics of the government and he thinks they could possibly be of help to him, so he doesn't want to get on the wrong side of them. But strategies of dealing with reporters will have to wait as he has not much time. He wants to contact Hall Green before he goes to church, so he immediately calls the solicitor's office and is grateful to get an appointment for that afternoon. He quickly passes the news on to Noelene and arranges to pick her up from work. Then with his cassock under his arm he runs to get his car.

# Chapter 4

(Thursday 14th September 1967)

Richard is nearing the end of the service when he notices a couple of men outside the church door. One has a large camera slung round his neck. He assumes it is the press, and so realises he is going to have to tell his small weekday congregation something of what happened during the night. He thinks it would be better if they hear it from him rather than from the men waiting outside. He decides to make an announcement. Just before pronouncing the blessing from the altar he says:

'I am sorry to have to tell you that last night the police came to search the Rectory.' There is an audible shocked gasp from someone in the congregation. 'However,' he continues, 'they would not tell me what they were looking for and, in any case, Noelene and I have nothing to hide. I hope soon to be able to tell you more, but in the meantime I trust you will hold the parish and Noelene and me in your prayers because, as you can imagine, it is all very upsetting.' He then says the blessing and heads for the vestry. Out of habit he gabbles off the post Communion prayer while at the same time pulling off his vestments. He still has his alb over his head when there is a knock on the outside vestry door. He frees his head and with the alb trailing from his other arm opens the door. Three young men are clustered there and the one in front speaking rapidly says:

'Ah Reverend! I spoke to you on the phone this morning. Can you please tell us what happened last night, and we would also like some photos? Do you mind putting your robes back on for the photos? It will emphasise your role as a minister.'

This time Richard is a little better prepared for them. So, with some confidence he tells them, 'Later today I shall be taking legal advice and until then I'm not going to make any comments. I will be happy to give you a statement once I've seen my solicitor.'

Another in the group pipes up, 'Just tell us please, did the police take anything from your home?'

The man with the camera is taking photographs, and the flashes momentarily blind Richard. Rubbing his eyes, he answers:

'I said, I've got no comment to make now and I'm sorry you've come out here for nothing. Now, if you will excuse me, I need to see my parishioners who are obviously shocked and upset about what has happened.' One of the reporters starts writing furiously in his notepad. Richard thinks he has already said too much. In his mind's eye he sees the headline: 'Congregation shocked and upset.'

He quickly peels off the rest of his vestments and gently but firmly pushes his way through the press group who follow him round to just outside the main door of the church where the small congregation are gathered in nervous conversation.

As he gets to the door one of the church stalwarts, a large barrel-like elderly lady, Agnes, bustles up to him and takes his hand.

'Oh Richard, I'm so sorry. Is Noelene alright?'

At this kind expression of concern, a lump comes to his throat but swallowing hard he retains his composure.

'She's bearing up well, but as you know she doesn't show her feelings very easily.' Richard thinks he is lucky to have many wonderful people in his congregation and that people like Agnes will stand by him whatever happens. The rest of the congregation, except for one, gathers around their priest. Eileen, who has a son in the army, is the one who has quickly moved away and is already in the car park unlocking her car.

Another parishioner asks anxiously, 'But Richard, what is going to happen now?'

'I really don't know. I haven't been charged with anything and I will be seeing a solicitor later today.' The press is circling the group at the door, like vultures trying to pick up scraps of the conversation and taking photos, until Agnes angrily rounds on them.

'Oh, can't you go away? We are having a private conversation here.'

Richard intervenes, 'It's okay, Agnes.' Then turning to the pressmen, 'Gentlemen, I told you I would give you a statement later today and I will keep my promise. Now if you don't mind, I have private pastoral issues to see to, so would you please leave us now?' He turns back to the parishioners and indicates towards the door. 'Perhaps we can go and talk in the church.'

Except for Agnes the others say they need to get on with shopping and other chores. With some guarded expressions of support, they drift away while Agnes and Richard go back into the church. They sit down in one of the back pews.

Agnes says, 'Please let me know if there is anything I can do. As you know I have friends in the Progressive Party and the Black Sash[11] that I know will be only too willing to help, so don't hesitate to contact me.'

This expression of support brings out strong emotions in Richard and he desperately feels like hugging her and crying on her shoulder. However, he restrains himself, partly because he assumes the pressmen are peering in at the church door.

'Thanks Agnes, that's truly kind of you.'

'Actually, long before today, I had wondered when the police might investigate you, because you have been very brave in speaking out against the government, and it's not just words, you have also done things to break down barriers, like when you invited that black minister Reverend Ndlovu to preach here. You are clearly becoming a thorn in their side you know, and I feel proud to have you as our rector.'

'Oh Agnes,' now choking on his words and wiping away a tear. 'It's times like this when we need good friends.' They

---

[11] Black Sash: A largely white women's organisation opposed to apartheid.

sit in silence for a few moments. Richard begins to feel extremely uncomfortable knowing the reporters are still at the door. He wants to get away, so he looks at his watch and exclaims:

'My goodness! Look at the time. I still haven't cleared away the Communion things, and I've got quite a lot to do today so I think I had better get on. Thanks again for what you've said. I really do appreciate it.' He goes to the vestry while Agnes remains in church, kneeling in prayer.

When Richard emerges from the church the pressmen pounce on him again, but he manages a non-committal smile, thanks them for their interest and getting in his car drives away while the photographer is still snapping him in his departing car.

Later that day Noelene and Richard are sitting in leather armchairs in Hall Green's large plush office. The solicitor offers them cigarettes which they decline. He lights up one for himself and leans back in his chair. He is a slightly balding, portly man, and is dressed in a grey suit with a waistcoat. Behind him on the wall are rows of framed certificates. An arrangement of fresh flowers is spread out in a corner. On a table at his side he clicks on a tape recorder. Richard tells him what happened during the night, with Noelene adding to his story here and there. Amongst other things Richard mentions in passing:

'You know, they even searched the loft.' At this, Hall Green sits forward and picks up a silver fountain pen. Pointing with the pen he exclaims:

'Hey! I think it might be an idea if you check that loft.'

The couple look at him in mystified surprise.

'Whatever for?' Richard asks.

'Come on,' he says, 'Don't be naïve.' He wags the pen at them. 'These guys don't play by the Queensbury rules. You surely know that the SB[12] has been known to plant incriminating stuff on those they want to silence. You see,

---

[12] SB: Special Branch. Another name for the Security Police.

if at some future date they want further evidence against you, they'll know exactly where to find it.'

'Now that you mention it, I did notice that Retief was wearing plastic gloves when he went up in the loft. I thought it was just because of the dust up there.' He looks at Noelene. 'And that was the one time when they didn't seem to want us around, wasn't it?'

Hall Green raises his eyebrows and nods affirmatively.

'There you are. I would definitely check the loft. And if you find something, don't touch it, but give me a call immediately.' Sitting back, he continues. 'Now this is all really difficult. You see, I think they were hoping to find something more than just that news cutting. What they would have liked to have found were some papers describing bomb-making materials and sabotage plans, but you don't have anything like that, do you?'

'Most certainly not,' says Richard with a nervous giggle.

'So, as they didn't find anything else, I would suggest they want to scare you, so that you stop or tone down your opposition. Look, I'm not a member of your church, but I live in this town and you are well known for your outspoken opposition to the government and your association with black people. Now, if you are not frightened off, they might use that Mandela document as evidence that you are promoting the aims of communism, and they may issue you with a banning order.'

Richard and Noelene look at each other with shock.

Richard exclaims, 'But I don't understand... I've never had anything to do with communism.'

'Ah, but the 1950 Suppression of Communism Act and subsequent amendments are so broad as to cover anything.' Hall Green swivels round in his chair, stands up and walks over to a glass-fronted bookcase. Opening the bookcase, he glances along a shelf and then extracts a weighty-looking tome. Back at his desk he flips through some pages. 'Here it is. Umm...' He reads a bit to himself. 'Yes! It says here, it covers, "anything that promotes social, political or economic change in South Africa." You see they want to be able to pounce on anyone they don't like, and it is clear they don't like what you are doing in this community. Now if they do ban you, you should bring the order to me and we will then see what action, if any, we might take. That is as much as I can say. Now, if I were you, I would go home and give that loft a good going over. And let me know immediately of any communication from the court or the police.'

Noelene nudges her husband. 'What about the press?' She turns to the solicitor. 'Richard has been pestered all morning by reporters. What should we say to them?'

Hall Green presses a buzzer and his secretary enters, notepad and pen in hand. He quickly dictates a brief statement. While this is going on, Richard and Noelene sit there feeling like spectators. The secretary leaves to type up the statement.

Richard leans forward and asks, 'Um, how much do we owe you?'

Hall Green brushes his question aside.

'I don't charge the clergy for consultations, but if I have to make any representations on your behalf, I may have to review the situation.'

They thank him and leave for home, having picked up the press statement from the receptionist.


As they drive into the Rectory grounds, they see a large Chevrolet parked in the driveway under the flame tree where Richard usually parks to get some shade.

'Oh God. Not the police again?' Richard exclaims.

'No, it's Bishop Andrew,' says Noelene with some excitement.

Richard then notices the Bishop sitting on the veranda, writing in a notebook he is holding on his knee. He is a tall athletic man, having won national honours at squash, and still plays regularly to keep fit. He is wearing a dark suit with his purple episcopal shirt and gleaming white collar. As they get out the car he looks up and comes down the steps, two at a time, to greet them in a more restrained manner than is his usual wont. As he comes down the steps he says:

'One of your parishioners, Agnes Grant, phoned to tell me what happened. I drove over right away. I hope you are both okay?'

Noelene suddenly bursts into tears. Richard takes her in his arms and is choking back his own tears. The Bishop embraces them both in his long burly arms and they stand there for some moments at the bottom of the steps in a three-way hug. The trauma of the night and their lack of sleep have caught up with them, and their pent-up emotions are released in sobbing and crying.

Richard finally breaks away and, wiping his eyes, says, 'I'm sorry, Bishop.'

'Oh, don't worry. You've both clearly been through an awful experience. Where have you just come from? No, don't answer. Let us go inside where we can talk.'

Entering the Rectory, the Bishop sees the damaged front door.

'My God! Did the police do that? Surely that wasn't necessary?' They stand looking at the damage while Richard describes what happened.

'Well, get it repaired and make sure you send the account to them. But come on folks, let's go and sit down – and what about a cup of tea? I am sure you could do with one. Let us all go into the kitchen.'

Once in the kitchen the Bishop tries to take over by grabbing the kettle and filling it at the sink. Noelene intervenes, 'It's okay, I'll do that. You sit down.'

'I'm not very domesticated, but I can at least make a cup of tea,' and he switches on the kettle.

Noelene insists, 'No, please do sit down. I'll see to it.'

With a shrug of his shoulders, 'Okay Madam. I'll do as I'm told.' Sitting down he says, 'Now, please tell me, what happened last night?'

Between the two of them they describe how they were woken up and what happened.

The Bishop listens attentively and having asked a few questions says:

'You have both been very brave in your ministry here and I want you to know I will support every aspect of it. So, I hope you will continue your work just as before. But I do ask you to be particularly careful. In these difficult times we need good priests in our parishes preaching the Gospel and caring for their people. We do not want martyrs. By the way, tell me, what was this banned document?'

Richard tells him about the newspaper cutting. Before he has finished the Bishop interrupts:

'You see, that's what I mean about being careful. You didn't need to have that cutting, did you? You have read it. You know what Mandela said.'

Richard looks a bit taken aback.

'Yes, but it's a report that people all over the world have seen and, in any case, I never thought I was sufficiently high profile for them ever to want to search my home.'

'Ah, but you see, you are a soft target. They would not do this to someone like me or the Archbishop. But they can make an example of you.'

'That's what Mr Hall Green said and they have certainly scared us.'

'Yes, it must be quite terrifying, but I'm glad you've been to see a solicitor.' Then, with emphasis, 'Now you must let me know what the fees were, and I'll send you the money. By the way what did your solicitor say?'

They tell him Hall Green had not charged and what he had said.

The Bishop frowns, 'I don't know this Hall Green chap, but let me tell you the diocese has an excellent legal firm that we have used in the past in various—'

He is interrupted by a loud knock on the door.

'I'll deal with it,' says the Bishop, jumping up from the table and walking purposefully down the corridor.

Richard does not like the way the Bishop is taking over, but he is too tired to do anything about it. Noelene is feeling quite relieved and she sighs, 'Thank God we have an understanding and kind Bishop.'

Richard recognises the voice of the press reporter at the door.

The Bishop comes back, 'It's a reporter from the *Evening News*. He says you promised him a statement.'

Taking the solicitor's statement from his jacket pocket he tells the Bishop:

'The solicitor gave us this.'

'Give it to me. Let me see to it.' He returns to the front door and they can hear the Bishop arguing with the reporter and then casually dropping into the conversation the fact that he is having lunch with the paper's editor the next week. They hear him tell the reporter he will make sure the *Evening News* is kept fully informed of any further developments. Then they hear the door close and the Bishop returns to the kitchen, dusting his hands and saying:

'Well, you shouldn't have any further trouble with them. If you do, don't hesitate to call me. I see most of the newspaper guys at Rotary or social events that, unfortunately,' and he looks up at the ceiling in mock resignation, 'for my sins I must attend. I even *praat die taal* with the editor of the *Volksblad*.' He adds laughing, 'There you are; you didn't know I was fluent in Afrikaans, did you? By the way, the *Volksblad* people haven't been on to you, have they?'

'No, they probably didn't bother because this town is so English. I doubt whether they sell any papers here.'

'Okay. Now unless you have any important appointments you should take the rest of today off. You've had to cope with enough for one day.' Then in an authoritative tone:

'Will you both kneel down, and I'll give you a blessing.'

Noelene and Richard kneel on the rug in the passage, and the Bishop prays, laying his hands on their bowed heads. That done, he helps them both up, gives them a hug and heads for the front door calling over his shoulder:

'Now don't forget. Let me know if anything further happens.' The door closes behind him.

Noelene says, 'I am absolutely dead on my feet so I'm going to have a lie down.'

Richard decides to follow the solicitor's advice and to search the loft immediately. Having found nothing, he joins Noelene and collapses on their bed utterly exhausted.

Normally if Richard lies down, he dozes off immediately. Although very tired, his eyes are now nervously stretched wide open as he lies on the bed. Noelene, however, soon nods off. Suddenly Richard twitches with fright as the bedroom phone rings. Noelene also sits up sharply. It is with some relief that he hears the voice of Stan Henderson, one of his Church Wardens who works in the city. Stan tells him he has picked up an early edition of the *Evening News* and there on page two was a picture of Richard outside the church.

'I wondered whatever had happened and was shocked to read that the police had searched the Rectory.'

'Well it really was very frightening I can tell you.'

'What does this government think it's doing? Just because you don't tow their line they now have to send in the heavy mob. By the way, how's Noelene?'

'Like me, she is feeling pretty shaky. In fact, she is just having a lie down.'

'Please give her our love and you go and have a rest as well. We can talk again later because I think the parish must stand behind you. So, if there is anything I can do, please let me know.'

'I will, Stan, and thank you very much for phoning.'

'Don't mention it. This bloody government: and they call themselves a democracy and a Christian democracy at that! It beggars belief.'

Stan rings off and Richard has barely put his head on the pillow before the phone is insistently ringing again. This time it is a friend from his university days who is now a freelance reporter in Johannesburg. Richard asks him to hold on while he unplugs the bedroom phone and goes to take the call in his study so that Noelene can get some peace.

On resuming the call Richard hears his friend say, 'I saw your news and then noticed that an Afrikaans paper reckons... where is it?' Richard can hear pages being turned. 'Ah! Here's the relevant bit. It says, "*Gedure die soektog het die poliesie op ANC papiere van ontstoken afgekom.*" What papers were those?'

'My God!' Richard is shocked into silence for a moment. 'That sounds terrible. Doesn't "*ontstoken*" mean revolutionary?'

'Ja, it's something like that. But I don't associate you with being a red-hot revolutionary.'

'Well it creates that sort of image of me doesn't it? And good Lord, it's only an overseas news cutting of Mandela's statement at his trial. It's not... oh, I don't know, plans to blow up pylons or something.' As soon as he has said it, he realises he must be a lot more careful about what he says on the phone.

His friend responds, 'Ja, you may think it is nothing, but our government has created in the minds of most whites that anything to do with Mandela or the ANC is terrorism, intent on killing all the whites.'

'Good God, I suppose you are right. Well, thanks for letting me know. Now I know what I'm up against.'

The call leaves Richard very worried as he imagines the sort of fantasies people might begin to have about what he is involved in. He decides he must phone Noelene's mother and his parents, as they will no doubt also get the news and it would be better if they heard it from him rather than from some sensational news report.

He first calls Noelene's mother and she is full of concern for her daughter and Richard. She is also furious and describes the government as having created a police state.

Richard's call to his own mother is totally different. When he tells her what has happened, all he gets is silence. He thinks he has lost the line and says, 'Mother, are you there?'

'Yes.' There is a pause. She is clearly shocked. 'I don't know what to say.' She adds plaintively, 'I'll tell your father. He can talk to you when he comes home. Mrs Latham is here having tea with me. I will have to go. Goodbye.'

'No, wait, Mother,' he exclaims urgently, to stop her hanging up. 'I also wanted to say that some papers are exaggerating what happened. You must believe me. I am *not* involved with the ANC and I have not done anything unlawful. So please don't believe any lurid news reports you might come across.'

There is silence again. Then she repeats rather abruptly:

'I'll tell your father. He can talk to you.'

Richard is dismayed, but not too surprised. He knows his opposition to the government causes consternation amongst his family, and that this is going to hit them like an earthquake, particularly if they hear a biased report. His parents have always tried to uphold a squeaky-clean reputation. The family own *Atwell's Emporium* the largest departmental store in the little East Griqualand town where they live, and where they are pillars of that white community.

He does not have long to consider his mother's reaction before the phone is ringing again. He hopes it might be his mother or his father calling back. It is not and, for the next hour he is unable to move from the phone, as one call follows another. He realises the news is getting around fast and is encouraged by the number of calls from friends and colleagues, near and far, expressing their concern and wishing him well. He is also pleased for the opportunity to put the record right for these callers.

After about six calls the phone rings again and by now he is expecting another sympathetic friendly voice. He lifts the phone to answer, but before he can utter a word a woman's voice yells down the phone:

'You bloody kaffir lover. You've got it coming to you.'

There is a click as the phone goes dead. He sits there stunned for some moments, his trembling hand holding the handset in mid air. As his brain clears, he recalls hearing about other opponents to Apartheid receiving abusive anonymous calls and he had always thought it would not overly upset him. However, now that it has happened, he is feeling shocked, angry, and helpless. He likes to please people and is extremely upset that someone should be so venomous towards him. He puts the phone back on its cradle and thinks, *what have I done? Oh damn, perhaps she read that bit about me being an ANC revolutionary*. His thoughts are interrupted by the phone ringing again. He lifts the receiver very gingerly, as though it is something dangerous. This time, however, it is Father Tom, his Roman Catholic colleague and friend. Choking with emotion, Richard can barely utter more than a few words.

Tom picks up Richard's distress and says, 'It's okay. I'm coming around right away.'

Richard puts the phone down and decides he is not going to take any more calls. Having replaced the handset he takes it back off the cradle and leaves it lying next to the phone, which is something he has never done before. He can hear the dialling tone buzzing away like an irritating horsefly. He wonders if he has done the right thing. One of his ideals as a priest is always to be available to people who need him. Even on his day off he has never taken the phone off the hook. After a while, the buzzing stops and there is silence. Now he is worried that perhaps he has caused the phone to be cut off.

Just then, through the study window he sees the stocky figure of Father Tom with his mop of wind-blown hair, stumping up the pathway to the veranda. Richard goes to the door to meet him. As usual Tom is wearing an ill-fitting suit that has seen better days, and a dog collar yellowing with age.

Tom holds out his hand in a warm handshake. 'How's it, old chap?'

'Ag, it's just so good to have friends like you at times like this.'

'How's Noelene?'

'Oh, she was trying to catch up on some sleep, but I think I heard her moving about.' They go through to the kitchen where Noelene is standing by a boiling kettle. Tom greets her with a hug and then flops down on the rickety old chair next to the fridge where he always likes to sit.

'I'm brewing tea for Richard and me, but would you like something stronger?'

'Aye, something stronger would be great, but I have to hear confessions this evening and it won't do to breathe alcoholic fumes over the humble penitents,' he says with his customary loud guffaw.

Richard perches on the kitchen table and tells him and Noelene about the hate-filled phone call. Noelene takes a shocked intake of breath. Richard also mentions that he has taken the phone off the hook and wonders aloud if he should go and put it back on. Tom immediately raises a restraining hand.

'No, leave it. I often take the phone off for all sorts of reasons, some of them not as holy as you might think. I always reckon that if it is anything important, people will always call again. In any case, from what you have said, it seems you need a break from the bloody phone.'

They tell Tom about the search and he chortles away over the stupidity of some of the books that had been taken away.

Richard asks him, 'Have you ever been searched by the SB? After all, you are also involved with black people.'

'Oh no,' he says laughing. 'Remember, I'm Irish and they know they can at any time refuse to renew my resident's permit. But you are a South African and they can't bear it when their own people go against them.'

'Ja, but what about "*die Roomse gevaar*"? They see the Roman Catholic Church as dangerous.'

'There is that. But, you see, that's my point. They've already blackened our name and most of our white clergy are from overseas, so they see us as outsiders. They sideline us as ignorant foreigners who don't understand the situation.'

Tom stands up, 'Well that was a lovely cup of tea. Thanks, Noelene. Now you two, look after yourselves. Remember,' and he does a little jig as he goes down the corridor to the front door singing, 'We shall over cu-um one day ay ay ay ay.'

# Chapter 5

(Sunday 17th September 1967)

It is the first Sunday after the search. Richard is getting ready to go to church to conduct his main Sunday service. Normally it is something he does almost out of habit, but today he is feeling very fragile and nervous. Since the search he has not been sleeping well. He lies awake at night, going over and over in his mind, amongst other things, the papers he had in his KwaBophela file. The notes he kept there included some critical comments on government policy and he wonders what the police would make of it, especially his summaries of his conversations with Simon. He hopes he has not written anything that may get his friend into trouble. He worries about what the police might do next. Now he just hopes he will be able to hold himself together sufficiently to face his congregation. He is not at all sure how they will react towards him, despite having received several sympathetic phone calls. From what he has been able to ascertain, the English language press – read by most people in Pemberton – has been quite critical of the draconian powers the police have to invade private homes. Nonetheless he fears some people in his congregation might now be afraid to have anything to do with him.

He leaves the house for the short walk to the church with his cassock over his arm and the file with his sermon notes clutched in his other hand. He has been careful to prepare a sermon that has no obvious political implications, something he has never been afraid of in the past.

Entering the vestry, he is greeted by the two schoolboys who are today on the servers' roster. The boys do not appear to show any awkwardness with him, and he soon overhears them chatting amongst themselves about who is likely to get into the Springbok cricket team. When the Lay Minister enters, he greets Richard with a warm handshake,

'Hey man, I only got back from Cape Town yesterday and haven't yet been able to speak to you. I want to say how sorry I am to hear of what you've been through.'

Richard feels emotional tears welling up, but conceals them by blowing his nose. Through his handkerchief he manages to say, 'Thanks, Bill. Please remember us in your prayers.'

'Ja, of course. Anyhow, it looks as though you are now bringing in the crowds. The church is just about full already.' He turns to the servers.

'You will have to put extra wafer breads out. I reckon at least another forty.'

Richard is astonished. He goes to the door and peers into the church. Turning back to Bill, he exclaims:

'Hell's bells! You would think it was a confirmation or some special service.'

When Richard follows the procession into church, he feels everyone is watching him. Conducting worship is second nature to him, but today is different. He feels tremors in his stomach and clutches his sweaty hands together to stop them shaking.

When the organ music for the introit dies down, Richard stands up in his stall to read the notices of parish events for the week. While doing so he is touched to notice that several friends from outside the parish are present. Some of them are sitting with Noelene. That pleases him immensely. He also spots some locals who only come at Christmas and Easter, and momentarily wonders if they have come out of curiosity. These, his friends and a more than full complement of regulars appear to account for the increase in the congregation. At the end of the notices he swallows hard to control his feelings and speaking slowly and deliberately, thanks those in the congregation who have supported him and Noelene over the past few days. He adds that, contrary to an implication in one news report, he believes in the rule of law and is not involved in any seditious covert activities. He then glances at the hymn board and announces the first hymn.

During his sermon Richard spots a man in the congregation who he does not recognise. Seeing this man disturbs him and for a moment he stumbles over his text. He nervously fiddles with his notes to find his place. Although he regains his concentration and continues preaching, he finds his eyes keep picking out this stranger. His thought is that the man is possibly a police spy.

The rest of the service passes normally, and the congregation are now filing out of church and milling around in the sunshine outside. Most people stop by Richard for a moment to shake his hand and some offer words of encouragement.

A parish counsellor slaps an arm around him and whispers in his ear:

'Don't let the buggers get you down.'

Richard laughs, 'Thanks. I'll try not to.'

A rather severe looking lady comments, 'I can't understand why the police waste their time on things like this when there are real criminals around.'

Richard is not too sure how to take that comment, but lets it pass. What he finds particularly pleasing is that Sergeant Chris Lotter of the local police is in church with his family. As he comes out, the tall sergeant leans towards Richard and brusquely comments.

'You know, some of the things the Security Police do make me ashamed of being a policeman.' Before Richard can thank him, he strides off to his car with his family following on behind.

There are also a few who avoid the rector by slipping out quickly and shielding themselves behind those he is greeting.

A retired British Army Major strides up to him and says in a commanding voice, 'Excuse me being blunt, but why don't you leave politics to the politicians? I thought your job is to preach the Gospel.'

Richard responds, 'Well, I'm afraid putting the Gospel into practice involves politics, but that is a big issue and perhaps we can talk about it again.'

The Major grunts and stalks off while Richard makes a mental note to visit him in the near future.

Almost at the end of the queue Carl, a young parishioner, emerges and grabs the minister in a hug.

'Ag Richard, I phoned to tell you we support you one hundred per cent, but unfortunately your phone was engaged. Liz and I have been praying for you and Noelene, and our hearts go out to you. It must be awful to be under suspicion. But listen, you must let us know when you are free, and we must go out somewhere so you can forget about your troubles. Tell you what – we'll take you to the Rotunda in Hopedale. They serve terrific meals there and the cabaret is usually fairly good.'

Richard feels a bit embarrassed at Carl's effusive support.

'Thanks, Carl. My diary is very full, but I'll let you know.' The thought flashes through his mind that it is hard to believe Carl can afford to take them to the Rotunda which is one of the most expensive restaurants in Hopedale.

As the last of the congregation dribble out, Richard looks around for the stranger he saw in church. He is nowhere to be seen. Pushing his worries aside he wanders towards a group of his friends who are talking with Noelene, but he is intercepted by the church treasurer, Beth, who asks to have a word with him. People are still thronging around the entrance chatting in small groups, so Beth leads him to one side. In almost a whisper she says, 'I'm afraid I've got some bad news. But first, how are you coping?'

'Oh, we are getting by. But what's this bad news?'

'I'm afraid the bad news is that Bert Chapman phoned me yesterday to say they are cancelling their pledge and won't be attending church here any longer.'

'Oh, no.' Richard heaves a tired sigh. 'Ja, come to think of it, I noticed Laura wasn't here today. Did he say why?'

'When I asked him, he simply said; "I think you know why".' She pulls a face, 'I know money isn't everything, but you know their giving is substantial and if we don't have their financial support, we are going to have real difficulty in paying our diocesan assessment. That's besides losing two important parishioners.' Then in a more upbeat manner she continues, 'But you are good at pacifying people when something upsets them. I think a visit from you early this week might be able to get them to change their minds.'

'Okay, I'll see what I can do.'

# Chapter 6

(Monday 18th September 1967)

The next day Noelene is at work and Richard is sitting in his study gazing out the window, not sure what he should be doing. He is finding it hard to live with the fears that now stalk him. Despite the support he received the day before, his mind is preoccupied with the mystery man who was at the service. After some time, his reverie is broken by a knock on the Rectory back door. On answering it he is met by the smile of Simon, who is standing there with extended arms.

'Hi Richard, my friend.'

'Hey, Simon.' Richard extends his hand in the traditional African handshake of clasping hands and then thumbs. 'It is good to see you. But I've told you, you don't need to come to the back door. Come in, come in.'

'I don't mind and, in any case, a black man knocking on your front door might draw attention, so perhaps this way is best.'

Richard ushers him in and, shutting the door, embraces his friend.

As they break apart Simon says, 'So, man, I see you are now one of us.'

Richard frowns in puzzlement. 'What do you mean?'

'You are also being tormented by the police, just like us.'

'How did you hear about it?' Richard asks with quizzical look.

'Oh, one of my members works as a housemaid here in Pemberton and she brought me Friday's newspaper after her employer had thrown it out. Anyhow, now you know a little of what it feels like to have them hassling you.'

'I must say it was a very unpleasant experience. And it scared the hell out of me.'

'That's right. That is how they rule, by fear. But you mustn't let them scare you. You know what the angels said when Jesus was born...' He holds his hands up as though he is the angel loudly announcing the words. 'Fear not. I bring you tidings of great joy.' Then more sombrely as he drops his arms, 'Ja, I know it's easier said than done and perhaps it's easier for me having less to lose than you. Also, we've got used to it.'

'Well isn't that part of the iniquity of the system. You've got used to the hardships they impose; and whites, are so used to our privileged position that we are not even aware of it. But we are nattering on here. Why don't we sit down and have a cup of tea or coffee? Which would you prefer?'

'Coffee would be great.'

Simon flops down on a kitchen chair and Richard starts making coffee while telling him about the search and some of the innocent items they decided to take away, to much unrestrained laughter from Simon. He is a bit concerned, however, about the KwaBophela and Twenty-One and Three files they took and what was recorded in them. When Richard tells him he responds:

'Well it doesn't sound as though there is anything there that isn't common knowledge. But I have just had another thought. You know, I always have to be watching out for informers and I just wonder if you've got a spy in your congregation.'

'Ja, that has occurred to me too. Like yesterday – there was a stranger in church who slipped away without me meeting him. But I don't think I told you that a few weeks ago one of my youth leaders, a bloke by the name of John van de Westhuisen, phoned me to say he had had a call from a Major de Wet who said he was from the security police—'

Simon sits up and interrupts pointing a finger, 'There you are.'

But Richard continues, 'This major asked John to meet him at the entrance to Princess Park in Hopedale. It was all cloak-and-dagger stuff, very strange. John said he wanted me to know before the meeting because he was a bit worried about what might happen. Well, when John came home that day, he called round. He told me the major and another officer had picked him up in a chauffeured car and had driven off into the country at high speed. He said he was really nipping straws because all they told him was that he had nothing to worry about, but that they had something important to discuss with him. For the rest they drove in silence. I think all this was a tactic to impress John and make him feel vulnerable and defenceless. Somewhere in the country they turned off into an old quarry and stopped. He said the major was then very matey and complimented him as being a loyal South African from an upstanding family. I think they also said something about his grandfather having opposed the English in the Boer War. They said that being a respected citizen of Pemberton, he was just the man they needed to give them information regarding an important patriotic undertaking to keep the community safe.'

Simon bursts out laughing, 'So that's what they call informing, a patriotic undertaking,' and he gives a sarcastic grunt.

'Well John is not stupid, and he soon realised that is what they wanted of him. He said the atmosphere changed when he told them it was not the sort of thing he would want to do. The major then mentioned some debts that John had, including his mortgage, and that should he be prepared to be one of their men he would be richly rewarded—'

Simon interrupts again chuckling, 'That's it. I was waiting for it. Bribery! That's how they get people to do their dirty work.'

'Well, although taken aback at all the information they had on him and scared as to what they might do next, John is fortunately a strong guy and insisted he didn't want to be involved. They did not tell him who they wanted information on, but he suspected it was me. John is far too good a friend and loyal churchgoer to be involved in anything like that. Once he had made his position clear they drove him back to the park and it seems that was that.'

Simon chips in again, 'You see, they have tried it with one member of your congregation, so they could well have tried it with another, and this time, perhaps with some success.'

'That's exactly what's been in my mind. You see, there is a new young couple in the congregation. Well, Noelene and I feel very uneasy about them. This chap Carl, he is not too bright, he has been very ingratiating and makes out as though he is a great friend of ours, although we have only known them for a few months. Well, he and his wife have showered us with gifts that are completely over the top and we have been invited out to dinner with them but, so far, fortunately have been able to make excuses. Only yesterday after church he again asked us to go out with them.'

'*Yebo*, well I would be careful of this chap, but there may be others as well. You know, I've heard it said the police always try to have more than one informer working independently on the same case. Neither knows about the other, and so they can play the one off against the other. In that way they keep them both on their toes. At least, that is the way they operate in KwaBophela. So even if this Carl is an informer there may well be another one as well.'

'Good Lord, the SB aren't stupid, are they? It's bloody frightening. I won't know who to trust.'

'No! The actual informers are often stupid, but not the guys higher up. So, I don't want to scare you, but I think you must be careful who you confide in.'

'Ja. The solicitor also warned us to be careful, so thanks for the advice.'

'Well, I just wanted to let you know we are praying for you and Noelene.' He takes Richard's hand and they say the Grace together. Then, draining the dregs from his cup, he stands up.

'I've got to be going.' Then he stops. 'Hey, I nearly forgot to tell you. The people at Twenty-One and Three think your idea of a children's party is great. Mrs Mazibuko says she will tell all the mothers. She says I must thank you for your kindness.'

'Gosh, that had completely slipped my mind.' Richard is silently thoughtful for a few moments. 'I wonder if we should still go ahead with it.'

'Why do you say that?'

'Well, I was just thinking of those children. It would be terrible if the police pitched up here during the party and caused trouble. Just think how disappointed and upset the children would be.'

'Hey come on, man. You don't know those children. They suffer disappointments every day of their lives. How do you think they feel when they come into Pemberton with their parents and they see the swings and they are not allowed to play on them? How do you think they feel when they see white kids with bicycles and expensive toys when all they have to play with is old cotton reels and clay animals they make themselves? Do you know that after lunchtime some of the older children from Twenty-One and Three go to Pemberton High and rummage through the rubbish bins to pick up the sandwiches and food the white kids throw away? Sandwiches which probably their mothers had to make for those spoilt white kids. Hey, you're getting me quite angry now—!'

'No, no, no,' Richard interrupts, feeling chastened. 'Of course, I'm not suggesting we cancel the party.' Secretly, however, Richard is wishing they had never had the idea of a party. 'It's just that I now feel scared of doing anything.'

'Look, you and Noelene are doing the right thing. The Bible says, "Blessed are those who are persecuted for righteousness sake." Jesus might have said, "Blessed are those who give parties for poor children who are never likely to have a party." So come on man, I'll stand by you. And think of it – they will be even more stupid than I think they are if they try to stop a kiddies' party. Just think what the newspapers would make of that, hey?'

'Ja, of course you are right. I'm just being a coward.'

Simon gives him a friendly slap on the back.

'No, you're not. You just need a bit of time to think about it and you'll know what is right. Talk to Noelene, see what she says.'

'Oh, I know what she'll say. She has got her heart set on this party. There is no way she will back down now.'

'There you are then. Now I really must go.'

'Hey, can't I give you a lift somewhere? I've got nothing pressing.'

'No, that's okay. When I decided to come and see you, I thought I would also visit some members of my church who work as housemaids further up your road. Now remember, if God is for us, who can be against us? So, you see they don't stand a chance.' He gives Richard a big hug. '*Sala kahle* my friend.'

Richard responds, 'Thank you very much. You are always so good to me. *Hamba kahle* and God bless you.'

Seeing Simon off, Richard notices that the post box at the Rectory gate is bulging with mail. Some of the larger items protruding from the posting slot make it look like the bill of an overfed bird. He collects the pile of envelopes and papers and carries them to his study. At his desk he begins to go through them. While doing so, on one envelope he recognises the handwriting of his brother Ian who shares the management of *Atwell's Emporium* with his father. Richard suddenly remembers that when he phoned his mother, she said his father would call back. He had not. He immediately slits open the envelope. He takes out a typed page and reads:

*Richard,*

*What do you think you are playing at? Don't you realise that we are likely to lose some of our best customers because of your crackpot activities? Ever since you went to university you've had these highfalutin' ideas and now it has got you into trouble. I hope you have learnt your lesson.*

*You would change your tune if you had the munts working for you, like I do.*

*Dad is furious and I think you owe Mom and Dad an apology because they must suffer the shame of facing the people in this town.*
*Ian.*

Richard feels devastated and decides he must speak to his father right away. The receptionist at *Atwell's Emporium* answers the phone and says she will try to find his father. After keeping him waiting for a long time she returns to say his father is busy and cannot come to the phone. Richard takes this as a further snub. In the past his father has always been only too willing to take his calls, whatever he was doing.

*Okay,* says Richard to himself. *If he will not speak to me, I will write to him and it won't be a formal typed letter.*

Going through the mail he comes across a vitriolic anonymous letter that adds to the hurt he feels. There is also a long critical letter from the Anti-Communist League, with a wodge of their leaflets all supporting the government as the only bastion against the spread of Communism in Africa. Although there are many messages of consolation and praise from friends and people for whom he has a high regard, it does not ameliorate the pain he feels from the rift with his family. He decides that writing to his parents may allay some of his hurt feelings. In the letter he apologises for the embarrassment he has caused them and explains that anyone who opposes the government is likely to be targeted by the Security Police. He adds that he is sorry if his views, which are shared by many who have phoned or written to him, including their own parish priest, cannot be shared by his parents. He concludes by expressing appreciation for all they have done for him in the past and hopes that despite their differences he can remain in contact with them.

Having posted the letter to his parents Richard feels a little more at ease and busies himself by putting all the mail relating to the search in a special file, determined, in time, to answer each one individually.

# Chapter 7

(The days following 18th September 1967)

Richard has remembered the church treasurer's suggestion, and a few days later he is walking up the path to the Chapmans' sprawling residence. On either side of the path are immaculately mown lawns bordered by colourful flower beds. At the side of the house a flowering climber on a trellis half conceals a swimming pool. It all looks like the front cover of an up-market gardening magazine. He rings the doorbell and hears it chiming a melody in the recesses of the house. It is late in the afternoon and he has noticed Bert's shiny black *Wolseley* in the driveway, so he knows he is home from work. Bert appears at the door. He is tall and thin and walks with a distinct limp, carrying a war wound in his hip. He has clearly not yet changed from work and is still in an expensive-looking light summer suit.

'Ah, Richard! Now why did I know you were going to call?'

His remark takes Richard aback.

'Well, er, um, well yes. I suppose you would have expected me to come, but in any case, I was due to visit you and Laura, and your call to Beth just made me bring it forward.'

'Whatever,' Bert says dismissively. 'I think though that it's all a bit too late. But come in and let's talk about it.' Bert stops for a moment, and craning his neck looks down the path and whispers, 'By the way, are you being followed?' He chuckles at what he thinks is a joke, making Richard feel more uncomfortable.

Richard follows him into their lounge dominated by a huge Tretchikoff painting over the fireplace. In the corner is a cabinet crammed with Bert's bowling trophies, and on the walls hang Laura's certificates for prize-winning floral arrangements. A large lampstand throws a pool of light over

Laura who is working on a piece of embroidery spread out on her lap. She looks like an aristocratic lady from a Jane Austen novel. Richard has never liked her but has been obliged to tolerate her because of the power she exercises in the parish. Seeing her he is vaguely aware of a feeling of repulsion as he notices her overdone make-up, her powdery cheeks and thick bright-red lipstick. Looking over the top of her half-frame glasses she nods coolly in response to Richard's greeting.

Bert shoos a large cat off a chair and invites Richard to sit down. There are cat's hairs on the seat, and Richard knows his trousers will be covered with them, but he pretends not to notice as he sinks into the chair. Next to the fireplace is a bar behind which are rows of bottles. Bert goes to the bar and Richard expects to be offered a beer as has happened on previous visits. Instead, Bert perches on a barstool and takes a cigar from a large box.

'You don't smoke, do you, Richard?'

Before he can say anything, Bert continues talking while snipping off the end of his cigar with a little silver tool.

'Laura is the one who feels strongly about this, so I'll let her do most of the talking. As you know I am not as involved as she is. I do my sideman's duty once a month and that is pretty much my lot because of my bowls commitments. But as you know Laura never misses a Sunday, besides being president of the Woman's Guild and organising the fete and other things, don't you dear?'

'Yes, and frankly, Richard, I'm extremely disappointed in you.'

The ice in her haughty tone sends cold shivers down the minister's back.

'Well, I'm sorry you feel that way. But can we perhaps start at the beginning. What is it that has so disappointed you?'

'You might not appreciate it Richard, but I've been a member of St. George's for over fifty years. I was baptised and confirmed there, and it has been my spiritual home ever since. Father Martin once said to me, "Laura, you *are* St.

George's". But since you came, I have been feeling increasingly unhappy. You have brought politics into the church. It was never like that in Father Martin's day, although the native problem has always been with us.'

Richard raises his eyebrows and answers in a sympathetic tone:

'But Laura, things change and move on and I know change is difficult, but the Anglican Church as a whole, is now realizing that Christian witness requires us to speak out on political issues.' Laura gives a little snort, but Richard continues. 'It is not just me. I am saying the same things that the Archbishop of Cape Town and others are saying. The church has to be relevant to day-to-day life.'

She retorts sharply, 'Oh! So, wasn't it relevant under Father Martin? I think what you are suggesting is an insult to very holy priests like him.'

'No, no. I agree with you. Father Martin is a very holy man. I have a really high regard for him and feel privileged to be following in his footsteps.'

She grunts. 'Then why are you changing everything? It is not only your anti-government sermons, but you also started this new liturgy thing. Fancy addressing God as *you!* You have no respect for God and no respect for our rulers.'

Richard feels insulted by her accusation, but controls his feelings as he answers rather pedantically, 'In using contemporary language many people come into a closer relationship with God rather than—'

At this point Bert interrupts, waving his cigar in the air making swirls of smoke. 'Let's cut to the chase here. We have all heard those arguments about modernising the services and politics and religion. We will be here till the cows come home if we get into that. I think what really disturbed Laura, and me for that matter, was when you had that Bantu minister to preach. No priest that I know of has ever done that and Father Martin certainly never did. He knew it was his duty to be in the pulpit himself every Sunday. But you had this black sambo come along, who is not even an Anglican, and he then had the effrontery to advocate communism from the pulpit.' Richard is shocked but keeps silent while Bert goes on. 'I ask you, what a ridiculous thing for a so-called Christian minister to do! I mean, isn't communism totally opposed to religion? After that, I am not surprised that the police have been on to you and searched your home. If I were them, I would also want to know what is going on in the Rectory and who you are inviting there. The police search just confirmed our own misgivings about you.'

'I'm sorry Bert, but if you don't mind me saying so, I think you misunderstood that sermon. It's a couple of months now since Simon preached here, but I cannot recall him saying anything of the sort.'

'No, I'm not wrong. I can remember distinctly. He said that the Bible says we must share our wealth and have equality. Now that's communism, although he was sufficiently devious not to mention the word.'

'Ah! I remember now. He was quoting from the Book of Acts and saying that at the very beginning of Christianity, that is what the early Christians did, and that apartheid was contrary to their vision and that that was the challenge—'

Bert breaks in, talking over Richard:

'Look, I might not know the Bible as well as you do, but in any case, I'm sure those words can be interpreted in many ways. As far as I am concerned, that is communism, a philosophy that is totally unrealistic. We have to live in the real world of law and… and…' Sitting forward, Richard makes as though he wants to respond, but Bert continues. 'Just hear me out,' he says, holding a hand up to silence Richard. 'And doesn't the Bible say render unto Caesar what is Caesar's and unto God what is God's. That surely means being obedient to the state and the state's laws, or don't you believe that?'

Pointing with her embroidery needle for emphasis Laura chips in.

'That is exactly where you have gone wrong, Richard. You are attacking the government all the time and, in that way, whatever that native said, you've allied yourself with our communist enemies who want one man one vote and all that nonsense, which I think is what that minister was driving at. Let me tell you, if it wasn't for our strong government, before you can say Jack Robinson, the reds will have taken over the country and we will have to be smuggling Bibles into South Africa like they now have to do in Russia.'

Reeling under their attack, Richard tries to offer a defence.

'I'm sorry, but I think you have misunderstood me and the Reverend Ndlovu. Let me explain this—'

Bert interrupts again and, from the height of his barstool, proceeds to lecture him.

'No, Richard. I think we have understood you perfectly. Laura is right. You young people don't realise the danger this country is in, and it is especially dangerous when a person in a public position, like you, gets taken in by wishy-washy liberalism that aids and abets the reds.' He gives a loud laugh and, in a sing-song voice repeats, 'Aids and abets, the reds. You know, I should be a poet. Anyhow, that is not the only thing. I don't think you realise just how much you have upset our way of life. I believe some people told you long ago, you are paying that boy who does the Rectory garden far too much. That is just the sort of thing liberals do that makes the communists rub their hands in glee, because it creates unrest amongst the blacks. Because you pay your garden boy too much, other boys start causing trouble. And it is not as though your boy is worth it. The rose trees Laura donated to the Rectory haven't been pruned for ages and the last time I looked they were surrounded by weeds and looking a mess. That's the thanks we get for our generosity.'

'Well, I'm sorry. I didn't realise those roses were donated by you. I'm afraid, I'm no gardener, but I'll certainly ask Alfred to clear the ground around the roses.'

Laura puts her embroidery down on a table at her side and starts getting up.

'He'll probably pull all the roses out. Natives don't appreciate beautiful things. You would have thought that

Noelene would have taken an interest because she could have cut roses for the house. Mrs Martin used to have beautiful arrangements.'

Richard feels anger begin to rise in him although he has been determined to keep calm, but before he can say anything, Laura walks towards the door with her head in the air.

'In any case, you will have to excuse us. We are going out tonight and I still have to get ready.'

'Can I make an appointment when you've got more time so that we can talk this through?'

'I don't think it will make any difference. Like Laura says, our association with St. George's goes back a long way and our decision to leave has not been taken lightly. In any case, whatever we say, I am sure you will continue to preach against the government and frankly we've had enough of that now. So,' he shrugs his shoulders. 'No hard feelings, but I'm afraid, this is the end of the line.'

'I really am sorry that you feel like that and sorry to be losing you from the family of St. George's.' Richard stands up, struggling to control his anger and just manages to maintain his pastoral role. 'I hope you will find a place of worship that is to your liking so you may continue your Christian pilgrimage. Also, on behalf of St. George's, I want to thank you both for all you have done for the church. I am sure a lot of people are going to miss you.'

Standing at the door, as a parting shot Laura says with some venom, 'You can tell them, we didn't want to go, but you have made it impossible for us to stay. So goodbye.'

Richard reaches out in an attempt to shake her hand, but with a swish of her skirt she turns her back on him and walks out, leaving him standing there feeling foolish with his hand extended in mid air.

Bert levers himself off his stool and leads the way to the front door. On the veranda he does at least accept Richard's handshake, but with a grimace on his face says, 'She's terribly upset by all this. You have taken away a large part of her life you know.'

At this point Richard responds strongly, allowing some of his anger to surface.

'No, I haven't. It is not my decision but hers and yours.'

'Look, I'm not going to go over everything we have already said. You have forced us out. That is the truth of it. Now I think you had better go.' He turns away from Richard and walks off to where a climbing rose runs up the side of the veranda. He taps his cigar ash into the rose bush. Turning towards where Richard is descending the steps he says, 'Ash is good for roses, but I don't suppose you know that.'

Feeling horrible, but trying to retain as much dignity as he can muster, Richard walks slowly to his car. Once in the car he pounds the steering wheel with his fists in his rage. He is angry that they spoke about Simon in such insulting terms and that he was too weak to challenge them more strongly. He feels particularly humiliated because he suspects they saw his visit as an attempt to beg them to change their minds. As he drives away, however, the thought occurs to him that Simon's sermon clearly hit a nerve, and that gives him some comfort.

Early the following week, Richard takes a phone call in his study. On answering, a voice he recognises says, 'Hi Dick.' It is Robin Farmer the minister from the white Methodist Church. Robin is the only person who calls him Dick and he does not particularly like it.

'Hullo Robin.'

'How are you coping with all the hoo-hah?'

'Oh, so so.'

They talk for a few minutes about the search and its aftermath and then Robin says, 'By the way, I phoned because I have some news for you. Mr and Mrs Chapman turned up at the Manse yesterday saying they wanted to become Methodists…' He pauses, but Richard makes no response, so he continues. 'Of course, I asked what had caused their change of heart and when they told me I sent them packing. I told them in no uncertain terms, that if they wanted to change churches only because of your political views they were changing for the wrong reasons. I can tell you they were so surprised you could have knocked them down with a feather. I think they thought I would welcome them with open arms.'

Richard responds rather sombrely:

'Well, thank you very much for taking the line you did. The tragedy of course is that they do need to be part of a worshipping community that will help them deepen their faith beyond playing lady bountiful and running fetes and things.'

'Oh, I wouldn't waste any tears on them. They are the sort who think church is like a country club, and I doubt if anyone will be able to shift that view in them. Anyhow, I thought you would be interested to have that bit of news.'

Richard thanks him again and rings off. He thinks Robin's call should have cheered him up. In fact, it has made him feel worse because he knows he would have liked to have had the courage to tell the Chapmans some home truths like Robin clearly had. He also feels guilty in that during the time he has been in Pemberton he has not been able to affect any change in their attitude.

# Chapter 8

(Wednesday 27th September 1967)

Richard is drawing up the agenda for the monthly Parish Council meeting. He has been agonising over it because it is the first meeting since the search, and in addition there has been the letter of resignation from Laura and Bert. He finally decides that it will be best to confront the issues and to have the Council's views out in the open, so at the head of the agenda he writes, *Police search Rectory: Views and Fallout.*

That evening, as the councillors gather around a large trestle table in the rather dowdy-looking parish hall, the tension is evident. Usually there is a fair amount of banter and laughter, but tonight the greetings are rather terse. Beth, the treasurer, and Stan, who is churchwarden, are having a private whispered conversation on one side while the others are taking their places, most appearing to be preoccupied with the agenda sheets in front of them. Richard is sitting at the head of the table, nervously glancing at his watch and tapping his pen on the table. Precisely on the dot of eight o'clock he calls the gathering to order and everyone stands for the usual prayer. They have barely uttered the concluding *Amen* and are still taking their seats when Stan says he wishes to speak. Richard anxiously shuffles his papers as he wonders what his churchwarden is going to say.

Stan clears his throat and then speaks in rather solemn tones.

'This has been a very difficult time for Richard and Noelene, and I want to propose a vote of confidence in our Rector.'

Richard silently breathes a sigh of relief. Stan continues:

'I am sure Richard means well by putting what has happened on the agenda, but you know there has been quite enough careless gossip and uninformed talk going on in the town so I think we should just take the vote without discussion and then put it all aside and move forward with the running of the parish.'

Beth immediately says, 'I'll second that.'

There are some affirmative nods of approval. However, Richard feels he must intervene. In preparing for the meeting he had geared himself up to face the difficulties and is now afraid that this proposal, however well intentioned, might have the effect of pushing any contrary feelings underground. He feels he must stick to his agenda and says:

'That is very kind of both of you and I really appreciate what you have said. However, I do think it is important for members of the Council to have the opportunity to voice any views and concerns they may have about what has happened. A full discussion may also help to dispel some of the gossip that is going around. In any case, there is a letter of resignation here from Laura and Bert that will have to be read and which I think should be discussed.'

Stan says, 'Well Richard if that is what you really want. Beth and I just thought it would be a good idea to save you further distress in what I am sure has been a very trying time.'

Another member asks, 'Isn't the matter *sub judice?*'

Richard replies, 'I'm no lawyer, but as no charges have been made against me, I don't think it applies. So, I hope members will feel free to talk openly. Perhaps a starting point could be Laura and Bert's letter.'

There is a murmur of agreement. The secretary then reads the letter. After a few moments' silence, Kurt, who is always forthright in his views, speaks up:

'Ag, I wouldn't worry about them. After all, some of us won't be sorry to see them go with all their airs and graces. You would think she was a duchess or something.'

'The thing is,' says Beth. 'I know money isn't everything, but their giving was considerable and it's going to leave a big hole in our finances.'

Kurt gives the table a gentle thump with the palm of his hand.

'Oh, come on, let's stick to our principles. If they want to take their money elsewhere, good luck to them. In fact, perhaps I am not a very good Christian, but I would say good riddance.'

Richard, as chairman, intervenes.

'Okay Kurt, thank you. Of course, principles must take priority, but all of this, including me being investigated by the police, is going to have practical repercussions on the parish and I think we need to discuss them.'

A question is posed as to whether any other parishioners have left the church.

Richard answers, 'No one that I know of has formally left, but there are a handful of folk that I haven't seen in church since the search, but it's still early days and, of course, any absentees I notice I shall visit.'

Someone suggests a successor to Laura who could organise the fete, and Kurt says he will run the tombola which Bert used to do. During this discussion Richard has become aware that one member, Marjorie Hussey, who normally has a lot to say, has been silent and is fidgeting in her seat. So, he asks, 'Marge, what do you think?'

Kurt laughing interrupts, 'Ah, I thought you weren't here. I think it should be minuted that almost half an hour has passed without a word from Marge.'

Marge leans forward and says irritably:

'Don't be silly Kurt. As Richard has said, this is a particularly important matter. Whilst I do not agree with Laura, the parish rector is a public figure and what he does can have far-reaching repercussions. Don't get me wrong, Richard, but it seems you have broken the law even if we don't agree with those laws. Now what sort of message does that give to our young people? And I must tell you, although I didn't mention it at the time, that when my nephew Nick and his fiancée came to see you to arrange their wedding, Noelene asked them to wait in the lounge because you were busy on the phone. *Well*,' she says with emphasis, 'when they went in, they were shocked as a black man was sitting there reading the newspaper. They did admit that he was very friendly and polite towards them, but they told me afterwards they were worried they were getting involved in a church that was breaking the law.'

'Actually Marge, that was the Reverend Simon Ndlovu. As you know our parish has started supporting his work at KwaBophela and he comes to see me from time to time. You may also assure Nick and Julie that there is nothing illegal about entertaining a black man in the Rectory.' Richard wanted to go on to say something about Christian neighbourliness, but he tactfully keeps his thoughts to himself.

Marge's intervention has given an opening for another councillor, Durrant, to speak up, although he normally has little to say.

'Excuse me Richard, but I thought the newspapers reported that the police had found some banned papers. Now that *is* illegal and having banned material looks a bit as though you are involved in some clandestine activity; as though you are on the side of our enemies. Now Richard, I am not suggesting you are, but that is the way many people will see it. And several people in Pemberton have sons or nephews in the army fighting on the border. We need to support them and having papers that supports the ANC does not help. After all, our country's motto is *Unity is Strength*. In these difficult times we need to show that we are united behind them.'

Beth snorts, 'This government with its apartheid policy has surely by definition abandoned that motto.'

Marge replies, 'Oh Beth, you know what we mean. I am sure Durrant will agree with me. We are all for the blacks. It is the terrorists and communists that our boys are fighting against. The Bantu who work for you and me aren't interested in politics and things like that.'

Beth raises her eyebrows and Richard sees an argument looming, so he chips in, 'Let me make it clear here that the paper that was found in my study was a report in a reputable

British newspaper of Mandela's trial. In addition, I understand that despite being banned, that speech was also reported in at least one South African newspaper. Furthermore, Durrant and Marge, as you both know we pray regularly for our armed forces and for their families at home.'

Marge resumes, 'Yes Richard, I know we do. But you sometimes seem so anti-government that I wonder if it doesn't put people off coming to church, especially as there are also quite a few parishioners who work in government offices. They might think their jobs could be at risk by coming to our church.'

Richard immediately responds.

'Marge, I think that is a little unfair. It is not the people in government, but the policy they follow that I think is wrong. You may recall that when Dr Verwoerd, the person who is regarded as the architect of apartheid, a system that I think is a denial of the Gospel and I would even go so far as to say, is an evil system – when he was assassinated, I said from the pulpit that while I disagreed with him, he was nevertheless seen by his people as a great leader and I called on all of us to pray for his widow and family.'

Marge looks at Richard. Then with a shrug she says, 'Well, I've said my say and I think the Council needed to hear it.'

Richard nods vigorously, 'Oh, I absolutely agree and I'm glad you did, so thanks Marge. Do you wish to add anything, Durrant?' Durrant shakes his head.

After a pause, Cyril, one of the older councillors adds, 'Listening to the points made by Durrant and Marge I think, and I hope you won't mind me saying this Richard, but you are still very young and you do tend to be a little bit, how should I say, a little bit outspoken – you know what I mean? Perhaps you should be a bit more careful in what you say. And perhaps we should reconsider our support for that African minister—'

A chorus of no's interrupts his suggestion. Cyril looks around the table and then continues: 'Okay, I'm just thinking of the well-being of our rector and I'm also thinking of Noelene. I think all of us would agree that we don't want you getting into any more trouble.'

Richard is feeling increasingly uncomfortable. He hates it when people patronise him or Noelene. However, for the umpteenth time he restrains himself and does not respond. However, Beth speaks up:

'There is nothing illegal about supporting an African mission and as Richard has said in the past, KwaBophela is our neighbour and as Christians we are bound to show love towards our neighbour.' There are several nods of agreement. An awkward silence follows before Stan speaks up.

'I think we have aired this fully now and I propose that we move on. Richard, from what has been said, I don't think we need to take a vote. It is clear you have the support of the Parish Council, even though,' he looks at Marge, 'some may wish to qualify their support—'

Marge interrupts, 'I do support you, Richard. I think you are a good priest and I will always be grateful for the way you helped me when my dad died. I just wish you were a little less political.'

Durrant quietly adds, 'Yes, I also support you and pray regularly for you.'

Cyril reaches over and pats Richard on the shoulder.

Stan resumes, 'There you are Richard. I think all that needs to be said has been said. Would you please let Noelene know that you are both in our prayers?'

There are some further murmurs and nods of agreement but Richard, despite the support, feels despondent and tired. He is furthermore afraid that he may not be able to contain his emotions and so agrees that perhaps it is time to move on with the agenda.

# Chapter 9

(Early October 1967)

Since the search and Richard's letter to his parents, he has had little contact with his family. He has tried phoning from time to time, but only his mother will speak to him and then the calls are awkward. If he mentions anything about their strained relationship, she denies that anything is wrong and if he persists, she makes an excuse to end the call. He has also written again, and whilst his mother has responded to his latest letter, it was a bland missive restricted to news about the shop, their social lives, and his father's and brother's achievements on the golf course. Noelene has regular contact with her mother, who is very supportive of them, while Richard feels hurt and neglected by his family's attitude.

However, out of the blue a letter arrives from his cousin Marie and her husband Pieter. They say they are on a touring holiday and want to know if they may spend a night at the Rectory on their way south. It is a long time since Richard has had any contact with his cousin, but as children they used to play together when on holidays at their grandparents' home in the Cape. When Marie got married, Richard and Noelene were in England and so they have still to meet Pieter. He is a deacon in the Dutch Reformed Church[13] and Richard assumes they are government supporters and guesses that somehow, they know nothing about his difficulties with the Security Police. Had they seen the news reports of the search, he is sure they would not be asking to visit.

Richard feels this is at least some contact with his family and he and Noelene are determined that the visit should be

---

[13] Dutch Reformed Church: The church many Afrikaners and apartheid government ministers and supporters belonged to.

amicable and a success. They are both at home and well prepared on the afternoon when Marie and Pieter arrive.

Marie, a very demonstrative person, is dressed in flamboyant colours with wide sleeves and skirt. With a flurry of fabric, she jumps out the car and flings her arms around Richard.

'My goodness Richard you don't change a bit.' She then hugs Noelene. 'And Noelene, you are as beautiful as ever.' By now Pieter, in a more sombre khaki safari suit, has joined them and Marie introduces him.

The greetings done, Richard offers to help Pieter with their cases, and leading them into the house shows them to the guest room saying, 'When you've settled in, please come through to the lounge.'

In a few moments they are all seated in the lounge and catching up on old times. Marie is doing most of the talking.

'I think the last time I saw you was at your wedding just before you went overseas. That must have been about five or six years ago. We were not married then and from what I remember Pieter had just started work and couldn't come. Anyhow there wasn't much chance to talk to you at your wedding, so this is a lovely opportunity. By the way, I hope we're not keeping you from your work Richard. We know ministers are terribly busy people.'

'No. Normally I would be out visiting in the afternoon, but I'm glad to take a break from that today. But look at the time, it has gone five o'clock – what about having a drink? I have beers on ice, there's gin, brandy, whatever you like, and I'll try my best to provide.'

'My goodness,' says Pieter. 'I didn't know ministers were allowed to drink. In our church it is certainly prohibited, but you Anglicans are more modern about things like that. Of course, Marie and I enjoy an occasional cocktail, but when the dominee[14] calls, if I am having a drink, I have to hide it behind the settee.' They all laugh heartily. 'Yes, I'm not joking you know. It is true. I could

---

[14] Dominee: Afrikaans – Minister or Pastor

certainly never have a drink in front of him, let alone offer him a drink. If I did that, I think I would be kicked out of the church.'

Richard takes their orders, and while he is getting the drinks Marie excuses herself, 'Before I have anything to drink, I think I must go and powder my nose,' and she disappears down the corridor in the direction of the toilet.

Richard takes the drinks into the lounge while Noelene is in the kitchen getting some bowls of crackers and nuts, when there is a knock on the back door. Opening the door, she is greeted by Simon who steps in and envelops her in his customary hug. Coincidently, at the same time Marie is passing the kitchen on her way back to the lounge and glancing in is horrified to see Noelene in the arms of this big black man.

She screams, 'Oh my God, HELP!'

Richard and Pieter rush down the corridor towards Marie, while a startled Simon releases Noelene and takes a step back.

Noelene quietly mutters, 'Oh no.' She quickly tries to take charge of the situation. 'It's okay Marie, I assure you I'm not being attacked.'

Marie is trembling from shock, and Pieter clasping her asks urgently, 'What happened my love?'

'That... that native grabbed her.'

Richard takes a moment to realise what has happened. His heart sinks but all he can do is to rather lamely say hullo to Simon, who is looking very embarrassed.

Noelene continues trying to normalise the situation. She takes a couple of steps towards Marie saying, 'Look, I'm sorry Marie if you've had a shock, but I can explain it all.' She gestures towards Simon. 'Let me introduce the Reverend Simon Ndlovu. Simon is a good friend of ours and although it may look strange to you, I greet Simon with a hug like I greet all our special friends.'

Simon also apologises.

'Madam, I am truly sorry to have distressed you. I hope you will forgive me.' Moving towards her he offers his hand.

'No, no, don't,' cries Marie shrinking from him and clinging to Pieter.

'No,' says Pieter firmly. Looking daggers at Simon he adds, 'Don't you dare touch her.' Then turning to Noelene with a look of disgust he continues, 'You, should be ashamed of yourself.' Then ushering Marie down the corridor, 'Come on my love, we can't stay here. Let us get our things.'

Richard follows them but once the couple are inside the guest room the door is slammed in Richard's face. He calls through the closed door, pleading with them to stay, but gets no response.

Simon starts to apologise to Noelene, but she stops him.

'No, please don't worry. I suppose they have never seen anything like this.'

Richard returns to the kitchen and, with a mixture of anger and helplessness, says, 'They bloody well won't listen to me.' He pauses, then adds shaking his head, 'I don't think we'll be able to get them to change their minds.'

Noelene is adamant, 'Well, if that is their attitude, tough. If people don't like it then so be it.'

They are still standing in the kitchen looking at each other, not knowing what to do or say, when they hear Marie and Pieter going down the corridor. Richard follows them to the front door. From there he calls out after them:

'This is really not necessary you know. I wish you would just stop a moment so we can talk.'

He sees Pieter throw their cases in the trunk and, with a slamming of doors, their car roars out of the driveway.

Returning to the kitchen Richard says with resignation, 'Well that's their loss. I suppose we must let them go. That's the trouble with so many whites in this country. They are so narrow minded they don't know any better. Of course, the pity is that they are due to spend tomorrow night with my parents. Whether they will now I don't know, but one way or the other my parents will hear about this and it is not going to help.'

Simon speaks up, 'Hey man, I feel terrible. I seem to have caused you a lot of trouble.'

'No, no,' says Richard. He goes over and gives Simon a hug. 'We are always glad to see you man – and there are drinks and snacks that are now going begging! So, let's go and enjoy them. At least friendship across the colour bar is not yet illegal.'

Noelene adds as they walk towards the lounge, 'Yes, but this government has been very clever in making white people think that any personal contact between the races is a crime. That is clearly what Marie and Pieter believe.'

'*Yebo*, and whilst not yet really a crime, me hugging a white woman is definitely immoral in their book. After all. I'm supposed to be dirty and have a bad smell although I washed this morning and used a deodorant.' He playfully lifts his arms and sniffs his armpits. 'But I really am sorry over what has happened. The last thing I want is to cause dissension in your family.'

'Oh, forget it,' says Richard. 'I'm going to have a beer, what about you?'

'Okay.' He gives a chuckle. 'Let us drown our sorrows before they drown us.'

# Chapter 10

(Mid October 1967)

It is Sunday evening and Richard is preparing to go to church. Noelene is lazily stretched out on the sofa reading. She likes to support him as much as possible in his work, but she draws the line at Sunday Evensong. She enjoys her Sunday evenings at home, knowing it is unlikely anyone will call or that the phone will ring because everyone knows that Richard is in church.

On his way out, Richard peers into the lounge and, chuckling, says, 'All you need is a glass of wine and a bowl of grapes next to you and you would look like one of those decadent Roman empresses.'

She raises an imaginary glass, '*Vive la decadence*. Admit it, you're just jealous.'

'Ah! You know me too well. I must say all the services today have tired me out and I wish I didn't have to go to Evensong. Anyhow, they are going to get a short sermon and there is no meeting after the service, so I should be back at a decent hour. Enjoy your book, lucky you. I'll see you later, bye.'

About halfway through the service while the congregation are singing a hymn, Richard's attention is drawn to a slight disturbance at the back of the church. He notices that his neighbour Charles, Gwen's husband, has just appeared, grim-faced, at the church door. He is in shorts and flip-flops, clearly not dressed for church. Stan, the duty warden, goes to the door and Richard notices that the two men are in earnest conversation, with sidelong glances in the minister's direction. Richard realises it is something important so, while the singing continues, he walks down the aisle to the back of the church. Stan ushers Charles and Richard into the porch so they can talk in private. The volume of the singing drops a bit, as some in the congregation are distracted by what is going on.

In the porch Stan takes Richard's hand and says, 'I'm afraid we have bad news. Noelene has been attacked in the Rectory and has been taken to hospital. The police have been trying to find you and they managed to call Charles. He will take you to the hospital straight away.'

Richard is used to emergency calls with people being unexpectedly taken into hospital, but this is different. He is stunned.

'But… is she alright?'

Charles answers, frowning, 'They said it is serious, but they wouldn't tell me anymore, just that you should go to the hospital without delay.'

Manically Richard peels off his vestments, and shoving them into the arms of Stan, instructs him to tell the lay minister to take over the service.

'I can go in my car,' he says to Charles. 'You don't have to take me.'

'No, I'm taking you,' says a determined Charles. 'My car is right here ready to go,' and firmly taking Richard's arm they run to the car.

Soon they are speeding to the hospital. Richard asks, 'Do you know what happened?'

'I really know nothing Richard. The police phoned. All they said was that Noelene had been attacked by a Bantu man and she had been taken to the hospital. They said they had been trying to get hold of you but didn't know where you were. I told them I could get to you quickly and would take you to the hospital. As I drove out from our house, I noticed lights on in the Rectory, but I didn't see anything else. Gwen and I certainly did not see or hear anything, but then the Rectory is not exactly near our house. They said she had been taken to Pemberton Hospital.'

In no time at all they are at the hospital on the outskirts of the town. Charles swings the car round the driveway and, with the wheels crunching on the gravel, stops abruptly at the front door. Richard jumps out and, taking the steps three at a time, runs toward the reception office. There is a bell on the counter that he rings urgently, and a nurse immediately appears from a rear office.

'I've come to see my wife, Noelene Atwell. She was brought here this evening.'

'I'm sorry, Reverend Atwell, but no one has been admitted this evening. In any case I know you, so I would have remembered if Mrs Atwell had been admitted.'

By now, Charles has joined him and speaks to the nurse.

'You are quite sure about that? The police said she is here. You've got no patient by the name of Noelene Atwell?'

The nurse glances down a list of names in a register.

'No. Did they say it was something serious?'

Charles answers, 'Yes. The police said it was serious.'

'Well then she would have been taken to the Manor Hospital in Hopedale.'

'Oh no,' groans Richard, running his hands through his hair in despair.'

Charles says urgently tugging at Richard's sleeve, 'Come on. We'll go to Hopedale then. The police must have made a mistake.'

The nurse says, 'I'm terribly sorry, Reverend Atwell. I could phone the Manor to find out?'

But the two men are already at the door and Charles calls back.

'No thanks. We don't want to waste any time.'

They bundle back into the car and, with tyres spinning, turn onto the main road. Richard's mind is a jumble of thoughts and he feels shaky and confused. He finds it difficult to comprehend what is happening. A white glow emanates from the dials on the car dashboard and he notices that they are travelling at seventy miles per hour. He looks at the car's clock. It shows ten past three. Richard shakes his head. He thinks he is going mad. He then realises the clock has stopped and irrelevantly wonders why. They speed on in silence until the city lights come into view.

Charles says urgently, 'You visit the Manor, so you must know the quickest way. Can you give me directions?'

Almost in a trance Richard answers, 'Stay on the main road until the Bergvlei turn-off. Take that and you'll then see the signs to the hospital. When we get near there, I'll tell you where the emergency entrance is.'

Once off the main road Charles continues to race, exceeding the urban speed limit. As it is Sunday evening there is little traffic and, at intersections, if there is no cross traffic, he jumps the red lights. It is not long before he is pulling up behind an ambulance at the emergency entrance. They leave the car in an ambulance bay and both rush to the casualty desk.

Although the clerk is busy with someone else, she is immediately aware of the urgency and anxiety in the rushed arrival of the two men. She turns from the person she is dealing with, saying, 'Excuse me a moment.' She asks Richard, 'May I help you?'

'Yes, I've come to see Mrs Noelene Atwell who was brought in earlier this evening?'

'The name doesn't ring a bell, but I'll check.'

She looks at a list of names in a folder.

'No, there's no Noelene Atwell here, but just hold on a moment.'

She goes into an office and closes the door.

Richard thinks she might be checking the mortuary list, and with his hands on his head in despair mutters, 'Oh, please God, no.'

However, within a minute she is back.

'I'm afraid we have no record of a person by that name. Please tell me your connection to this person?'

Charles speaks up hurriedly saying, 'Mrs Atwell is Reverend Atwell's wife, and while he was at church the police called me – I'm a neighbour – and told me Mrs Atwell had been attacked in her home and was taken to Pemberton Hospital. We called there, but they didn't have her, so we came straight here.'

'Well, if her injuries were serious, she would have been brought straight here. When did this happen?'

Charles looks at his watch.

'Well, it is nearly an hour now since the police phoned.'

Richard chips in, 'Could she have been taken to another hospital?'

'No, we're the only admitting hospital in Hopedale on a Sunday. Let me call the police for you.'

She picks up a phone and, in a moment, says, 'Is that Pemberton Police Station? I'm phoning from the Manor Hospital in Hopedale. A gentleman,' she turns to Charles, 'What's your name please?' He gives his name and she continues, 'Mr Charles Pickering says the police called him about an attack on a Mrs Noelene Atwell about an hour ago and that the police had said she was taken to hospital…' There is a pause. 'That's right. She is the wife of Reverend Atwell. He is here with me…' After another pause, 'You are absolutely sure about that? Okay, just hold the line.' Then holding her hand over the mouthpiece of the phone the nurse turns to Richard.

'He says there has been no report of any attack. The officer says he would like to speak to you.' She hands the phone to Richard.

'Richard Atwell speaking.'

'Hello Richard.' He recognises the voice of Sergeant Lotter. 'Man, I hope I'm right in saying that there has been a terrible mistake here. I've had no report of any attack on Noelene. But I will go around to the Rectory immediately to investigate.'

'I appreciate that. I will also phone the Rectory from here to see what I can find out. Thank you.' There is a brief pause… 'Yes, goodbye.' Richard turns to the nurse. 'May I call my home to see if my wife is okay?'

She nods and Richard quickly dials the number. He can hear the phone ringing and ringing and ringing. He utters a quiet prayer.

'Please God, let Noelene be alright.' Suddenly he hears Noelene's voice. For a moment he is overcome with emotion and nearly drops the handset, but then steadies himself by slumping against the counter in front of him.

Noelene repeats, 'Hullo, hullo. Who's there?' She is just about to put the phone down when he responds.

'It's me, Richard. Are you alright?'

'Yes, why shouldn't I be?' is her surprised answer.

'Oh, thank God for that.'

'Richard, where are you? What's going on?'

He tells her about the phone call to Charles, and how they have ended up at the Manor Hospital. He adds that Sergeant Lotter would be calling at the Rectory in a few minutes.

She replies, 'I think that must be him now. A car's lights have just come up our driveway.'

Richard tells her that he will be home as soon as possible and puts the phone down. Leaning his elbows on the counter he drops his head into his hands. He feels quite weak from the relief that is flooding through him.

Charles puts an arm around his shoulders.

'Oh Richard, I'm so sorry to have put you through this.'

'No, no it's not your fault. Whew! I'm just so grateful she's okay.'

Charles is embarrassed.

'Well, I'm really sorry. It seems I was taken in by what now appears to be a terribly cruel hoax.'

'How could you have known? No, I am just so grateful to you. You have really been so helpful in the circumstances.'

Three days after that traumatic evening Richard is opening his mail. Amongst the letters he spots a rather grubby envelope with his address scrawled out in rough capitals. 'Oh no!' he sighs as he recognises the tell-tale signs of an anonymous letter. For a moment he wonders if he should just screw it up without reading it, but then with a shrug, tears it open. On a scrap of exercise book paper is printed:

IF YOU DON'T WATCH OUT, KAFFIR-LOVER, NEXT TIME THE ATTACK ON YOUR WIFE WILL BE FOR REAL.

He drops the bit of paper on his desk. For some moments he stares at the letter, numb with shock. Some of the letters they have received have been very scary, but none so far have threatened either of them with physical harm. Richard cannot bear the thought of Noelene being hurt or raped. He feels quite dizzy as these thoughts pass through his head. He grips the arms of his chair as though he needs something to hold him together. Then anger kicks in. In fury he smashes his fist down on the desk yelling:

'These cowardly buggers. I bet it's the bloody SB.' He jumps up from the chair and paces about the study in a rage, feeling helpless and confused. His emotion switches to despair and he shouts out pleadingly, 'What can we do?'

Suddenly the phone rings, causing Richard to freeze with fright. As he gathers himself, he is in half a mind to ignore the phone. Then muttering, 'Oh, what the hell,' he picks up the receiver and answers abruptly, 'Hello!'

There is a moment's silence at the other end and then a gentle voice says:

'Is that the Reverend Atwell?'

'Yes, speaking,' he says gruffly.

'Oh!' There is a short pause. 'This is Coetzee from C and G funeral directors. I'm calling about the funeral for the late Mrs Mary Geldart. I have the family here now. They tell me you have been in touch with them and they would like to know if this Friday at 3 pm from your church is okay with you?'

In a more polite tone Richard replies, 'I'll just check my diary.' While he is finding the appropriate page, he becomes aware that his manner was very curt when he answered the phone. 'Yes, that will certainly be okay, and I'm sorry Mr Coetzee if I sounded irritable when I answered the phone. I'm just having a bit of a bad day.'

'No, that's alright. I was a bit surprised because it didn't sound like you. Anyhow, let me confirm then that the service will be on Friday at three o'clock in the church followed by a private cremation.'

They conclude the call and Richard puts the phone down. Doing something that is familiar has helped to clear his head. He picks up the letter, crumples it into his pocket, thinking he will not tell Noelene. Then on second thoughts he realises that would be unfair because it concerns her directly. He wonders how he might tell her without frightening her unnecessarily. He eventually decides that, however frightening, they cannot avoid facing it and so it might be best to show her the letter.

Later when Noelene is home from work, he makes her a cup of tea and when they are seated in the kitchen, he takes her hand. She gives him a worried questioning look.

'Oh dear. Something has happened. So, what is it this time?'

'I'm afraid we had another of those letters today.' He takes the piece of paper from his pocket and smoothing it out places it on the table in front of her. For a few moments she just stares at it. He adds, 'I'm afraid we are not going to be able to ignore this one.'

Looking up at him and in a shaky voice she answers, 'Whatever can we do?' There is a long pause. 'I think we will have to tell the police.'

He holds her hand firmly, 'Yes, I have already thought we must do that. But it's not going to achieve much, because in the first place I'm convinced the SB are involved in this, and secondly, even if the police wanted to, they will never be able to trace where this letter came from. But you are right. We must let the police know. I thought perhaps we could ask the Bishop to take it up with them; in that way we go to the top and they might realise this is serious. In addition to that, in the short term I am not going out again and leaving you here alone at night. Either you will have to come with me, or we will have to arrange for someone to be here with you.'

Noelene looks at him in silence for a few moments.

'Yes,' she pauses. 'But that's going to be awful and such a bind, as though I need nurse-maiding.'

'But otherwise I'll be worried sick about you all the time,' answers Richard in desperation.

After a pause she says, 'Okay, I can see your point, but it's going to be miserable living like that. After all you have meetings most nights of the week.'

'I know it's going to be difficult, but I'm afraid we are going to have to do something and I was going to add that perhaps we also need to make some long-term plans. I was wondering if we shouldn't begin to consider leaving and going to England, or Australia perhaps.'

'No!' she says emphatically. Then, noticing his desperate shrug and the helpless look on his face, she continues with a frown but in a softer tone. 'That's a bit extreme isn't it? I really would not want that. This is our country – and my mother, and our friends are all here.'

'But what else can we do? I cannot see how we can continue to live here safely without compromising what we know is right. Anyhow, as I say, that is a longer-term idea which we don't have to go into now, but which I really think we will have to consider in the future.'

Although she doesn't like it, Noelene eventually agrees that in the short term she should not be alone in the house at night, and that she will arrange to spend evenings with parishioners or friends when Richard is out at meetings or church services. The Bishop also takes the matter up with the Chief of Police in Hopedale. As a result, Noelene and Richard are invited to meet a Brigadier Bezuidenhout at Hopedale Police Headquarters.

An attractive young woman in a navy-blue suit, looking like an airhostess ushers Richard and Noelene into the Brigadier's light, modern, luxurious office on the third floor of the police headquarters. The furniture is made of shiny-silver tubular steel, with soft furnishings in black leather. One side of the room is all glass, looking out onto Hopedale's main street. The Brigadier is a huge man and would certainly not be out of place in the *Springbok* rugby front row. His uniform, adorned with several ribbons and gold braid, makes him look even more impressive. He stands to greet them with a big smile, and when they are seated asks if they would like some tea or coffee. Both are feeling intimidated by the Brigadier's air of authority and, in their nervousness, they decline the offer. The Brigadier dismisses the young lady and, still smiling, opens the discussion.

'Reverend and Mrs Atwell, I have good news for you. We have decided not to take any further action against you regarding the material that was found at your home. Of course, we accept your statement that having that paper about Mandela was an oversight on your part. There were also no other proscribed materials amongst the documents the police requisitioned.' He points to a large brown paper parcel on top of a filing cabinet. 'In fact, I have a parcel here of all your papers and books which you may sign for and take with you today. Of course, the paper about Mandela we have had to destroy which is what you should have done in the first place, but never mind that now. As you English people say, that is all water under the bridge. You see, we police are not so harsh as some of the newspapers make out. I always like to see common sense prevail which, I think you will agree, is true in this case.'

Richard, feeling beholden to the man answers, 'Thank you very much, Brigadier. That's a weight off my mind.'

Noelene also utters a quiet, 'Thank you.'

With his elbows on his shiny desk and putting his fingertips together the Brigadier continues:

'Now, regarding the anonymous letter your Bishop passed on to me,' he places his index finger on a piece of paper in front of him. 'I have a photocopy of it here. Also, that sham phone call that caused you so much distress, let me tell you straight – we in the police force regard that sort of behaviour as cowardly and despicable and we take it very seriously. But you know there is only so much we can do. We wish we could track down things like that, but it is terribly difficult.' Then with some emphasis he continues, 'That doesn't mean to say that we won't keep our eyes and ears open. I can assure you that right now I have forensic experts examining that letter, but the chances of getting any leads, I'm sorry to say, are indeed slim. Also, the phone call was to another party, and you will appreciate that we cannot trace every call in Pemberton. However, I have spoken to the Pemberton police and they have promised me that on their regular patrols they will make a point of calling at your house to check that everything is in order. And if you have any ideas as to who is behind this, or if anything happens to give you concern, please let your local police know.'

Richard is sure the Brigadier knows that the phone call and letters are almost certainly from the security police, but naturally the Brigadier would not admit it. So, Richard says nothing.

As if sensing that Richard might want to say something, the Brigadier asks, 'Is there anything you would like to say, or do you have any questions?'

Richard and Noelene look at each other. Noelene shakes her head and Richard answers, 'No, I don't think there's anything else. These letters are just very cowardly as you say and when they threaten, like that one did, it's also very frightening.'

As if agreeing, the Brigadier adds, 'Yes, we do live in frightening times when we have to stand together to uphold our Christian values.' Then with a big smile and outstretched hand as he stands up, he says, 'I'm sure you will agree with that. Now, it has been good to meet you and, as I said, please do keep in touch with our officers in Pemberton.' Shaking their hands and brushing aside their thanks with 'Ag, we are always only too pleased to help,' he hands the parcel to Richard and shows them out of the office.

It is only when they are in the car driving back to Pemberton that Richard allows his anger to surface.

'The hypocritical bastard,' he mutters. 'He knows only too well where those letters came from, and if he doesn't know I'm sure he is happy to turn a blind eye. I bet we never hear anything from his so-called forensic experts.'

Noelene is a little more sanguine.

'Well, perhaps now that it has been brought to his attention, he may let them know to back off for a bit.' Richard gives a sceptical snort, but Noelene continues, 'Look, just think of it. If it carries on, and we complain again, this Brigadier chap is going to look pretty useless. Today he was able to play the gracious forgiving card by telling us that nothing further will happen as a result of the search. I thought he was very clever doing that, showing off his power. But he will not be able to do that next time. Then he is going to look pretty inept don't you think?'

'Um, maybe. I hope you're right.'

# Chapter 11

(Tuesday 21$^{st}$ and Wednesday 22$^{nd}$ November 1967)

Richard has just returned home from conducting a funeral when there is a knock on the back door, and he goes to answer it.

He is greeted by Simon. As they break apart from their usual embrace, Simon says, 'Hey man, may I use your lav'? I'm desperate for a pee. You know, there are no public toilets for blacks in this town.'

'Yes of course. You know where it is.'

Simon hurriedly disappears down the corridor.

Richard goes to the study where he puts away his funeral vestments. He can hear Simon singing in the toilet and envies the *joie de vivre* of his friend. After a while he hears Simon coming down the corridor, so he calls out, 'I'm here in the study.'

Simon comes in and flops down in an easy chair.

'So, how's life been treating the number one suspect of the Special Branch?'

'Well, I haven't seen you since the hoax phone call, have I?'

'What hoax phone call?'

Richard tells him about the hoax and their visit to the Brigadier.

Simon exclaims, 'My goodness, you are now hobnobbing with the big shots hey! But seriously, that phone call and the letter must have been scary?'

'Yes, and I'm afraid it's beginning to get me down.'

'Hey man, you mustn't let it get you down. They're just trying to frighten you. Of course, it's easy for me to say that. We get used to it, like being stopped in the street and being shouted at by some little snot-nosed cop who hasn't even got his matric.' Simon jumps out of his chair and starts to act out the scene; something he clearly enjoys and is good at. Drawing himself up with his arms akimbo he demands in a strong Afrikaans accent, 'Kom mon you kaffir, show me your dompass.' Then dropping to his knees in supplication. 'Certainly, my baas, certainly. I have it right here, my baas.' He takes his passbook out of his pocket and holds it above his head while looking at the floor. 'Here it is my baas, I'm a good boy my baas.' Then jumping up again to play the policeman, he pages through the passbook. 'Um, okay.' Then he laughs and points at the book. 'Gits, it says here, you are a minister. Well I never! A kaffir minister! Miracles will never cease. Anyhow, it looks as though your pass is in order.' Then in a very stern voice. 'But just you *pasop*[15]. I'll be watching you, minister or no minister. Go on, bogger off.' He throws the passbook down. Then, as himself, he scrambles on his hands and knees on the floor to retrieve the passbook. 'Thank you, my *baas*, thank you, you are a good *baas*.' He then collapses in the chair while Richard is in stitches of laughter. 'Ja, you can laugh. But I promise you it is no laughing matter. I ask you, for God's sake – a man being treated like that by someone half his age, let alone if that man is a minister!'

'I'm laughing at your act. You should be on the stage in a satirical show. I think you would show up the blatant incongruity of this ludicrous system we live under.'

'Ja, it is ludicrous, but also terribly tragic.' His face assumes a serious expression. 'A couple of weeks ago you know, my cousin got shot by the police. He was in Durban one evening just walking down the street when a cop shouted at him. He got such a helluva fright, because he didn't have his dompass with him, so he started running, thinking he would get away in the dark. But the bloody copper pulled his gun and shot him.'

'Oh no,' Richard exclaims. 'What happened?'

'He was lucky. The bullet hit him in the leg, so now he is hobbling around on crutches. The police excuse was that they were looking for a burglar in the area and he fitted the

---

[15] Pasop: Afrikaans – Beware.

description. In other words, he is black so he must be a burglar.'

With some anger Richard says, 'But that's typical of the cops. Shoot first and ask questions later.'

'That's right, and black lives are cheap. So, if you kill someone, well…' and he shrugs his shoulders, 'that's one less kaffir to deal with you know.' He pauses for a moment. 'Hey!' and he brightens up. 'Let's not get depressed. I came to tell you some good news. I think I told you about a co-operative that I wanted to start at my church. Well, my friend,' and he leans forward and slaps Richard's hand, 'it's up and running man. Just over twenty people have joined so far.'

'Hey that's wonderful. How does it work?'

'Well, every fortnight two of our church women take a bus to Checkers in Hopedale. There they bulk-buy things like sugar, mealie-meal, flour, beans, those jumbo tins of jam – that sort of thing. And these women are getting very good at it you know. They look out for special offers and bargains, and the other day they got a whole box of tins of condensed milk at less than half price, because some of the tins were dented in an accident, but none of them had holes so it was all okay. In the afternoon one of our members, who has a taxi, goes to fetch them. Members of the co-op can then come and buy stuff at the church at the supermarket price, with a little bit extra to cover our costs, rather than the high prices the shops charge here.'

'That's great. You have often talked about self-help programmes. Now you've actually got one going.'

'Ja, but you know, and this just shows how the whites have brainwashed us – the biggest difficulty we have in getting people to join, is that they say Europeans and Indians know how to run shops, but they are not so sure about blacks. I ask you; our own people have been taught to mistrust us. But we are slowly building confidence, and every week more members sign up as they see the savings people are making. And we have got great plans man. I've found a second-hand fridge that runs on paraffin. We want to get it so we can also buy things like meat and butter. But we need a bakkie or some sort of lorry to get it to the church and that, my friend, is where I hope you'll come in.'

Richard looks at him with a mystified frown. 'How can I help? I haven't got a bakkie.'

'No, but isn't Mr Baker who runs AB Builders a member of your church?'

'Ja, that's right.'

'Well, a member of my church – Alphaes – is one of his drivers. Now, could you perhaps ask Mr Baker if, after work one Saturday afternoon, Alphaes could use the bakkie to fetch the fridge for us?'

'Well, I don't know,' Richard says hesitantly. He pauses in thought. 'Andy Baker is a funny bloke you know, and there might be insurance issues as he won't be using the bakkie for work, but, ja, I suppose there is no harm in asking him.'

'That's my friend,' Simon says, slapping Richard on his knee. 'Look, we don't want anything for nothing. We are prepared to pay for the petrol and any damages.'

'Okay, I'll see what I can do. Look, I'm just going to have some lunch, so you must stay to have something to eat with me.'

Sitting at the kitchen table, eating salad and sandwiches, Simon is examining the *Sealatrix* salt-and-pepper containers. Holding up the salt cellar he says, 'Hey, this is good. You can keep the salt sealed so that it doesn't clog up in our damp climate. Where did you buy these?'

Embarrassment envelopes Richard.

'Um... you can't buy them in the shops.' Simon looks puzzled. Richard continues, 'I'm afraid it is something white women do. They hold a tea party and a *Sealatrix* representative comes and demonstrates their products to the ladies. They can then order what they want. They only sell through these tea parties.'

'Ah!' says Simon. 'I wondered why you were hesitant to tell me. Presumably a representative wouldn't go to a black gathering, is that what you mean?'

'Well they might, but I very much doubt it. It's another element of our apartheid society, and I feel bad that I can benefit from it whilst so much is denied to you.'

'No, don't feel bad, especially about such a small thing as salt-and-pepper pots. I'll get my own back on you when I get to heaven, because I'll be in a mansion while you will be in a little pondokie.' He slaps his sides with laughter. 'Remember the first shall be last and the last first,' and his laughter erupts again as he slaps Richard on the back. He then looks at his watch. 'Hey, I've got to be going. I'm forgetting that time flies.'

'Are you going to KwaBophela now or do you have other calls to make here?'

'No, I've got to get home. I'm meeting some of the mothers.'

'Look, I've got nothing on my agenda right now, so let me give you a lift.'

'Thanks. That will be wonderful as there are not many buses at this time of the day, certainly not to KwaBophela. So, from the main road I'd probably have to walk.'

Ten minutes later the two men are in the parish car heading out of town. They have barely left Pemberton when Richard notices a *VW Beetle* in his rear-view mirror coming up fast behind them. Being on a clear straight stretch of road he expects the car to overtake them. Instead it slows down, following behind them. In his mirror Richard can see two white men in the car. He tries to keep his eyes on the road and not to watch the following car too closely, but mentions it to Simon.

'Hey, you know, I think we're being followed.'

Simon looks back over his shoulder. 'Um, maybe. We'll see if they also turn off to KwaBophela.'

Entering the bends of the foothills they drive on for a further mile before coming to the turn-off. Richard notices that the other car also slows down and, as he makes the left turn, the VW follows suit. Once on the dirt road, the parish car kicks up clouds of dust that envelope the following car. Simon looks round again.

'If they are following us, we might have given them the slip in this dust – or else,' and he laughs heartily, 'they're eating our dust.'

It isn't long before they reach the entrance to the township and the warning signs by the Bantu Affairs office. To save Richard having to get a permit, Simon suggests leaving him there so Richard pulls up at the side of the road. As their dust settles, they notice that the VW has also come to stop about a hundred yards behind them.

'You know you might be right,' says Simon. 'I think they *have* been following us. Let's see what they do now.'

The VW remains where it stopped. The car is too far away for Richard and Simon to see what the men are doing. Richard is feeling quite frightened and assumes they are waiting to see what his and Simon's next move is.

'I know what I'll do,' laughs Simon. 'I'll go back and ask if they are lost and need directions.' He gets out of the car and starts to walk down the road. As he approaches the car it suddenly turns around and drives slowly away.

When Simon gets back to where Richard is waiting, he exclaims, 'Did you see? They were taking photos of us.' He chuckles. 'I gave them a big smile and said *cheese.*'

Richard, however, is more terrified than ever. 'I wish I could laugh them off like you.'

'Oh, don't let them worry you man. We haven't done anything wrong or broken any laws. If they want to waste their time following innocent people around, then it just shows how small-minded they are.'

'Well I'm going to head back home now, whether they are still on the road or not.'

'Okay. Thanks for the lift. *Hamba kahle* and remember – don't worry, and don't forget to have a word with Baas Baker.'

'No, I won't forget. I'll try to do it as soon as I can and will drop you a line to let you know. Or better still, it's the party for the children from Twenty-One and Three in a few weeks' time. I should be able to tell you then. See you. *Sala kahle*.' Richard turns the car around and apprehensively begins to head back. As he approaches the main road, he sees the VW waiting there, which confirms his fears. A man steps out and flags him down. He is tempted to put his foot down and speed away. Instead, although terrified, he pulls up behind the other car.

The man comes over to Richard and is soon joined by his companion. They are in khaki safari suits and both have handguns in holsters slung round their waists.

The first appears very casual by placing his hand on the roof of Richard's car, leaning against it and enquiring, 'Please tell me. What are you doing with that bantu in this location?'

Richard tries hard to be assertive.

'As you can see, I am a minister and I was just giving the Methodist minister who works at KwaBophela a lift home.' Thinking of Simon, it is as though some of his courage rubs off on Richard. So, he asks the men, 'By the way, who are you?'

'Never mind who we are. I am just telling you to watch out. Take this as a warning and keep away from here. White people have no business to be in a black area.' He slaps his hand on the roof of the car and turning to the other says, 'I've given him a warning so let's go.' The two men saunter back to their car.

With some relief Richard drives slowly past their car and continues home. Once off the dirt road he keeps glancing in his mirror, but the VW is not to be seen. He finds he is sweating, and his hands are nervously clenched to the steering wheel. He also castigates himself that he did not take down the registration number of the VW.

Arriving back at the Rectory he is met on the veranda by an ashen-faced Noelene. She has been waiting for him.

'Oh, I'm so glad you're home. I've just had the most terrible phone call.'

They clasp each other in a desperate hug. Noelene is shaking with emotion as though she is having a fit and then breaks into loud sobs. Richard struggles to control his own emotions for Noelene's sake and holds back on telling her what happened to him. After a few moments he suggests, 'Let's go in and sit down, and we can talk.'

Clinging to each other they go through to their favourite chairs in the kitchen – the place of many difficult conversations. They sit down facing each other across the table and Richard reaches out to hold her hand.

'Go on. Tell me, what was that call?'

Just then a saucepan on the stove starts to bubble over.

'Oh heavens! With all this I forgot about the potatoes. They'll boil to nothing.' She jumps up to turn the hotplate down. When she is seated, he again takes her hand. Her face is tear-stained, and she meets his gaze before looking down. Her free hand starts to twist the tablecloth between her fingers.

'I don't know if I want to tell you everything. It was just so horrible.' She sniffs and releases his hand to take a handkerchief from her sleeve. After blowing her nose and wiping her eyes she continues, 'It was a woman on the phone and the hatred she expressed was unbelievable and in the most awful language. I have never had anyone talk to me like that. She must have known you weren't here because she said, did I know that you were out having sex, *and* she used the "f" word, with kaffir women.' For a moment she chokes on her tears. Richard gets up, comes around the table and kneeling beside the chair hugs her. Clearing her throat, she continues, struggling to get the words out. 'She said, God was punishing us and… and... we didn't have children because... He would never give children to evil people like us,' and she breaks out in further sobs. Richard holds her tightly while she cries into her handkerchief, her whole body in convulsions.

After a while she gradually calms down and when she looks up at Richard, he sees rivulets of tears still streaming down her face as she says, 'I can't believe anyone could say anything like that.'

They remain there while he quietly strokes her back. Eventually he says, 'People who express those sorts of beliefs are hardly Christian. Certainly not the sort of Christians we want to be.' He pauses for a few moments as he has become aware that his knees are now aching from kneeling on the hard floor. He gets up and pulls a chair round to sit next to her and then tells her about his experiences on the KwaBophela road. 'It seems the SB is following our movements and have a pretty well-organised plan to wear us down. I think we must tell the Bishop. After all, he said we must keep him informed. Perhaps we could give him a ring tomorrow. Maybe you should speak to him. You seem to relate better to him than I do. He might be able to help us.'

That night they both sleep fitfully; the slightest noise disturbs them, and in the early hours Richard thinks he hears someone on their veranda. He gets up and having turned the veranda light on peers through a window but sees nothing out of the ordinary.

Shortly after breakfast Noelene phones the Bishop. Richard is standing nearby and overhears the conversation. He is pleased that Noelene appears to be finding the call reassuring. After a while she thanks the Bishop and hands the phone to Richard,

'He wants to talk to you.'

'Good morning Bishop.'

Richard can hear him but is confused by what he is saying. Then he realises the Bishop is talking to someone else. Suddenly the Bishop chips in:

'Just hold the line a sec Richard. I'll be with you in a moment.'

It occurs to him that the Bishop is at the same time on his other phone. He has always been impressed by the four telephones the Bishop has on his desk and his ability to conduct several calls at the same time. Now Richard overhears him saying:

'Yes, I want to speak to him now.' There is a short silence then, 'Will you tell him as soon as he comes out of church, he must phone me as a matter of urgency. Thank you.' Richard hears the click of a phone and then the Bishop is hurriedly speaking to him. 'Thank you for holding on, Richard. I was on the phone to the Archdeacon. As soon as he calls me, I shall get him to arrange for someone to take your services this Sunday. I told Noelene, that you must take an immediate break. You must get away for at least a week, away from the phone and away from the parish. I want you, as a matter of obedience to your Bishop, to book in somewhere well away from here. I suggest the clergy cottage at Hogs Back. With the schools doing exams that shouldn't be a problem, but, if it is, I am sure you will find a vacancy somewhere. Then you must let my secretary know of all your appointments, and she will make the necessary arrangements with the Archdeacon. Have you got that?'

'Wow, yes. But I really don't think this is necessary—'

The Bishop interrupts enunciating his words very deliberately.

'I said this is a matter of obedience. No buts about it. No, come on man, do it. You owe it to your wife and to yourself. It will give you both a good break before the run-up to Christmas. And be assured, I'll have another word with Brigadier Bezuidenhout.'

On the one hand Richard quite likes being told what to do, but at the same time he resents being bullied. However, he knows there is no point in arguing.

'Okay Bishop. Thank you. I'll see what we can arrange.'

'Good man! It's rotten that you're getting these anonymous calls. You are going to need to be strong to cope. So have a break and then keep me informed as to how things go. I'll tell my secretary she will hear from you later today. Goodbye.'

Richard feels a bit bewildered as he puts the phone down. Noelene is standing next to him. She knows the Bishop deals with his clergy in a high-handed way and how much it irritates Richard. She takes his hand saying:

'Well, as you've said in the past, he is a bit overbearing at times, but quite honestly, I wouldn't mind a break. All I'm doing at school now is invigilating and marking papers. And as I've told you, since the search the staff have been very supportive, except perhaps for one or two. So, I am sure I can get someone to take over my invigilating duties, and there will be plenty of time when we get back to mark the papers. After yesterday I really feel I need some recharging of the batteries.'

'Ja, but I find him very annoying the way he just takes over. I don't think the church wardens will be very pleased if I just drop everything. The parish will think one of us has had a breakdown or something. The Bishop shoots from the hip without thinking things through.'

'But that's not your responsibility. If he takes over then he must explain it to the wardens. When you phone his secretary, you could tell her that the Bishop or the Archdeacon must give the wardens something to read out on Sunday to explain our absence. Otherwise people will be wondering what's going on and since the search there is quite a bit of talk going on anyhow.'

'What will he say to the parish? "I have ordered Richard and Noelene to take a holiday?" That will surely start speculation. They may even think I've done something wrong and that holiday is a euphemism for suspension. And there is the Sunday pew leaflet. Who is going to do that? You know, come to think of it, I really think this is a big mistake, given what's happened recently.'

Noelene releases his hand and gives him a playful prod.

'Oh, come on. *You* know it's not a suspension and parish life thrives on speculation about the clergy. If we didn't give the old ladies something to natter about their lives would be extremely dull. As to the pew leaflet; well, the Bishop's secretary will have to see to that, and it won't be the end of the world if there is no leaflet on Sunday. Come on; let's be positive.' She gives him a hug. 'Let us make the most of this. Let's go and enjoy ourselves. If it's okay with you, I'll phone Hogs Back right away and then you can make the other arrangements. Um, I'm beginning to see the possibilities. Just think, in a few days' time we can be taking some nice long walks through the forests and then lounging around with nothing to do in the beautiful garden at the cottage.'

That reminds Richard of how, on a previous holiday they made love in the moonlight in that garden and his reservations begin to fade.

'Okay, it's now Wednesday; so if we go from Thursday to Thursday – how does that sound? Then we'll only be away one Sunday.'

'And if the cottage isn't taken, we could perhaps stay on an extra day or two and still be back for Sunday. So that is decided then. I'll find the Hogs Back phone number.'

# Chapter 12

(Late November)

Although their Hogs Back break does give Noelene and Richard some respite, the fear of what the SB might do next is seldom out of their minds.

A week after their return, Richard is picking Noelene up from Agnes Grant's home where she has spent the evening while he was at a meeting. He knows that she has become increasingly irritated by having to, as she describes it, be nurse-maided in the evenings. He notices that this evening she is particularly moody. During the drive home he asks, 'Your evening go okay?'

Noelene replies glumly with a sigh, 'I'm afraid this isn't working. I know it means you don't worry about me being alone, but really this is no fun for me. I feel I am imposing on people. Agnes is a dear and she would never say I'm imposing, but *I* feel I am.'

'Alright, but you've spent evenings with others that have been okay.'

'Actually, that's not true. It's just that I have not mentioned it before. I really have not been comfortable with any of the people I've been billeted on and it means I'm out most nights of the week when I've got things I want to do at home. People I've been to have been very kind, but seem to think they have to entertain me in spite of my telling them they can get on with other things and leave me to read my book or do some knitting. You know, Agnes even specially baked a cake for me as though my being there was some sort of special event. Then, when it started getting late, she would not go to bed, but insisted on staying up with me even though she was nodding off. I began to feel very embarrassed.'

'Ja well, perhaps we must try to arrange for you to go to some people more our age.'

'But that's not a solution either. People our age have families – like the Lotters and the Nicholsons – and I feel I'm intruding and imposing even more. They'll be helping their children with homework and getting them off to bed and won't want somebody else in the house.'

'You could offer to help the children with homework. Good heavens, they would be pleased to have a free teacher on tap.'

Noelene feels herself tensing.

'You're not seriously suggesting that are you? Look, I teach all day, I don't want to be teaching in the evenings as well. You are just not seeing it from my side. My point is that I feel I am imposing on people and I want to be at home. I've got my own life to live.'

'Okay, but then what's the alternative?'

'I don't know.'

Now Richard starts to get irritated.

'Look, can't you just try it a little longer and see how things go?'

'How much longer? It certainly doesn't look as though things will change in the foreseeable future. I certainly do not trust the so-called assurances of that Brigadier in Hopedale. You are now a marked man and our friendship with Simon and his family really seems to get to them. So, unless we cut off everything to do with Simon and Florence, and KwaBophela and Twenty-One and Three, and we are not going to do that, the threats and poisonous phone calls are going to continue.'

They drive on without saying anything further. The silence hangs between them like a heavy fog until they are nearly home, when Noelene says:

'You know, I think we just have to show more courage in the face of these cowardly acts. So, why can't I stay at home and lock myself in. Surely I'll be okay?'

Richard shakes his head.

'No, I wouldn't be happy about that. You are making things very difficult for me. Remember, as Hall Green said, these people play dirty, like the night Charles got that hoax call. Now if something really happened to you, I would never forgive myself, and just think what your mother would say. When we got married, I promised her I would look after you.'

'That's just it, you see,' she says with vehemence. 'Nobody thinks I can look after myself. My mother always thought I was a gullible little girl. She probably still thinks that and now you also think I need looking after.' There is a brief pause and then she shouts, banging the dashboard of the car with her fist. 'Damn it. I'm an adult, not a bloody child anymore.'

Richard is shocked at her outburst. He was unaware of the strength of her feelings. He is not sure how to respond, so he does not say anything.

After a few moments Noelene continues in a quieter vein.

'Look, life is full of risks. Just think about all the risks Simon faces every day and he takes it all with a wonderful sense of nonchalance and good humour.'

Richard does not like this at all. He jealously suspects that Noelene compares him unfavourably to Simon. What is more she continues:

'Let us suppose someone breaks in one night when you are there with me? What are you going to be able to do? We don't have a gun in the house, and I wouldn't want one, so I'm no safer with you than if I was on my own.'

'Oh, don't talk nonsense,' he mutters crossly.

Noelene explodes, 'Don't tell me I'm talking nonsense. You see, you are just proving my point. To you, I'm a silly woman who talks nonsense and needs protecting.'

'Oh Noelene, I didn't mean that,' he says with exasperation. They have now arrived home and he parks the car in the garage, angrily yanks up the handbrake and switches off the headlights and the engine. He tries to take her hand, but she pulls away and opens the car door. 'No don't go yet,' he pleads. 'Look, I'm sorry, but let us talk about it, please. This is a good place to talk.'

They are sitting in the dark garage in the dull glow of the car's interior light as Noelene has the door slightly ajar.

Richard continues. 'We can't go on like this. You are getting irritable and I'm worried, because I just don't know what they are going to do next.'

She snaps back at him, 'Well don't take it out on me by saying I'm talking nonsense, like I'm an idiot or something. You haven't a monopoly on worrying about all this. Of course, I am also worried, but we have got to stick together. It's not going to help if we start having a go at each other.'

'Okay, I'm sorry. Of course, you are right. I want to help you...' He pauses leaving the sentence unfinished as he feels her bristling next to him. 'Ag, that's not coming out right. I don't mean it in the sense that you are weak. What I mean is that we must help each other. Actually, if the truth be told, in this respect you are stronger than me. I'm more of a paranoid wreck, while you take a lot of this and still get on with things.'

'Then, why not trust me to be on my own in the evenings? I promise you I'll make sure all the doors are locked and I'll phone someone at the slightest indication of anything being amiss.'

'Okay. Look, we're both tired so let's get to bed now and perhaps we can talk some more tomorrow.'

Noelene makes sure they do talk about it the next day and eventually she prevails, and Richard reluctantly agrees to her staying at home in the evenings. As a compromise she agrees to his plan to arrange for some meetings to take place in the Rectory which in the past she had resisted.

# Chapter 13

(Friday 8th December 1967)

It is the afternoon of the party for the children from Twenty-One and Three. With the borrowed kombi Richard has ferried the children over to the Rectory. They are now all sitting, very subdued, in a large circle on the front lawn in the shade of two gorgeous flame trees. All of them are dressed in what appears to be their Sunday best – the girls in spotless if well-worn frocks, and the boys in khaki shorts and most with white shirts with a few even wearing ties. A few have shoes and socks, but most are barefoot. Two of the mothers are standing at one side with Richard as though they are there to keep order. This party is something the children have clearly never experienced, and they are overawed by the occasion. Noelene has been preparing cakes, biscuits, jellies, blancmanges, Cokes and ice cream with the help of a couple of women from the parish, one of whom is Agnes.

Noelene draws Richard aside and suggests, 'Why not play "Follow the Leader"? Hopefully, that will break the ice.'

Just then Simon arrives, and with his help the two men soon have a long line of children following them around the garden doing all the actions. Simon exaggerates all Richard's actions which bring shrieks of laughter from the children as they try to imitate him. After that Noelene starts them on the games she has arranged. While that is going on the women who have now been joined by the mothers, are setting the food out on the veranda.

When the children are summoned to the veranda, they are struck dumb by the spread of delicacies before them. Noelene had planned that they would help themselves to what they wanted, but all are too scared to touch anything. One of the mothers suggests to her that it might be better if the children sit on the lawn and the women serve each with a selection of items on a plate. Soon the children are scattered about and munching away happily. The adults circulate, replenishing the rapidly emptying plates while Simon and Richard are taking around bottles of Coke. Some of the children are not sure if the straw in the bottle should be eaten, but Simon demonstrates how to drink through a straw. There is much laughter as some blow instead of sucking, causing bubbles to fizz out from the bottles. That is followed by long queues at the Rectory toilets. The mothers help with the toileting and have to pacify one child who, when the flush is pulled, gets a fright and starts screaming.

After that, Richard's big moment arrives when he takes the children round to the back garden for the treasure hunt. Simon translates Richard's instructions and the children scatter to scramble under bushes, climb trees and turn over stones – all searching for the little parcels wrapped in red crepe paper. Whoops of joy can be heard as treasures are found and opened.

While this is going on, Richard becomes aware of a group of white boys in High School uniforms who are on their way home from school and are now standing at the Rectory fence, gawping at the scene. However, they soon get bored and wander off. As they do, one of them shouts back an obscene comment about snot-nosed little kaffirs, followed by raucous laughter from his friends. The effect on Richard is like a cold blast snuffing out the excitement he has been enjoying in the party. Worries seep into his head about what these boys might tell their parents, and how that will add to the stories that already circulate in the town about the goings on at the Rectory. Fortunately, the partying children don't seem to notice, but Simon does. He comes over to Richard and with a hand on his shoulder says:

'You know, we should feel sorry for those boys. Basically, they are afraid you know. That is what makes them say things like that. It's only empty bravado. They are afraid because they have been brought up to think of black people as devils, with the result that they see these innocent little children as potential impi hordes that will come and murder them and rape their women in the night. So, doing anything for black people is like giving encouragement to the enemy.'

'Ja, I'm sure you are right.'

'Of course, I'm right. But let's forget about them and enjoy ourselves with the kids.'

By now all the treasures have been found and they return to the veranda where ice creams are handed out. Then, with thunder rumbling in the distance Simon says:

'It looks like a storm is coming so I think we had better get these children home. In any case, it's nearly five o'clock.' He shushes the children and, as he likes any opportunity to make a speech, proceeds to thank Richard and Noelene and the helpers and leads the children in a hearty applause.

Going to start the kombi, Richard notices it has a flat wheel. On closer inspection he discovers that the tyre has a gaping slash in it. Somebody has clearly sneaked into the driveway with the deliberate intention of causing trouble. Richard's heart sinks and thoughts flash through his mind. Is it one of the boys who were watching over the fence? Or could it be the men in the VW who stopped him on the road to KwaBophela?

Grim-faced, he goes back to tell the other adults of his discovery. They are shocked that someone could be so mean.

After some discussion Agnes says she will pay for a taxi to take the children back. She is thanked and one of the mothers offers to walk up the road to hail an African taxi while Simon and Richard change the wheel. In the meantime, Noelene phones the police to report the incident.

It is not long before a taxi, already half full of people, stops at the Rectory gate. There is much good humour as children are passed in to pile up on the adults' laps until there is really no space left. When Agnes wants to pay the driver, he refuses saying he wants to contribute to the party. Furthermore, he promises to return as soon as possible to take the rest of the children.

He has just left when a police van arrives. An officer, who Richard doesn't know, has been sent to investigate the incident. Richard shows him the damaged wheel and the officer takes out a notebook. He looks around at the remaining children who are now nosily running around the lawn. He pedantically takes down the vehicle registration, Richard's name and the Rectory address. He then asks, 'What are these Bantu children doing here?'

Richard is not sure how to answer. Just then Simon, who has been fitting the spare wheel stands up and looks at Richard who draws courage from his friend's presence and replies, 'I'm sorry, but what has that got to do with the damaged tyre?'

'Well, it might have been one of them that damaged the wheel.'

Richard replies with some exasperation.

'Officer, these are little five- or six-year olds! None of them would have the strength or the wherewithal to cut a tyre like that. In any case they have been under our supervision all afternoon.'

The officer notices the smile on Simon's face. Pointing his pencil towards Simon he asks, 'Is this your garden boy?'

Despite his fears and anger, Richard now sees the funny side to what is happening.

'No. May I introduce you to my colleague the Reverend Ndlovu?'

Simon holds out a hand to greet the officer who avoids him by peering down at his notebook and writing. With a smile and a shrug of his shoulders Simon puts his hands in his pockets.

After a moment, the officer turns to Richard, 'Have you any idea who might have done this?'

He answers cautiously, 'Not really. There were some High School boys who passed here and shouted some obscenities at us—'

'What is that?' the officer interrupts.

'Some obscenities, some swear words.'

'Oh, ja okay.' The officer makes more notes and then asks, 'Do you know these schoolboys, and could you identify them?'

'I know the names of one or two but not all of them. They often pass here, so I think I could identify most of them.'

Simon intervenes, 'Actually, I really don't think it was those boys. None of them—'

The officer snaps at Simon.

'Look here. I am investigating this matter. I will decide who are suspects.' He pointedly turns to Richard. 'Did you see anybody near the kombi?'

Richard includes Simon by facing him as he answers.

'Well I didn't, did you, Simon?' He shakes his head, so Richard continues. 'You see we were involved with the children and someone could easily have sneaked up the driveway without us seeing.'

While the officer is making further notes, Simon speaks to Richard making sure the officer can hear.

'It seems you live in a dangerous place you know. Even though you are a minister and you generously hold a party for poor children; like the Bible says, you give to the poor, and then somebody hates you so much for doing that they come and commit a criminal act in damaging your car. Well,' he says shaking his head, 'all I can say is, I'm glad I don't live here.'

The sarcasm is not lost on the officer, who snaps his notebook closed and sullenly says to no one in particular, 'We will let you know if we find out anything.' He turns and marches off to his van at the bottom of the drive while the two ministers, looking at each other, are barely able to stifle their giggles.

Just then the first big drops of rain begin to fall so the remaining children are ushered onto the veranda, and Richard goes to find some rain macs for Simon and himself so that they may complete changing the kombi wheel.

# Chapter 14

(Mid December 1967)

Richard had forgotten his promise to enquire about the bakkie, but having been reminded by Simon at the children's party he calls round at the Bakers' home late one afternoon the following week. Andy is sitting on his veranda with bare feet, no shirt, and with his potbelly hanging over his shorts. Alongside him on a table are a tankard of beer and a bowl of salted peanuts. As Richard walks up the path from the front gate Andy calls out:

'Hullo Richard. Nice to see you, especially as this is getting to be your busy time of the year, is it not?' He turns and calls out to his wife through the open front door. 'Darling, Richard is here. Do you mind bringing out another beer?' and without getting up he stretches out a foot and hooking it around the leg of another chair pulls it up for the minister. 'Man, it's been a hot day hasn't it? You know your predecessor, old Father Martin, he always did his visiting in a black suit. The poor old chap must have been so hot. It's nice to see ministers like you going with the times and wearing shorts and safari jackets.'

'Ja, it was difficult for those chaps, because that is what was expected of them in those days.' Richard sits down and continues. 'But not everyone is changing. Have you seen the dominee when he visits Pemberton? If he wore a safari suit, it would create a scandal amongst his people.'

Andy's wife comes out with a *Castle* lager and a glass on a tray. Richard stands up and greets her.

'Oh, don't get up,' she says as she puts the tray on the table. 'I hope you'll excuse me as I'm busy in the kitchen. I'll leave you two to talk.' She disappears through the door.

Richard decides to broach the subject of the bakkie right away.

'Andy, I've come to ask you a favour. You know we have this link with the Methodist Mission at KwaBophela and that we help them from time to time.'

'Umm no, I don't think I know about that,' he says, frowning and shaking his head. 'Perhaps it was mentioned on a Sunday when I wasn't there.'

Richard tells him about Simon's church, the co-operative, their need for a fridge, and how Andy might help.

'Ag, man,' he replies, 'I don't know if I can help you. You see, the insurance only covers the bakkie while it's being used for my business.'

'Yes, I told Simon the insurance might be a problem.'

'Well it is you see. And in any case, I don't know if I can trust that driver of mine. Ag man, help yourself to peanuts,' and he slides the bowl over towards Richard. 'He is not very reliable you know. Just last week he came to tell me there was a dent in the back of the bakkie. He says someone must have bashed into him when he was parked at the hardware store, because, he said, when he came out, there was the dent. Well,' and he pauses as he quaffs his beer, 'I think it was just an excuse. He probably backed into a tree or a lamp post or something. Now, you see if something worse happened and the bakkie was out of action, my whole business could grind to a standstill, and I really can't afford that. So, Richard, I hope you understand. I'm not just being difficult you know. I really would like to help you, but I'm afraid in this case my hands are tied.'

'Ja, okay. I can see that. I just thought it was worth coming to ask on the off chance that you might be able to help.'

'And I'm glad you did man. You know me, if I can help, I will. Like, you may not know it, but I promised Stan I'd bring those trestles over to the church hall on Saturday for the fete…' He pauses a moment as he realises, he has just contradicted what he said about the insurance. Then, with a frown he tries to redeem himself. 'You see strictly speaking I shouldn't do that, because that's also got nothing to do with my business. But you see, the difference is I will then be driving the bakkie, not that good for nothing black.' He smiles at the minister, feeling quite pleased with his explanation. Then he points at Richard's nearly empty glass. 'Now, what about another beer?'

Richard declines and says he needs to be getting on as he must get ready for a Confirmation class after supper.

Andy jokes, 'No rest for the wicked hey!'

Driving away, Richard reflects on the visit with a heavy feeling inside. He sees the insurance issue as just an excuse, and that really it is Andy's typically white attitude towards his black driver and being involved in doing something for black people that is the fly in the ointment. Thinking more generally about the situation in South Africa he wonders if it is possible to undo the decades of prejudice that go back to the days of slavery. He becomes really pessimistic as he considers the near impossibility of being able to effect change in well-meaning people like Andy, who are totally unaware of their deep racial prejudices.

Over supper he tells Noelene about the bakkie problem. His depression begins to affect her as well, until she suddenly brightens and suggests:

'Hey, you've got that minister's discretionary fund. What about using some of that to hire a bakkie for a day? Then you can go and collect the fridge for Simon.' Seeing the worried expression on Richard's face she adds, 'Look, I don't want to tell you what to do, but don't you think that's an idea?'

He hesitates and then says, 'Yeah, but I must admit I am becoming increasingly nervous about going to KwaBophela these days and whether the SB will carry out their threats.'

She frowns, 'Yes, it is scary, and I also worry whenever you go to KwaBophela. The thing is, if we kow-tow to the SB we will end up never being able to visit Simon and Florence again. I guess these people can't stand the fact that we have black friends…' She pauses for a moment. 'But look, you won't be doing anything illegal. Hey, I've got another idea. I am full of good ideas today! What about taking someone with you – like Stan? He's a liberally-minded person. At least talk to him about it and see what he says.'

'Yes, I could do that. I suppose I'm a coward at heart,' he says in a mournful tone.

'That's nonsense. How many white priests are willing to stand up in the pulpit and expose the injustices in our society like you do? How many have the courage to go and visit places like KwaBophela and Twenty-One and Three and then encourage others to go there too to see for themselves? Come on, you have shown tremendous bravery, that's why the SB is now on to you. You are a priest doing God's work and of course it will be tough sometimes. But if you back down you will end up doing nothing. We just have to hold on to the positives of what we are doing.'

'Ja, you are right as always, my love. I am becoming terribly negative. Okay, I'll speak to Stan. That way I'm also letting at least one of the church wardens know how I'm using that fund.'

After Evensong the following Sunday, Richard is with Stan in the vestry where the church warden is counting the collection.

'Stan, could I have a brief word?'

'Sure Richard. You look worried, what's the trouble?'

'No trouble. I just wanted to ask a favour.' He tells Stan about Simon's need for a bakkie to collect a fridge and that Andy Baker couldn't help. He explains, 'So I was thinking of using some of the money from the discretionary fund to hire a bakkie and to fetch the fridge for them. Do you think that is a reasonable use of the fund? And... and this is the favour. Would you like to come along to keep me company? You did say some time ago that you had never been to KwaBophela, so this could be an opportunity.'

'Well yes. By the way, it is only two weeks to Christmas. You are surely not planning to go before Christmas, are you?'

'No, but I was thinking of going early in the New Year when things are relatively quiet in the parish.'

'Great! I've got some leave early in January so that would be just fine. As far as the discretionary fund is concerned, it's your fund. You don't have to ask my permission or anyone's permission for that matter on how to use it. It's up to you.' Then glancing down at the small piles of coins on the table in front of him, he continues, 'And the way the church finances are going, we may not be able to make that planned donation to Simon's church, so if we help them in this way it could compensate for that.'

'Well I hope we will be able to make our donation in addition to this.'

'Oh yes, I hope so too, but we'll have to see. By the way, on the bakkie issue, nobody hires out bakkies here in Pemberton that I know of, but I have noticed a bakkie hire place on my way to work, just as I drive into Hopedale. I think it is called *Botha's Bakkies*. We could go there in my car and then you won't have to use the parish car.'

'Thanks. That will be a help. I'll let you know when I've made the arrangements.'

Richard leaves the vestry and wanders off down the road to the Rectory feeling slightly relieved. He does have some nagging thoughts that he was not quite honest with Stan about why he asked him to come along.

He duly fixes a date with Simon and Stan, and phones to reserve a bakkie from *Botha's Bakkies*.

# Chapter 15

(Tuesday 9th January 1968)

Early on the morning when Richard and Stan are to collect the fridge, the Rectory phone rings. It is Stan on the phone.

'Ag Richard, I'm terribly sorry, I'm not going to be able to make it today.' He coughs a couple of times. 'I'm feeling really crook. I dosed myself up last night in the hope that I would sleep it off, but I'm afraid I feel worse today.'

'Ja, I can hear you sound pretty bunged up. Well I'm sorry you can't come but I hope you are soon okay.'

When he puts the phone down Richard wonders what he is going to do now. He would like to cancel the trip, but Simon would be expecting him and there is no way he can let him know without going there to tell him in person. So, he reasons he might as well go anyhow.

Richard collects the bakkie and driving out of the vehicle renting yard he is not feeling at all comfortable, partly because he is driving an unfamiliar vehicle, but mostly because of his fears. The manager at *Botha's Bakkies* had asked where he was going and he very self-consciously told a lie, saying he was collecting some donated furniture from a farmer in the Pemberton district.

He constantly glances in the rear-view mirror, but there doesn't seem to be anyone following. It is a beautiful hot sunny day and he is driving through the gentle lush countryside that he loves, and so he tells himself to stop being paranoid and to try to enjoy the outing. Merino sheep are peacefully grazing on the rich grass, beyond which lies a blue strip of a lake with weeping willows dotted on its shore. After passing through Pemberton he continues through pine-covered hills. It is only when he turns off on the KwaBophela road that the pleasant country scene ends. Now the red earth shows through between tufts of brown grass. Here and there are some aloes and a few dusty bushes.

He stops as usual at the Bantu Affairs office to get a permit. The clerk is today particularly chatty and helpful. Richard explains what he will be doing and that he will be returning to KwaBophela later in the day and asks whether he will have to get another permit for his second trip.

'No, that won't be necessary. I will make this permit out to cover the whole day.'

Richard is anxious to get on, but the clerk is taking his time filling in the necessary forms, and he pauses a number of times to chat about the hot weather, and to complain that he can't turn the fan on because it blows all the papers about.

Eventually Richard emerges from the building and notices two well-dressed black men standing next to the bakkie. As he approaches, they greet him, and one asks if Richard wants to sell the bakkie. He explains to them that it is not his to sell and then gets in and drives off, thankful to be on the move again.

Arriving at the Mission, he sees his friend running up the hill to greet him. Simon explains that Florence has got tea ready for them.

Some chairs have been placed outside the Manse in the shade of a tree, and Richard is invited to make himself comfortable, but in fact it only increases his feelings of unease. He is feeling tense and impatient to get the job done. Simon is his usual ebullient self, chatting and laughing. After a while, Florence emerges from the Manse with tea and warm crispy jam scones, which she has taken from the oven only minutes before. Eating a scone Richard notices that a little group of pre-school children, some of them naked, who had been playing under the tree, are now gazing longingly at the scones. It makes Richard feel even more uncomfortable. He remarks, 'Simon, the tea and scones are lovely, but I do think we must get moving to get that fridge. I don't even know how far we have to go.'

Simon laughs, 'Hey, what's the hurry man? Have you got some meeting or something to go to?'

'No, I've got the bakkie for the day. I was just wondering how far we have to go.'

'Oh, it isn't far, so we've got plenty of time. The chaps that are coming to help us will be here soon and then we will go.'

It is at least another thirty minutes before a group of three men turn up. Then there are introductions, catching up on news and plenty of joking. After another attempt by Richard to hurry them up, they make their way to the bakkie and with Simon in the cab with Richard, and the three helpers on the back, they set off.

Simon directs Richard back to the main road which they cross onto a dirt track. Richard is driving at a snail's pace as the bakkie bumps and bucks over ridges and tussocks of grass. Even going slowly, Richard can hear the grass of the raised middle between the tracks brushing the underside of the vehicle. He hopes there are no unseen rocks that might cause damage. He reflects to himself that at least this is not Andy Baker's vehicle. After what to Richard seems like ages of twists and turns over the veld, they finally arrive at a trading store set amid a clump of tall blue gum trees surrounded by a small drab cottage and some huts. At one side, a windmill's vanes are slowly turning in the breeze with a clanking sound, pumping water into a small dam where a group of women are doing their laundry. Over the front of the store a huge sign with peeling paint announces *Seedats Store*. Next to it is a faded sign advertising *Joko Tea*.

They drive into a dusty clearing at the front of the store.

'Here we are,' shouts Simon and jumps out of the cab. With elaborate arm gestures and much shouting, he directs Richard to back up towards the entrance of the store. Having finally parked, they all go in. Coming in from the bright sunlight Richard's eyes take a moment to get used to the gloomy smoky atmosphere inside. The store is full of people milling around, several women are sitting on the floor, some with babies tied to their backs, while others are at a counter getting their purchases. He feels very self-conscious, being the only white person there. The shop is quite large, with a counter running around three sides. In front of the counter at one side are piles of cattle hides, pelts of wool and bags of produce. The hides together with the rank smell of sweaty people makes Richard feel a bit queasy. Behind the counter are rows of storage bins, large jars of various products and, reaching to the roof, shelves with bolts of material. In a raised pulpit-like structure in a corner sits a large Indian man that Richard assumes to be Mr Seedat. His glasses are sitting low on his nose and he appears to be writing in a ledger.

There are loud greetings all round and Richard is introduced to several customers as though he is some sort of celebrity. Mr Seedat also reaches down from his eyrie to shake the white man's hand. After the introductions, Simon and some of the men become involved in animated conversation. They are talking in Zulu which leaves Richard feeling excluded. He then begins to feel embarrassed, noticing that the group keep looking in his direction. At the same time, he is impatient as he has not yet seen the fridge and would like to get it loaded so they can be on their way. He interrupts the group to ask Simon.

'Is there a problem?'

'No man, no problem,' Simon laughs. 'They are just talking about you being the minister whose Bible was taken away by the police because they thought it was subversive.' He slaps his thigh and roars with laughter while the others provide a chorus of laughs. He continues, 'They are saying that for once the police were right. They had better watch out, because the Bible is a dangerous book when you take it seriously,' and here he and the others laugh even louder. Some come over to Richard and shake his hand warmly for the second time, now with admiration and congratulations. Richard feels a pleasant sense of pride seeping into him and enjoys basking in the adulation. He likes being admired. He momentarily imagines himself as a figure of hope to the oppressed people of South Africa.

While Richard is daydreaming, Mr Seedat has been issuing instructions to one of his workers, who leads Simon and his group out through a door at the back. They beckon to Richard to follow. In a shed at the back of the store stands a mammoth fridge covered in dust and rusting at the corners where the enamel has chipped off. Richard wonders how they are going to move it, as it looks as though it must weigh a ton. However, one of the men fetches a trolley onto which they can lift the fridge. With it precariously balanced they carefully trundle it out to the bakkie. There an argument breaks out amongst the group and Richard gathers from the elaborate gesticulations that several suggestions and counter-suggestions are being made, as to how to load the fridge. Eventually they call for reinforcements from some of the shop's customers and, with a cacophony of shouts and grunts, they manage to lift the fridge onto the bakkie, which sinks down on the back axle under the load. There is then further chatting and finally, with handshakes all round, they are ready, much to Richard's relief, to take their leave.

He inches the bakkie back along the track. There is now even less clearance under the vehicle, and he shudders each time he hears a scraping sound and worries that the vehicle's silencer will be torn off. He is concentrating so hard on driving that he is almost oblivious of Simon sitting next to him, until he feels a friendly slap on the shoulder.

'You know pal, you are a really good friend to me and my people. I know I can trust you. Can I talk to you about something that's worrying me?'

Amid his fears, Richard again feels a sense of pride that this fellow minister should want to consult him.

'Okay, go ahead, but you won't have my full attention, because I have to concentrate quite hard on getting over these bumps.'

Simon continues, 'It is something very confidential, but here in the bakkie nobody can hear us, so you see, it's a good time for me to talk.'

Now warning lights start flashing in Richard's brain as Simon carries on.

'You see, I've wanted to talk to you about this for some time. A young man in my congregation has come to me to ask for advice. He is a member of a secret *Umkhonto we Sizwe* cell in KwaBophela.'

The shock of hearing that name nearly causes Richard to steer into a bank at the side of the track. The colour has drained from his face, and despite the heat he feels shivers of alarm racing through his body. *Umkhonto we Sizwe* is the armed wing of the ANC and is regarded by the government as a terrorist organisation.

Simon appears to be unaware of the effect his words are having on his friend, and he continues:

'This man has told me that for a long time he didn't want to have anything to do with them, because he followed Luthuli and Gandhi in believing in non-violence. However, after a while he began to think he could not stand by as a Christian and not do something. So, he joined them to try to be a moderating influence. He told me that some of the young hotheads wanted to plant a bomb at Hopedale station.'

Richard takes a shocked sharp intake of breath, but Simon carries on.

'He said he argued them out of it. He told them it would be a stupid move, because if a lot of whites were killed, the defence force and the police would take revenge and there would be wholesale slaughter of our people. And of course, he was right. We would have had a Sharpeville massacre right here in KwaBophela.'

Richard is feeling stunned and wishes he had never heard any of this, but he cannot find the words to stop Simon who keeps on talking:

'He said, he told them that blowing up pylons and power lines and perhaps a reservoir or something like that, where no people are injured, would put more pressure on the government. It could even cause some overseas investment to dry up, and that might force the government to consider change. He says that is the policy they have been following. They did blow up a pylon and bring down the electric lines, but that was quickly repaired, and the police hushed it up, so it wasn't even reported in the papers. Now some of the younger members are getting impatient, saying they must do something more drastic and he thinks sooner or later they will get their way. So, he is wondering if he should continue to be one of them, and he wants my advice. What would you do if you were in my shoes?'

Richard is in a cold sweat. He is terrified by what he has heard. He knows that people get life sentences and are even hanged for being involved with stuff like this. What is more, anyone knowing anything about terrorism is legally bound to report it to the police or risk serious punishment. Richard knows he will not betray Simon's confidence, although he wishes he had never raised this subject.

Simon interrupts his thoughts.

'Hey, you are very quiet. Come on pal, you must have some ideas?'

'Man, I don't know. I would be dead scared knowing anything about *Umkhonto we Sizwe*.'

'Yea, but I'm his minister. Must I, like Pontius Pilate, wash my hands of him?'

Then another frightening thought occurs to Richard.

'Are you sure he is not an informer trying to trap you?'

'No, no, no. Whenever anyone talks to me about anything political, I always have that thought in the back of my mind. And whilst I could not be one hundred per cent sure, I am ninety-nine per cent sure this guy is genuine. Hey man, I know him from when he was a little piccanin, and he has always had a high sense of fairness and justice and has always been totally loyal to his tribe and his family. I don't think he could ever take a bribe, and that's what those despicable creatures do. In any case, we know who the informers are in KwaBophela. They are so stupid they stand out like sore thumbs. The one day they are in rags, the next they are strutting about in new suits, and they think we don't know where they get the money from. No, this man is not one of them,' he says, shaking his head.

They have now left the track and crossed the main road and the driving is a little easier as they near the Mission.

'Look, I really don't know what to advise you, but I'll think about it and I'll pray for you as you talk to this man. But please Simon, be careful. You are getting into deep water. This is...' Richard pauses not quite knowing what to say. Then he adds, speaking slowly with emphasis on each word, 'This is really terrifying stuff you know.'

'No man, we're used to it,' Simon responds lightly. 'Normal life for us is always dangerous. We can be walking along the road minding our own business, and then a cop stops us. The next minute, we find ourselves in jail.'

Their arrival at the Mission signals the end of that conversation although Richard is left with tremors in his stomach at the information he now knows.

Simon jumps out of the cab and starts shouting to a group of men nearby to come and help carry the fridge down to the church. Soon the bakkie is surrounded by people – men, women, and children who have materialized as if from nowhere. All are curious, some are in awe, and it is as though they have brought back some sort of trophy. There are plenty of helpers, so Richard follows the group of about seven or eight men, as slipping and sliding on the loose gravel, and with a cacophony of shouted instructions, they slowly manage to carry the heavy fridge down the hill followed by the crowd. Once it is installed in the church Richard says to Simon:

'Okay, I'm going to be on my way now, as I've still got to take the bakkie back to Hopedale.' At that Simon calls the people, who are now crowded in the building, to silence. He proceeds with a speech, first in Zulu and then switches to English, and with his hand on Richard's shoulder says:

'And all this is because our good friend here, Reverend Richard Atwell, has paid for the transport and been our driver today.' Applause breaks out while he shakes Richard's hand. As the clapping dies down, sounds of approval from the gathering can be heard, and several people come up to Richard to shake his hand and to express their thanks, some in English and some in Zulu. Richard's fears are momentarily dispelled by a pleasant warm feeling as he smiles and nods to each person thanking him.

Finally, he can make his escape. Simon walks up the hill with him. Clustered around the bakkie are a small group of children on their way home from school. Some have small satchels; others are carrying a slate and a battered exercise book or two. Although their school uniforms have seen better days and a few of the children are barefoot, they all look very neat and tidy and greet their minister respectfully.

'*Sawubona Mfundisi.*'

Amongst them Richard recognises Simon's youngest son, Moses, who comes over to Richard and, shaking his hand, shyly speaks to him in precise and deliberate English, 'Good afternoon Reverend Richard.'

Richard responds, 'Good afternoon. How are you doing at school?'

'I am doing very well thank you Sir.'

Simon then speaks up, 'You are going to be a *mfundisi* like your father, aren't you?'

His son answers modestly looking at the ground.

'I hope so Father. I shall study hard at school to one day get my matric so that I can be called to be a *mfundisi*.'

'That's good, my Son. Now run along. I am just saying goodbye to the English *mfundisi*.'

Richard moves quickly towards the bakkie, gets in and starts the engine, terrified that Simon may hark back to their earlier discussion.

Simon calls out, 'Thank you pal, and *hamba kahle*.'

'Yes, *sala kahle*,' Richard returns the traditional farewell.

As he turns the bakkie and drives off, his relief at getting away is tempered by the weight of the information he now carries. He is further troubled when on the way back the terrifying thought occurs to him that one of the men helping them may have been the MK cadre Simon was talking about. In that way he could be accused of associating with terrorists.

# Chapter 16

(Wednesday 10th Jan 1968)

The next day Richard arrives at church for his midweek service. He notices that the outside vestry door is open, which is unusual. He usually unlocks it, and he assumes one of the wardens has come to do some chores in the church. Stepping into the vestry he momentarily freezes with shock. Vestments are lying scattered on the floor; drawers have been tipped out and the safe door is standing ajar. The church has been burgled. His immediate fear is that the burglar or burglars might still be in the building. He quickly retreats. Standing outside he wonders what he should do.

Looking around he cannot see anyone in the vicinity. Shading his eyes from the sun's reflection he peers through a window, but all appears normal in the church. He thinks he must do something, so he cautiously approaches the vestry again and this time shoves the door wide open against the wall to ensure no one is hiding behind it. Then, picking up a heavy brass candlestick as a weapon, he quietly opens the door into the church, and gingerly surveys the building. Not a sound can be heard, and everything looks as it should be. Still thinking someone might be hiding in the church he enters slowly, holding the candlestick aloft. Moving down the nave he peers under the pews. Here and there in the aisle he notices blobs of black candle wax that he cannot recall seeing before. Nothing else has been disturbed, so he makes his way back towards the altar. There he notices that the altar candles are missing. He returns to the vestry where he sees what has happened to the candles. One candlestick is on the vestry table and the other is on a ledge in front of the open safe. The candles are completely burnt down with wax stalactites hanging from the rim of the holders and running into smudgy black pools of now solid wax. The curtains are drawn, and he assumes that the burglars came during the night and used candlelight rather than the bright electric lights, which might have alerted passers-by. He glances into the safe where, to his surprise, he sees that the silver communion vessels are all still there.

Richard is early for the service and no one has yet arrived. He thinks the first thing he must do is to report the break-in. He walks quickly round to the florist's shop next door to the church. There he explains to Mrs Owen what has happened and asks if she would please phone the police. She does so immediately. Replacing the phone after the call she says, 'They say they'll be around in a few minutes.' Then she adds, 'Have they got away with a lot?'

'It doesn't look like it. Of course, I haven't yet been able to check everything as I've left things as they are in case the police want to take fingerprints.'

With a shudder she comments, 'Oh, what is the world coming to, that people will stoop to stealing from a church?'

'I don't know. Anyhow, thanks for phoning, but I think I had better get back.'

Re-entering the church grounds, he sees a parishioner, who is early, peering in at the vestry door.

'Whatever has happened?' she asks.

He tells her about the burglary and that he has called the police. He adds, 'I hope we will be able to have our service, but we will probably start a little late.'

Just then Sergeant Lotter drives into the church parking area. He is accompanied by another officer whom he introduces as from the CID. The two officers go into the vestry and Richard hears the sergeant exclaim:

'Wow, they must have brought a very big crowbar to smash the safe open.' After a pause he calls out, 'Richard, will you come and look here?' Richard goes into the vestry and the sergeant points to the open safe. 'Is anything missing out of there?'

'Nothing that I have noticed. That's what puzzled me. All the communion vessels seem to be there, just as I left them.' Then Richard notices something else, 'Ah,' he exclaims. 'The registers aren't there.'

Sergeant Lotter points to the table.

'Aren't these them?'

'Oh, yes.' As he reaches to pick one up, the CID man stops him.

'No! Don't touch them. We might get some fingerprints.'

Sergeant Lotter adds, 'We don't want you sorting things out here yet, but from what you can see is there anything missing?'

Richard glances around, 'No, it's all a mess. I expected the communion silver to have been taken, but everything seems to be here, and we never keep any money in the church.'

'You are lucky. I bet they were disturbed so they made off. Well if you would like to leave us here, we will see if we can find any clues.'

'I was just going to conduct a service. May I take one of the communion chalices and the cruet of wine, then we will be able to have Communion?'

'Ja, it doesn't look as though any of that stuff was touched, so take them. I'll just have a quick look in the church and then you can let the people in.'

After the service Richard returns to the vestry where Sergeant Lotter and his colleague have completed their work. They are packing up a case of equipment and the sergeant says, 'I'm afraid we haven't been able to get anything usable. It looks like these chaps were wearing gloves. They certainly seem to know what they were doing, but that doesn't fit with them being disturbed and making a quick getaway. In any case, who is going to disturb them here? The church is well away from the road.' He pauses. 'Umm, I don't know. It is a mystery. Well you can tidy up now and I will be interested to hear if anything is missing. It looks like they were after something special. You see, if it were blacks, they would have taken the silverware and the tape recorder. They would have got good prices for those. Frankly, I'm puzzled.'

The mention of the tape recorder brings to the forefront of Richard's mind the anxiety he was trying to suppress. He glances up at the shelf where he keeps the audio tapes. They are not there.

'Oh no,' he mutters, realising this is probably the work of the SB searching for some evidence against him. He tells the sergeant, 'It looks as though my tapes have gone.' Richard rummages around amongst the vestments on the floor to see if the tapes have been thrown down somewhere, but they are nowhere to be seen.

Scratching his head, the sergeant wonders aloud, 'Who would steal tapes when there was all this other valuable stuff to be taken?' Then he seems to have another thought and asks, 'By the way, what was on the tapes?'

'Only some modern hymns I recorded for the youth services.'

The sergeant gives Richard a meaningful look, then glancing out the door to see where his colleague is, he whispers, 'I think I know what you are thinking. I am afraid all I can do is send in the usual report on the burglary, but I can assure you, I will have a private word, off the record you see, with my Captain. But I don't think it is going to make any difference. That branch of the police is a law unto themselves, and you know, frankly they make me sick.' He goes to the door, puts his cap on and turning back to Richard adds, 'Oh yes! If you find anything else missing, please let me know.'

# Chapter 17

(Wednesday 10th January 1968)

Later, on the same day as the burglary, Richard is attending an evening meeting of the Diocesan Mission Committee in the Hopedale Cathedral Centre. The meeting has gone on longer than usual but is now finally breaking up just before eleven o'clock. Above the hum of conversation and the scraping of chairs as the members stand and gather their papers, the chairman calls out:

'Can anyone give Nosipho a lift home?' After a slight pause he looks at Richard who has his head down, hoping the chairman won't notice him. 'Ah, Richard, you go in that general direction, don't you? Would you please take her?'

'Oh! Er... yes,' he answers with some embarrassment, wondering if he can think of an excuse. He turns to her, 'Where do you live?'

'I'm just about a mile off the main road on the old Glendale road. Going to Pemberton you pass that turn-off. You see, I don't think I'll be able to get a bus at this time of night, and taxis are terribly expensive.'

Richard reluctantly agrees, hoping his reluctance is not too obvious.

Nosipho is an attractive young woman who has just joined the Mission Committee. As they drive along, she tells him she used to work as a nursing sister at St Luke's Mission hospital just outside Hopedale. Now she has set up a small clinic at Glendale as there is no doctor for the thousands of African people living in that area.

Richard is only half-listening to her. He still has the morning burglary on his mind, with the suspicion that it was the work of the SB. So, he is doubly nervous about being alone with a black woman out in the country in a car late at night. Although there is little traffic around, when they turn off onto the old Glendale road, he notices the headlights of

Steyn opens the grilled door at the back of the van and commands, 'You heard the officer, get in.'

Nosipho reaches into Richard's car for her handbag that is lying open on the seat after the other officer's inspection.

'Leave that,' shouts Steyn and he springs towards Nosipho, grabs her arm and drags her roughly away from the car.

'I only want to get my handbag.'

'Well you can't. Get in the van.' He pushes her into the van, slams the door and locks it.

Richard feels he should reprimand them for being so rough and rude, but he is too terrified to get any words out. He fears that Nosipho must think him a coward at the lame way he has behaved.

'Now you can get back in the car and drive me to the charge office and don't try anything funny because I'll be right here next to you.'

Richard obeys with difficulty. He is shaking so much he has trouble getting the key into the ignition slot, but finally manages it and restarts the car. He turns the car around. The officer stops him from driving off.

'Wait! Wait for the van and then we can go.' He is watching over his shoulder. When the van's headlights pierce into the car he instructs Richard, 'Okay, we can go. Keep your speed between forty and fifty until we get to town so that the van can keep up with us.'

Once they are on their way, the officer becomes quite chatty.

'These Renault cars are bloody good you know. I had one and it never gave any trouble even though I drove it a lot over rough farm roads. This is a new model isn't it?'

'Yes.'

After a while he talks to Richard again.

'Look, don't get me wrong. I'm sorry I have to apprehend you, but you know as well as I do it's the law of the land. Now, I know there are lots of white men who like to have a bit of black pous now and again and it seems these young Bantu girls can give a chap a really good time, but however nice, it is just not right. That's why I have to do my duty.'

After this little speech he is silent for a while.

Richard finally manages to say, 'In my case it is not like that. We were not doing anything illegal. We were at a meeting in the Anglican cathedral, and if you phone Canon Wilson he will be able to verify that he asked me to give Nosipho a lift as there would have been no buses this late, and we left barely twenty minutes before you stopped us, so there was no time to do anything wrong and, in any case, I had no intention of doing anything wrong.'

'Well, that's your story. You can put that in your statement at the charge office.' Then, as a new thought suddenly occurs to him, in a surprised tone he asks, 'By the way, are you a minister then?'

'I'm an Anglican priest.'

This is met by an uneasy silence while Richard wishes he had worn his clerical collar to identify himself. He thinks it might have commanded a little respect from these policemen, and he might not have landed in this situation.

Finally, the officer says, '*Jislaik* man, I didn't realise. I am sorry. I didn't mean to offend you by what I said.'

Richard does not respond. They have now reached the city limits and the officer begins to give directions to the police station where they soon pull up in front of a pair of barred gates. The officer leans out his window and shouts at a black constable sitting on a box just inside the gates. The constable jumps up, opens the gates and, standing to attention, salutes as they drive in. Richard is directed to a parking space in a dark gloomy yard. He stops the car and switches off the engine. This is not the entrance Richard used when he and Noelene came to see the Brigadier. That thought leads Richard to think it won't do any harm and may help if he mentions that contact.

'By the way, last month my wife and I were invited to a meeting here with Brigadier Bezuidenhout.'

The officer looks at Richard with raised eyebrows and, after a pause, cocks his head to one side and asks, 'Do you mind telling me what that was about?'

'It was in connection with some anonymous threatening letters I have been receiving.'

'Who would do a thing like that to a minister?'

'I don't know.' Then, feeling a little more courageous he adds, 'But I've got a shrewd idea as to who is behind it.'

'And who is that?'

'I don't think I should tell you.'

'Did you tell the Brigadier?'

Now Richard is not feeling so sure of himself.

'Well, not really. No.'

The policeman seizes his chance to reassert his authority while at the same time thinking he might impress the Brigadier by getting some new information on a case that was before his boss.

'You know, you are not allowed to withhold information from the police. If you think you know who did this, it is your duty to tell me.'

It is too late but now Richard regrets saying anything and feels he has dug himself into a bigger hole than he was in before. He answers nervously, 'Well, I've got no proof, so perhaps it's probably nothing.'

The officer feels he is on to something and says sternly, 'Look, if you don't tell me, I could also charge you for withholding information from a police officer.'

'Okay.' He pauses. 'I think it is the Security Police because in the past they searched my home, but of course I have no proof, so really it is nothing.'

'Ah! Well we'll see about that.'

All this has taken place while they are still sitting in Richard's car. Now the officer says to Richard, 'By the way, I am Warrant Officer van de Walt and you are the Reverend…?

'Reverend Atwell.'

'Okay Reverend Atwell. I'm afraid I must ask you to hand over your car keys and then will you please follow me.'

Richard passes the keys over to the policeman and gets out the car. He is in a daze, but with a jolt becomes aware that the van with Nosipho, although it drove in behind them, is now nowhere to be seen. As he follows van de Walt, despite his confusion and fear he manages to ask, 'Where is the lady, Nosipho?'

'Ag, don't worry about her. The girl will be taken care of.'

Richard wonders what that means, and feelings of guilt that he has not spoken up for her are piled on to all his other feelings. He is led down a long corridor which smells like a stationery store. They pass two other policemen and one jokes, 'Ah! Van de Walt strikes again.'

Van de Walt ignores them and shows Richard into a small office that is bare of any furnishings except a table and two chairs. He tells Richard to sit down while he calls down the corridor to another policeman who brings in a file of forms. Van de Walt takes down Richard's personal details and his statement as to why he was with a Bantu woman on the old Glendale road. The officer's writing is very laborious, and Richard has to repeat himself a number of times. The term *Anglican* also defeats the officer so Richard spells it out for him. The time this takes increases Richard's anxiety and irritation.

Eventually van de Walt says he is going to make some enquiries and he calls in another policeman to wait with Richard. Richard hopes that at last he is going to phone Canon Wilson and that he will soon be released.

The policeman who was summoned stands at the door with his arms folded, looking bored. Suddenly Richard is desperate for a pee. He asks, 'May I go to the toilet?'

'Okay. Come with me.'

They turn a corner into another long gloomy corridor with an iron barred gate. Attached to the officer's belt is a huge bunch of keys. He unlocks the door and points to a loo.

'I'll wait here for you.'

There is no door to the toilet which stinks of urine. He gets his fly open just in time before the stream comes gushing out. When finished he pulls the chain. There is a loud clank, but nothing happens. He tries again with the same result.

The officer calls out, 'Ag, leave that. It has got to be fixed.'

Richard follows him back to the office where he sits down. He looks at his watch. He should have been home at least half an hour ago and realises Noelene will be worried as to what has happened to him. He asks the officer, 'My wife will be worried that I'm not yet home. May I phone her?'

'You will have to ask Warrant Officer van de Walt.'

Richard keeps looking anxiously at his watch. There is nothing else to do. After over half an hour the door opens and van de Walt comes in.

'Look,' he says as he scratches his head. 'I'm afraid we can't let you go tonight. As you mentioned to me, your name is on the Security Police files. When I spoke on the phone to the Major, he said he wants to talk to you. Apparently, he thinks you can help them with some investigation they are involved in. Now, he can only see you in the morning, so I'm afraid we are going to have to detain you here.'

Naively Richard asks, 'Can't I go home? I can come back in the morning whenever you want me.'

'I'm afraid that is not possible. Now first of all you have to hand over your watch, your wallet, and that ring,' he points to his wedding ring, 'and I need to take your fingerprints. Then Officer Voster will show you to the cells.'

Richard tries again, 'But is that really necessary?'

'It is the procedure.'

'Can I at least get a message to my wife that I won't be coming home tonight? She will be terribly worried by now, probably thinking I've had an accident.'

The sergeant hesitates for a while and then says, 'Well, I'll see what I can do.'

Richard hands over the requested items. In the meantime, Voster has been out and is returning with the fingerprint equipment. Richard feels intense embarrassment at having to submit to this process. Having taken the prints, the policeman points to a grubby looking rag and a jar containing what looks like car grease.

'You can use some of that to clean your hands.' He then leads him back to the barred gate where the toilet is. Again, he unlocks, and they descend some steps and enter a dank dimly-lit corridor with barred cell doors on either side. He pushes open a door to an empty cell.

'This is where you sleep. Now you must give me your belt and shoelaces.'

'Why is that?'

'It is the regulations.'

Telling himself to be brave, Richard enters the cell, removes his belt, sits down on a bunk, and takes off his shoes. He cannot believe it is necessary to take out the laces.

'Look, must I really give you the shoelaces?'

Voster answers with some irritation, 'You will do as you're told.'

'Okay, okay, I was just asking.' He pulls out the laces and hands them over.

Voster drops the items into a bag, walks out of the cell, swings the door closed with a loud clank and locks it. Through the bars he says, 'The light will go out in about ten minutes.'

The sound of his footsteps grows softer as he struts off down the corridor. Richard hears him mount the steps, the rattle of keys and the shluck of the lock in the gate. Then there is silence except for some muffled sounds from one of the other cells that sounds like someone snoring. A moment of panic grips him. He jumps up and with his trousers sagging, lunges at the door, grabs the unyielding bars and cries, 'No, no, no.'

A slurred voice calls from one of the other cells.

'Ag, shrud up.'

Strangely Richard finds some slight comfort in that response. At least he is not alone. Hitching up his trousers he glances around at his bleak surroundings. The walls are unplastered but the brickwork has a covering of whitewash. In the corner is a zinc toilet with no seat or lid. The bunk is a concrete base on which there is a thin stained mattress with two folded blankets. The floor is also concrete and looks as though it has a film of dampness over it. There is a strong smell of *Dettol*. High in the ceiling is a single light bulb behind a wire grill.

Feeling devastated, he sits down on the mattress with his head in his hands. He cannot believe he is in this situation. He is still sitting like this when the light goes out. The darkness terrifies him further and he remains sitting there, feeling unable to move. After a while, his eyes become accustomed to the dark. He can discern a dull glow coming through a barred window high up on the wall. Eventually he forces himself to get up and spread the one blanket on the mattress, from which a slight smell of vomit emanates. He feels his stomach heave but manages to control himself, and after a while begins to think he is imagining the smell. He thinks he must try to get some sleep. Taking off his jacket he folds it to use as a pillow. He lies down staring at the dark ceiling. The mattress is lumpy and uncomfortable. He feels cold but finds that he is sweating. He always says his prayers before sleeping and, remembering his routine, he gets up and kneels on the hard, cold floor. He tries to pray, but finds his mind keeps straying. His head is full of a jumble of thoughts, flitting between fears of what might happen, what has happened, whether van de Walt has phoned Noelene, and what has happened to Nosipho? He thinks that whether they notified Noelene or not, she is going to be terribly anxious. He hopes she will phone the Bishop even though it is the middle of the night, and perhaps he might be able to use his influence to rescue Richard from this awful plight. Of course, the Bishop would get on to the Diocesan solicitors and the thought occurs to Richard that he might have demanded to see a solicitor. It is too late now, but he determines to do so in the morning. He begins to castigate himself for not being more assertive. He thinks of Simon and imagines he would have spoken up in no uncertain terms, while he himself has allowed these young policemen to get away with their atrocious behaviour. Feelings of being a coward increase his despondency. His whole body feels taut and his head is throbbing. Eventually, exhausted, he asks God to forgive him and to help him in the mess he has got himself into. He lies down on the bed, wriggling around to try to get as comfortable as possible.

Gradually he becomes aware of shouts in Zulu that sound as though they are coming from quite far away. Of course, it then occurs to him; the police cells are segregated, and the shouts must be from African prisoners. He supposes that is where Nosipho must be. After a long time, he drifts into a half sleep.

When he wakes, he is not sure if he has slept at all, but then realises he must have dozed off because he has dreamt that he was apologising to a stern-faced Bishop Andrew for getting himself into trouble. He lowers his legs over the side of the bunk. His body feels tired and stiff. The horror of his situation closes in on him. He sits on the edge of the bunk with his head in his hands, and tears quietly roll down his cheeks.

# Chapter 18

(Thursday 11th January 1968)

Richard is still sitting on the bunk when suddenly the light comes on. He hears the hollow sounding clank of the barred gate. From one of the other cells there is a groan and then a flood of swearing. In the light the walls seem awfully close as though the space has shrunk during the night. Through his watery eyes he sees lines of scrawled graffiti, snatches of the history of previous occupants. Forcing himself, he gets up, wipes his eyes with a handkerchief, and clutching his trousers goes to peer through the bars. Whatever is happening is taking place down the corridor out of his sight. Turning back, he notices for the first time a small metal shelf fixed in the corner. On it is a plastic bowl, a jug, and a grey-looking cloth. He feels dirty and the possibility of a wash slightly raises his spirits. He goes to the jug, but finds it is empty. Just then he hears footsteps, and a very young-looking white police officer appears.

'I see you are awake. You'll get some breakfast in a little while.'

'My jug is empty. May I have some water to have a wash?'

'I'll tell the boy,' and he walks off down the corridor.

Not having his watch, Richard has no idea of time and that adds to the disturbance he feels. There is only a glimmer of light through the window so he assumes it must still be very early. He feels totally helpless. All he can do is sit and wait while his mind scatters over what has happened to him over the last twelve hours. He tries but fails to arrange his thoughts rationally. The one thought he can hang on to, which he keeps repeating to himself, is that he must demand to see a solicitor.

The dull light in the window grows gradually brighter and, in the distance, the increasing hiss and intermittent roar of traffic can be heard. The world of everyday life is resuming but Richard feels acutely cut off from it. Eventually the officer returns with an African man dressed in convict's garb, carrying a tray. He unlocks the door so that the convict may place the tray on the shelf. The convict takes the jug and wanders off while the officer relocks the door and marches away. Despite all his anxieties, the thought strikes Richard that even white prisoners have black servants to attend to them.

He does not really feel like eating but picks up the tray and, sitting on the bunk, inspects what he has been given. There is a bowl of mealie-meal porridge swimming in what looks like skimmed milk; a slice of brown bread with a white smear of what he guesses is margarine, and a cup of coffee. He decides he must eat something, but the cold porridge makes him want to vomit and in any case a fly has flown in and settled on the porridge bowl. He brushes the fly away, but it keeps returning so he gives up. He tries eating the bread which tastes slightly stale. It feels very dry in his mouth, but he manages to wash it down with the sickly-sweet lukewarm coffee that he has managed to keep away from the fly's attention.

After a while, the African convict returns with the jug of water, which he passes to Richard through the bars. When Richard is alone again, he tries to have a wash. Splashing the cold water on his face he feels the stubble of his beard and guesses that razors would not be provided. Completing his brief ablutions, he sits down on the bunk. While waiting, he starts gearing himself up to be more positive.

Finally, the young policeman he saw earlier appears. While he is unlocking the cell, Richard attempts to be assertive:

'Look, I'd like to see my solicitor.'

'You'll have to ask the sergeant,' is the abrupt reply. The officer continues, 'Here, you can have your belt and laces back and then you must come with me,' and he tosses the items onto the bunk.

At last things are happening and Richard feels hopeful. He tries to lace his shoes quickly, but it is difficult as his hands are shaking so much. The officer at the door becomes impatient:

'Come on, come on. I haven't got all day.' Richard finally completes the tasks and with his jacket over his arm follows the officer. He is taken back to the little room he had been brought to on the previous night. A policeman is sitting there, apparently waiting for him, with a file and some sheets of paper scattered on the table.

'Ah, Reverend Atwell. I am Sergeant Botha. Please sit down.'

Richard sits down opposite him. The policeman who escorted him stands at the closed door as if on guard.

Richard decides to speak up straight away.

'Sergeant, I believe I have the right to legal representation, so I would like to phone my solicitor.'

The sergeant holds up his hands. 'Hey, hey, hey, slow down. We are coming to that. What I must tell you is that we are now holding you under the *General Law Amendment Act No 37 of 1963* which provides for a person to be held for questioning. Now, there is no charge against you, so you see there is no need for legal representation.' He shrugs his shoulders. 'In a short while you will be taken to another station, where Major Beukes wants to question you about certain matters of state security. So, there is really nothing more for me to say. Oh, yes. I must give you a receipt for the things you handed over last night,' and he passes one of the sheets of paper to Richard who is staring at the sergeant in complete bewilderment.

'What is all this about?'

'That I am unable to say, but the Major will explain it all to you.'

Richard persists. 'Now, last night I asked Officer van de Walt to phone my wife to tell her what had happened. Did he do that and what did she say?'

'I'm sorry, I cannot comment on that.' He turns to the officer at the door and hands him the file and a large envelope and stands up. 'I think they are ready to go, so you can take Reverend Atwell to the van.'

Remaining seated, Richard tries again.

'But what is this all about? I should be told. You can't just keep me without legal representation or at least telling me why I am being held.'

'But that is exactly why we are holding you under the provisions of the 1963 Act.' The sergeant looks at Richard with a pleading expression. 'Now, please do not make things difficult for us, because I really cannot answer any of your questions. But don't worry, it will all be explained to you. Now the Major is expecting you and we do not want to keep him waiting, do we? So, the sooner you get on your way the better.'

'Well, where am I meeting this Major?'

In an exasperated tone the sergeant answers, 'As I said, I can't answer any of your questions, so save your breath Reverend Atwell and please do as I say.'

'This is certainly not right,' mumbles Richard as he stands up. 'This Major will have a lot to explain to me.'

He follows the policeman out to the back yard where he had been brought in last night. He notices his car is still parked where he had left it. He is led to a police van where another officer is waiting in the driver's seat with the engine ticking over. Richard never thought he would ever have to be taken anywhere in what is known as a Black Maria – although it is not black but green. His escort tells him to get in. At least he isn't pushed in like Nosipho was last night, but he still feels embarrassed at being transported like a criminal. The van has been standing in the sun and the stuffy heat hits Richard as he climbs in. Inside the smell reminds him of old socks and it is gloomy as the only light comes from louvered ventilation slits in the metal sides of the van. Crouching down he makes himself as comfortable as possible, using his folded jacket as a cushion on the wooden slatted benches that run along either side. The officer locks the back door of the van. Richard hears him getting in with the driver, a door slams and the van moves off. Richard cannot see where they are going because all that is visible through the louvered ventilation slits is the passing road surface. He tries to follow the direction of the journey by noting the turns the van makes but is soon totally confused as to where they are or in what direction they are travelling. In any case it is difficult to prevent himself from being thrown from the seat when the van swings around a bend, so he wedges himself in a corner and hangs on to the slats of the seat for more stability.

The sinister nature of what is happening to him begins to bring back the desperate fear he felt in the prison cell. He feels like crying out but realises it would be pointless as any cry would be drowned by the throaty roar of the van's motor. After a while he becomes aware that the noise of traffic and the sounds of the city have diminished, and the van is travelling faster so, he concludes, they must have left Hopedale. Because he cannot hear much passing traffic, he guesses they are not on the main motorway, but he still does not know which road out of Hopedale they are on. At least now the air is circulating in the van and the heat is not so intense. It all helps him to think he must try to do whatever he can. He holds a cupped hand over his ear to the wall of the cab in an attempt to pick up any conversation from the two policemen, but all he can hear is the rattle of the motor and the whistle of the tyres on tarmac.

Eventually the van slows down, and Richard hears the scrunch of gravel as they pull off the road; they come to a stop and the motor stalls. Now he can just hear the driver asking, 'But where do I go? I can't see any road.'

'You dom kop,' the other responds. 'They don't advertise it. Just drive slowly through these bushes and then you'll see the track.'

The van is restarted, and they move slowly forward. Suddenly the vehicle tilts to one side, then jolts back and, even hanging on, Richard still bumps his head on the side. Branches brush against the van and some twigs and leaves protrude through the ventilation slots and break off, falling into the van. They travel a little faster. Then the van stops again and the motor is switched off.

Richard hears the driver say, 'Should I hoot?'

The escort responds irritably, 'Don't be stupid. We don't want everyone for miles around to hear us. Just wait. They have seen us and will soon open the gate.'

After a while there is the sound of heavy gates being opened and they move forward. Finally, the vehicle comes to a stop and he hears the officers getting out of the cab. There is a rattle as the back door is unlocked. The escort commands, 'Come on, get out.'

Richard shuffles himself out of the van. His eyes take a moment to adjust to the bright sunlight. Shading his eyes with one hand, he glances around. He sees that they are in a large compound and have stopped in front of what looks like a rambling old farmhouse. To the side of it are several rondavels and out-houses scattered around. The whole complex is surrounded by a high boarded fence topped by razor wire. Before he is able to take in everything, he is told, 'Come with me.'

He starts to walk but is feeling so stiff and unsteady that he stumbles. Stopping for a moment to regain his balance, he stretches himself, while the officer turns and looks at him with a frown.

'Come on,' he commands, and Richard follows him up the veranda steps. At the same time as they reach the top of the steps the front door opens and a rather podgy middle-aged clean-shaven man with a bald head comes out. He is casually but smartly dressed in shorts and an open-neck shirt. He looks like a farmer. He offers his hand.

'Good morning Reverend Atwell. I'm Major Beukes.' Unsure of himself Richard goes along with the handshake. 'My goodness! You look as though you had a bad night. I suppose you would like to freshen up, so I'll take you straight to your room.' The Major's speech and manner is slow and relaxed, and Richard begins to think his fears might have been unfounded. He follows him into the cool dark gloom of the house. Rounding a corner in the corridor the Major opens a door.

'Here's your room. Please make yourself at home.' He points to the far side of the room. 'That door over there leads to a bathroom. I think you will find all you need and there is an electric razor in the bathroom cabinet if you would like to have a shave. Your wife is also sending some fresh clothes and they should be here by this afternoon. If there is anything else you need, please tell me. I think you probably would like to have a shower, so I'll leave you and will call back for you when you have had a chance to settle in.'

He closes the door. Richard is left feeling totally baffled and speechless. It is all so unexpected and confusing. The one minute he is a prisoner in a police van, the next it appears he is being welcomed as a house guest. Feelings of relief are tempered by nagging fears. Richard is a man who likes to be in control and now he feels he is being moved around at the will of others. The phrase 'settle in' sounds particularly ominous, as though he is there for an extended stay. It is confirmed by the fact that Noelene is sending some clothes. He is glad to know they have contacted her, and he wonders how much she knows about what is happening. At least, she is aware that he has not been killed in an accident. But he feels completely cut off from the people he knows and from the life he has been living, as though he has entered a parallel world. It is all very unreal.

He looks around the room which reminds him of a motel room. It looks comfortable and functional, but that is it. He takes a few steps and glances into the bathroom. The clean white towels and the gleaming chrome of the fittings confirm his thoughts that it is just like sanitized motel accommodation.

Despite his fears and bewilderment, he decides that a shower and shave will boost his morale.

Having showered he does feel more positive, until he faces the reality of having to dress in the same grubby underwear and clothes which he thinks still smell of the police cell. As ashtray. 'I decided there and then that I owed it to him to ensure that nobody else should be killed like he was. So, I decided to become a policeman. Having a degree helped me because I rose through the ranks quite quickly. I also spent some time in America, in Alabama actually, learning how the police did things there. That was a major influence on my philosophy of life. I came to see the Negro as epitomised by their songs and their music, like "Ol' Man River, he just keeps rolling along". For them, life is all about lazing around and doing nothing, just letting nature take its course. You see, the black man is a child of nature. He's got no sense of individual property like we have. He thinks he can just take whatever he comes across. He doesn't have to work for it, because to him it is all part of the given-ness of the world.'

Richard is sinking into the warm comfortable chair, and finding it very hard to keep awake. His eyelids keep drooping, his head feels heavy and he is beginning to nod.

'Ag, I'm so sorry, I'm being boring. I see you are beginning to doze off.'

That snaps Richard out of his torpor. He wasn't aware the Major was watching him so closely. He feels at a great disadvantage and apologises, 'I'm terribly sorry. It is just so warm, and I haven't had much sleep. May I have a drink of water? That will help me.'

'Certainly, certainly. I could offer you something stronger, but that won't help you stay awake, so we'll keep the cocktails for this evening.'

As if by magic there is a knock on the door and a uniformed officer appears.

'Would you bring the Reverend a glass of water with ice please?'

Richard realises then that there is a button somewhere under the desk which the Major operated to summon the officer. A carafe of iced water covered with a white cloth is brought in with two glasses and placed on a drinks cabinet at the side of the desk. The Major gets up; the ice tinkles into the glass as he pours the water and hands it to Richard.

'Thank you very much,' says Richard feeling even more obliged to this man.

Sitting down again the Major continues speaking:

'Now, where was I? Oh yes. You see, lazing around and sucking a piece of straw is part of the nature of the black man. You can't change that,' he says shaking his head. 'Now the white man is not like that at all. He likes to find out things for himself. He likes to improve himself. Why do you think all the important scientific developments happened in Europe, whereas the natives of Africa were still in the dark ages until the white man arrived? And look at those countries where blacks now rule. Absolute chaos! So, I believe that we whites are a bastion of civilization here in South Africa.' Sitting forward with his elbows on the desk he becomes quite intense and taps his pen on the desk as if to press each word home. 'We have and must continue to develop this country. We owe it, not only to ourselves, but also to the black people you know. We must show them better ways of living. I think that is why God led white settlers here in the first place.' Then gesturing towards Richard with the pen. 'That is why I can understand people like you. You want to help the blacks.' Lowering his voice he assumes a wistful, sad tone, and slightly shaking his head continues, 'Where you go wrong is that you see the blacks as though they are white. In a way you are colour-blind, and a person who is colour-blind can never see things as they really are. Treating the blacks as if they are whites is like trying to get a baboon to recite Shakespeare. It will never happen. You may be able to teach him certain tricks, but you can't change his nature.'

Despite his tiredness and fear, Richard is shocked by the Major's comparison and feels he must show some dissent.

'But black people are still people. You cannot compare them to animals. It would be like comparing a baboon with a... a... with a trout.'

'No. I think my comparison is a valid one, if perhaps a little overstated. Let me tell you this. Although my church doesn't like it, I have read Darwin's *Origin of the Species*, and it makes a lot of sense to me. I have heard of bishops in your church who accept the theory of evolution and who explain how evolution can be reconciled with the Bible. I agree with those bishops. Over millions of years we have all evolved from the apes. But the whites have evolved much faster than the blacks. Even before Darwin, the naturalist Linnaeus drew attention to the vast differences between Europeans and blacks. The blacks are much closer to the apes, not only by skin colour but also their frizzy hair, flat noses and thick lips. Their reasoning powers are still in a developmental stage. And, like animals they also resort to violence more quickly. Now those are facts, and we can't bluff ourselves that they are the same as us. They are still evolving and, perhaps in a few hundred years' time, they may catch up, but right now there is a gulf between us.'

Richard's feeling of being at a disadvantage increases as he has not read Darwin and only knows vaguely about Linnaeus. Also, despite taking regular sips of water, all this philosophising is making him feel even more tired and so he says nothing more, having little energy or inclination to pick an argument with Beukes.

'Now, as I said,' the Major continues, 'we whites have certain duties and responsibilities. You see, Russian and Chinese communists have infiltrated Southern Africa and they want to extend their power here. They are using the blacks as their puppets to ferment revolution and to destroy white power so that they can then move in and set up a Marxist state here.' He notices that Richard is looking doubtful and shaking his head. 'You look as though you don't believe me. You see we have a lot of information that for security reasons we unfortunately can't divulge to the public.' Beukes raises his eyebrows and points at Richard with his pen. 'If you knew some of the things I know, it would make your hair stand on end. But it is of course common knowledge that there are military training camps just outside our borders where young black men are being trained in guerrilla tactics. And communist propaganda is influencing many black people, and especially the black movements like the ANC. For example, I have heard young umfaans say that they are determined to take over white jobs like those of train drivers, even if they make a mess of it and drive the trains into the sea. Those were their very words. You see, they do not care what the consequences will be as long as the whites are overthrown. And that is just what the communists want so that they can step in. Now it is our duty to stop them or the whole of South Africa will go up in flames.' He pauses while looking thoughtfully at the ceiling. Then he looks down at Richard. 'This leads me to the question of why you are here. I want you to listen to something.'

From a drawer he takes a small tape recorder. He slots in a cassette and presses the start button. There are a lot of crackles and noise. Then, in between the noise, Richard hears snatches of an African man speaking. He hears the word *Umkhonto*, but the rest of the sentence is drowned out by what he thinks sounds like the straining revs of a car engine. The Major presses the pause button and almost whispering says, 'Did you recognise that voice?'

'No, I can't say that I did. In any case, it is an awfully bad recording.'

'Ja, I apologise for that, but it doesn't matter. Perhaps you will recognise this voice.' He plays another bit of the tape and Richard is stunned when he recognises his own voice saying, 'You must be careful'. The blood drains from his face, he feels himself going cold, and he looks up at Beukes who is watching him closely.

'Well, that's me, but... I don't understand.'

There is an uncomfortable silence. Then the Major explains, 'That's right. You see, unfortunately in the police we sometimes must do things secretly in order to carry out the work of protecting our nation. That vehicle you hired was fitted with a hidden tape recorder. Unfortunately, it did not work very well. It seemed to pick up your voice better than the Bantu you had with you. But we heard enough to know that he was talking to you about *Umkhonto we Sizwe*. Now, you can help us by telling me what he told you.'

In shock, Richard does not know what to say. He is overwhelmed by fear and hopes Beukes does not notice how frightened he is. If they think he is involved with this terrorist organisation he will be in great danger. He could get a life sentence. For a few moments he feels paralysed, staring in a transfixed way at Beukes who meets his gaze. Then he blurts out, 'I've got nothing to do with *Umkhonto*, I promise you.'

Leaning back in his chair and folding his arms the Major replies sardonically, 'I'm not accusing you of anything. All I'm after is what was said in that bakkie.'

Richard realises that he must be incredibly careful. He has no idea what Beukes has up his sleeve. He might have been able to glean a lot more from the recording than he is letting on.

'Well, it was a... a general conversation.' He pauses for a moment searching his mind as to what to say. Then he blurts out with emphasis, 'Neither of us has anything to do with *Umkhonto.*' After another short silence he adds, 'But we both know from news reports that they are carrying out violent acts and we were saying, as Christians, we disagreed with violence.' Richard feels as though Beukes is staring him down, so he takes refuge in a drink of water.

'Oh come, come Reverend. You do not expect me to believe that was all that was said. Look, let me tell you something more. We already know that *Umkhonto we Sizwe* is operating in the KwaBophela area. Now this Bantu minister will be sure to have his ear to the ground. Also, from what we know about him, he is the sort of person who would be trusted by an organization like *Umkhonto* and the people would speak to him and tell him things. It also seems as though he trusts you. So, you see, you are in a key position.' He pauses, looking at Richard as though waiting for a reaction. When Richard does not respond he looks at his watch. 'But look, it's nearly lunch-time. I'll tell you what. You go and have your lunch, think about what we have talked about and have a siesta this afternoon. Then later we can talk again.'

Despite feeling at a great disadvantage, Richard summons up the courage to ask, 'Major, I would like to know how long I'm going to be kept here, what my legal position is, and what my wife knows, because you told me that she is sending some clothes for me.'

In an exaggerated gesture the Major throws up his arms as he exclaims:

'Oh, I do apologise.' He continues, 'The sergeant at the charge office should have told you. You are here for questioning under the *General Law Amendment Act of 1963*. Now, the questioning process can take many days or only a few hours. It all depends on you. As far as your wife is concerned, she was notified that you would be away from home for some time as you are a witness in matters of state security and that, if she so wished, she could hand in some clothes for you. This she has done, and the parcel is even now on its way here. You should have it later this afternoon.'

'But why am I being locked in my room?'

'Reverend,' he answers with a pained expression and he talks even slower. 'You have been on spiritual retreats. In a retreat, as you know, you are forbidden to talk. Silence is kept. That is a good thing because it prevents the retreatant from being distracted by other things, and he can focus on what is really important. Now, I regard your stay here as something like a retreat. A time for you to be alone with your conscience, and to reflect on the higher values like honesty and good government that holds back the atheistic forces of nihilism and chaos. Not to be troubled by outside things, but to have the time to know what God wants of you in relation to the things we have talked about. By restricting your movements, we are helping you to reflect on those things. Perhaps you can relax and think of your stay here in that way.' He stands up. 'Now you must return to your room. Lunch will be brought to you. And let me assure you that despite the nonsense the papers write about us putting drugs in people's food in order to get them to talk – well, that is all nonsense. We do not do that. You will find it is all good wholesome food. I hope you enjoy it.'

The door opens and an officer is there to take Richard to his room. With some effort Richard heaves himself out of the chair. At the same time, he says, 'I would also like to know if my Bishop—'

But Beukes interrupts and moving towards Richard pats him on the shoulder.

'Ag man, you are worried about too many things. Let me assure you, everything has been taken care of. Your Bishop also knows what is happening. You go and have your lunch now. Have a good rest this afternoon and later we will meet again, and you can then ask me any further questions.' He waves his hand in a dismissive action in the direction of the door and with a frown says, 'So go on, and try not to worry.'

Richard feels he has little choice, and, in a moment, he is back in his room.

The thought that his food might be drugged hadn't occurred to him, but now it is troublingly in his mind and it reminds him just how vulnerable he is in this situation. But he also has a growing feeling of anger. It occurs to him that being secretly recorded is really a dirty trick and then Beukes had the cheek to suggest that he should reflect on the value of honesty. He is also worried about how the SB knew he was going to be hiring that bakkie. The only people who knew were Noelene and Stan Henderson. Thoughts flash through his mind. Surely Stan is not an informer! Or is he? Did he feign illness so as not to come that day? Isn't it always the one least suspected? But surely not Stan! If he can't be trusted, then who can be trusted? On the other hand, perhaps the Rectory phone is bugged. He had wondered about that for some time.

He goes over to the window. All that can be seen is a bare dusty yard that stretches to the palisaded fence. There is nothing growing in the yard except for a few weeds and tufts of straggly grass. Above the fence he can see a wooded hillside, but that is the total view. A Jackie Hangman is perched on the fence. It drops down to the ground for some prey and then returns to its perch. There is a knock on the door, and an officer enters with a tray of food, which he places on a small table in the corner.

Although Richard thanks him, the man leaves without uttering a word of acknowledgement. Perhaps this *is* like some sort of silent retreat. He is reminded that on retreats he had enjoyed going for long walks. He grunts, thinking that he won't be taking any walks here.

With the lunch is a set of cutlery, wrapped in a paper serviette. Obviously, they are not worried about him harming himself with the metal cutlery. The thought of suicide was there when they took his belt and laces away, but now it is even more prominently in his mind and he feels disturbed by it. He has heard how detainees have sometimes killed themselves in desperation. At least the official line has been that these were suicides or accidents. He, however, has assumed that those who have died in detention were killed as a result of being tortured. Cold shivers of fear course through his body.

He stands in the middle of the room with these thoughts for a few moments. Then, shaking his head vigorously he thinks to himself, *'Come on, I can't let that sort of thinking get hold of me. Of course, Beukes is a policeman and as such he believes in government policy. But he seems a nice enough chap and has a job to do. He is like a genial Afrikaner Oom[17].'* He glances around the room. *'And this doesn't look like a jail, even if I am locked in. It is certainly not the cell I was in last night.'*

Drawing courage from these thoughts, he goes to the table and takes the cover off the food. He thinks that doctored or not, the food looks good. Not at all like the awful stuff he was given in the police cells. In any case he decides he must eat to keep his strength up and to try to remain as normal and calm as possible.

He sits down, says grace and starts eating. He tries to steer his thoughts away from the tape recording, but without

---

[17] Oom: Afrikaans: Uncle.

any success. His mind keeps going back, trying to recall exactly what was said in the bakkie. What he is certain of is that Simon mentioned contact with a member of *Umkhonto we Sizwe*. That is clearly what Beukes wants to know. Richard's thoughts run on and he becomes aware that what Beukes wants is the identity of the contact and that is something Richard doesn't know.

'Ah,' he says aloud and then checks himself thinking they might be able to hear him. Now being careful to keep his thoughts to himself, he concludes that Beukes can't know very much, because otherwise what was the purpose of his questioning? So, most of the conversation must have been drowned out by the noise of the bakkie. These thoughts bring him some relief. He decides that he will stick to his story that it was just a general conversation. But with relief comes renewed anger at how underhand the SB have been, and new fears as to how far their tentacles can reach because they could be in cahoots with the bakkie hire firm. He also wonders what other recorders are hidden, perhaps in the Rectory, or even in the church.

These reflections are interspersed by terrifying thoughts about this mysterious place of detention. He has noticed that whenever anyone enters his room, he never hears a key turning. It appears it is only locked on the inside, like child locks in a car. Also, there don't appear to be any African servants. The only people he has seen so far are all white police officers. Clearly, they want to keep everything in-house to maintain the secrecy of the place.

After lunch he tries to have a nap, but his head is too full of everything that has happened. There is so much rushing around in his brain and yet he feels paralysed. It is as though time has stopped. After glancing at his watch several times, he realises that it has stopped. *Of course*, he thinks to himself, *I didn't have it with me last night, so it hasn't been wound up.* Not knowing the time increases his confusion.

After winding his watch, he tries again to relax and, hopefully, to have a sleep. But Beukes' words: 'We know he was talking about *Umkhonto we Sizwe*' keeps going through his head. He also wonders what other surprises Beukes might spring. The tape recording has really shaken him. Then it occurs to him that perhaps Beukes was bluffing, perhaps they have been able to decipher the tape and are now pumping him in the hope he will reveal further information. With shock he remembers Simon saying that the young man had mentioned a bomb plot at Hopedale station. He wonders if Beukes knows that. *If so, is he trying to catch me out? Could they implicate me in something like that?* He also recalls reading somewhere that it is treasonable to withhold any information to do with terrorism. These thoughts rattle around in his head and nervous tremors course through his body like waves. He decides that he is going to have to be very careful in what he says to Beukes as he might be digging himself into a deeper hole. The last thing he wants is to get Simon into trouble.

Midway through the afternoon there is the customary knock on the door and an officer brings in tea and a parcel. Opening the parcel is something of a relief, not only for what it contains, but because doing something tangible takes him out of his thoughts for a moment. The parcel contains the promised clothes and toiletries. He immediately feels in the trouser pockets and searches through everything for a possible message from Noelene, but there is nothing. Changing into fresh clothes lifts his spirits for a moment. He feels the need for some exercise, and paces up and down the room, whirling his arms and doing a bit of running on the spot. It is a hot day and he starts to perspire, so he stops his physical jerks as he does not want to get his fresh clothes sweaty.

He stands at the window, gazing at the bleak scene outside, not knowing what to do. Time seems to be passing so slowly. He moves from the window to sit on the bed. After a few moments he thinks he hears something outside so returns to the window. Peering through the burglar bars he sees that nothing has changed. He wanders back and forth between the window and sitting on the bed.

At last he is summoned back to Beukes' office. This time the Major is smoking a cigar and the drinks cabinet is open. Seeing Richard, he stands up and offers him a drink. Richard has already decided to stick to soft drinks to ensure he has a clear head.

'Thanks, I'll just have an orange juice.'

'Oh, but you surprise me. I know you enjoy a Becks beer and I've specially got some on ice for you because we like our guests here to feel at home.'

'No thanks,' he utters nervously, frightened by the detail of Beukes' knowledge of him.

'You see,' says the Major sitting down and indicating to Richard to be seated. 'I've been doing my homework on you. That does not surprise you does it? After all, you know we have been taking an interest in you.'

There is a knock on the door and the Major asks for the orange juice. While waiting for it to arrive he makes small talk, asking if Richard had a good lunch and a siesta.

'Well I'd prefer not to be here,' he answers cautiously. 'My watch has stopped, so could you please give me the time?' Once he has reset his watch he tentatively asks, 'It would help if I could have something to read, at least a Bible and a Prayer Book.' Mentioning a Prayer Book reminds Richard that over the last twenty-four hours he hasn't been able to say Matins and Evensong, so summoning up further courage he adds, 'As you know so much about me you will know that Anglican priests are required to say Morning and Evening Prayer every day and, by the way, aren't prisoners given a Bible?'

The Major laughs waving his cigar in the air.

'A man with spirit! That's what I like. Well, let me be honest with you. You have caught us out. There should have been a Bible in your room. I don't know what could have happened to it, but I will see to it that you get one.' There is a knock on the door. 'Ah, here is your orange juice.' He reaches for an ice bucket on a stand at the side of his desk. 'Some ice in your drink?'

'No thanks.'

He hands Richard his drink and raises his glass.

'*Gesondheid*, or as you English people say, cheers,' and he downs a draught of his drink and then drawing on his cigar leans back in his chair.

'Well, you've now had a chance to recall that conversation you had in the hire vehicle. What else can you tell me about it?'

'Well, nothing really. That's all I can remember.'

The geniality of the Major's demeanour disappears, a frown creases his forehead, and he appears to be studying the liquid in his glass. Then putting down his glass and leaning forward he says:

'Reverend Atwell, you know that *Umkhonto we Sizwe* is intent on terrorism and murder. They will think nothing of killing hundreds of people, whites and blacks. We know there has been talk in their organisation of setting off a bomb in the Sasol oil refinery or even in a crowded city centre or at a big rugby match. We know they have these things in mind, and we must be vigilant if we are to prevent such a tragedy. So, information from someone like you can perhaps save hundreds, who knows, perhaps thousands of lives. That is why I want you to think very carefully about that conversation you had which I am sure you will be able to recall. After all, it was only the day before yesterday that you had that conversation and, in any case, I know ministers are trained to remember what people tell them, especially important things.'

'Really, Major Beukes, I can't think of anything else,' he says rather sheepishly.

There is a long silence while the Major scrutinises Richard. Finally, he continues, 'Well, I really didn't want to do this, but I wonder if it will help to concentrate your mind.'

Waves of fear wash over Richard and he feels slightly dizzy as he wonders what is coming. The Major opens a drawer and takes out what looks like a folded white handkerchief. He places it on the desk and carefully unfolds it.

'Do you recognise this?'

Richard lifts himself slightly from his chair to get a better look.

'Well, yes. It's a packet of Durex,' he says stating the obvious, but being totally mystified as to what condoms have to do with the conversation with Simon.

'These were found in your wallet by Warrant Officer van de Walt. Why were you carrying condoms to a Mission Committee meeting?' he adds with more than a hint of sarcasm.

'But I wasn't. That cannot be mine. I have never carried condoms, ever, in my wallet.' He pauses and there is a desperate silence. He looks up to see the Major has a hint of a smile and is shaking his head as if in disbelief. Richard adds, 'They couldn't have been in my wallet. If those were found in my wallet, they must have been put there by somebody else.' Richard is now feeling extremely confused and anxious. He wonders what is going on.

'Oh, Reverend Atwell,' the Major says with a pained expression. 'Don't please accuse us of planting evidence. You see, if this was put in your wallet by someone else it wouldn't have your fingerprints on it.' With his hand under the handkerchief he carefully turns the packet of Durex over so that Richard can see the black marks of the fingerprint powder. 'We compared these with the prints the sergeant took from you at the charge office and they match exactly. Now, I put it to you that you didn't check the contents of your wallet when I returned it to you this morning precisely because you, a minister, would have been embarrassed for me to know that you were carrying such things around with you.'

'Honestly, I didn't have them anywhere on me and I don't know how my fingerprints got to be there.'

'Whatever you say,' he says with a loud sigh. 'I have got hard evidence here,' and he glances down at the Durex. 'You see, before I stepped in, van de Walt was going to charge you with intent to commit an offence under the Immorality Act.' He pauses for a moment and then continues. 'Just think of it for a moment. You, out late at night, with a young black girl in the car, on a lonely stretch of country road, with condoms at hand. It only points to one thing. On top of that the sergeant has a signed statement from the Bantu girl that you made improper suggestions to her.'

Richard gasps in disbelief.

'What! I don't believe it!'

'Okay,' the Major continues, shrugging his shoulders. 'Maybe it is your word against hers, but with these condoms and the evidence of where you were apprehended, he's got more than enough to bring a change against you. I was jealous of him you know, because in my investigation, more hard evidence is what I need. That is why I stopped him…' he pauses and then adds, nodding his head, 'for the time being. Of course, if you can tell me more about that conversation with Bantu Ndlovu, then you can forget about van de Walt's charge. Now, if you will excuse me, I have an important phone call to make. We can continue our talk tomorrow.' The door opens and an officer appears to escort Richard to his room. He stands up to go, but the Major has a parting shot. 'Oh yes, your request for some reading matter. You will now find a Bible in your room, but as far as any other reading matter is concerned, I don't think you will have time as you have quite a lot to think about, haven't you?' With that he picks up the telephone receiver and swivels round, turning his back on Richard.

Back in the room Richard notices an open Bible on the table. It is as though it was there all the time. But no, Richard thinks, *Surely, I would have noticed it. And it wasn't there when I had my lunch.* He wonders if his perception of things is getting muddled. He asks himself, how did Beukes get a message to someone to put it here? He wonders if their conversations are being monitored. He feels totally exposed and vulnerable, and again remembers Hall Green's comment that the SB do not play by the rules. He mutters silently; *they are trying to wear me down*. He is mystified as to how his fingerprints could have got on to that packet of condoms. He feels disoriented. In a panic he says to himself; *they are catching me out at every turn*. Then it suddenly occurs to him, *van Zyl, the bugger! He must have stolen those Durex from my wardrobe when they were searching the bedroom*. He recalls now that a day or two after the search he had noticed that the condoms were not there and had assumed they were somewhere amongst his socks and handkerchiefs. In any case, he had bought some more, and with all the upheaval had forgotten about the ones he thought were missing. Now he figures van Zyl must have taken them just in case this sort of occasion might arise when they could be used to blackmail him.

Again, Richard finds himself pacing up and down the room with short, jerky, tense movements.

That evening he does not feel very hungry even though the dinner they bring looks quite appetising. His mind is racing all the time and he is not thinking too clearly. The one hopeful thought that he comes back to is that it seems as though Beukes wasn't bluffing when he said he has no real evidence from the conversation with Simon. So, Richard thinks; *I must stick to my story that I know nothing further. I cannot possibly betray Simon. If, as Beukes is threatening, they bring an immorality charge against me, then surely Canon Wilson will be able to give evidence that he asked me to give Nosipho a lift. The Bishop has also said the diocese has good legal people – they would hopefully get me released*.

The fact that he is innocent does not enter his mind and any positive thoughts keep getting lost in his fear. Then he sees the Bible again and decides he must read it. He sits down at the table with the open Bible at the side while he picks at his dinner.

Out of the corner of his eye he notices someone has pencilled an asterisk next to a verse. He picks the Bible up and reads it. "Let every person be subject to the governing authorities..." He slams the Bible down in anger. He is familiar with Saint Paul's exhortation in his epistle to the Romans that they should obey the governing authorities. He thinks; *these people really are naive if they think that means I should do the SB's bidding.* Then another frightening thought occurs to him. *They are trying to brainwash me. I must get a grip on myself.* He remembers being taught at theological college that saying the prayers of Matins and Evensong each day is designed to give the clergy support and structure to their lives. Although he does not have a Prayer Book, he pushes aside most of his uneaten dinner, kneels at the side of the bed and starts reciting as much of Evensong as he knows by heart. He also reads the sections of the Bible that he recalls are set in the current lectionary. The whole process takes him ages and he has to repeat parts, as his mind keeps straying to the events of the last twenty-four hours, but he finally gets through it.

After a shower he puts on the clean pyjamas Noelene had sent, with the result that he feels a little better. He lies down and tries to go to sleep, but restlessly tosses and turns even though he's very tired. The heat of the day has hardly dissipated, and although his window is open there is not a breath of wind and it feels as though there is no air in the room. Eventually he drops off to sleep.

How long he has slept, he does not know, but he is suddenly woken by the most awful screams. He sits bolt upright, reaches out for the light switch, then remembers he is not at home. It is pitch dark and it takes him a few moments scrabbling around to find the light switch. He turns the light on and jumps out of bed. Terror grips him. He can feel his heart beating in his chest. The screams seem to be coming from a room at the back of the house. He goes to the door and turns the knob, but it is still locked. He hears a man with an African accent desperately calling out:

'Stop, please stop, stop, please, please!' The screaming subsides to a low moan. Someone is clearly in severe distress. It sounds as though someone is being murdered. Then the full horror of the place dawns on him. This house, hidden away in the countryside, far from anyone, is an SB detention and torture facility. All the veneer of hospitality he has been shown is simply to mask the real purpose of what is nothing less than a hell hole. Now the high palisaded fence round the perimeter brings to his mind pictures of Nazi death camps. He falls to his knees at this horrific thought, crying out, 'Oh God no, NO!'

The fact that the screams have died down is no relief. With shame he realises he has been so terrified that he has lost control of his bowels. Warm poo is sliding down his inside leg. He carefully gets up, holding the leg of his pyjama trouser to stop his faeces from falling on the floor. He hobbles over to the toilet to clean himself. He thinks he is becoming deranged. Removing his pyjama trousers, he can't help the poo from falling out. In despair he sits down heavily on the toilet. His nice clean pyjama trousers are soiled. The smell makes him feel nauseous. He sits there for some time in desolation. Eventually in a daze, and with some effort, he rolls off wads of toilet-paper and begins to clean himself and the floor. He then tries to wash his pyjamas in the bath but gives up and stumbles out of the bathroom with a towel loosely around his waist.

At the door of his room he cups a hand to his ear and listens for any further screams. However, he hears nothing. In a desperate panic he bangs repeatedly with his fists on the door shouting, 'What's going on? Someone, please tell me?' He bangs his head on the door. There is no response. He falls against the door with his hands clutching and pulling at his hair. After some time, he gets up, turns, then stumbles over the towel he has dropped in his panic and falls to the floor grazing the palms of his hands. He lies whimpering on the hard-wooden boards. Eventually he crawls to a corner of the room. Sitting on the floor he pulls his knees up to his chin. He sits there shuddering, almost unable to breathe because of the sobs that rise through his chest. He thinks he is going mad, and hysterically whimpers to himself, 'Will I be next? Please, please, don't let it be me!' He sits there crouched down, mewing like some sort of cornered animal. Eventually exhaustion takes over and there on the floor he falls into a troubled sleep.

# Chapter 19

(Friday 12th January 1968)

When he wakes, he notices that the room light is still on, but now there is also daylight streaming through the window. He looks at his watch. It has just gone six o'clock. His body aches and his knees and elbows are sore and red where they have been in contact with the hard floor. He has a dull headache above his eyes, which do not focus very well. Groaning, he stretches himself and moves the towel covering his legs. His nakedness puzzles him for a moment, but gradually that fact brings the dreaded thoughts of the horrendous events of the previous night back to mind. He drops his head to his knees in an anguished moan. Was it a nightmare? He lifts his head, looks around the room trying to clear his head and exclaims aloud:

'Oh God!' After a pause he cries out in anguish, 'Oh God, my God, why hast Thou forsaken me? What am I to do?' He starts sobbing like a little child. Eventually there seems to be no more sobs left in him. He lifts his aching body and steadies himself by leaning with one hand against the wall. Bending down he picks up the towel and shuffles off to the bathroom. Over the hand basin he washes his face. Out of the corner of his eye he sees the shame of his pyjamas lying in discoloured water in the bath with scum covering it. Doing anything requires a great effort, but he forces himself to run fresh water and to complete the washing of his pyjamas. He then has a shower, feeling as though he must cleanse himself from the fear and shame of the night. Having showered, he drapes the pyjamas over the shower head so they may drip dry into the bath. He hopes they will soon be dry as he does not want Beukes or any of the others to know he has disgraced himself.

Having just finished dressing, his breakfast is brought in. Sitting down in front of his porridge it strikes him that the timing seems to be too exact to be coincidence. It is as though they know what he is doing and waited until he was ready before bringing his breakfast in. Leaving his breakfast, for which he really has no appetite, he gets up, and starts scouring the room for peepholes or hidden cameras. He scans the ceiling, searches the walls and the light fittings and looks behind the curtains, but all in vain. He feels claustrophobic, as though imprisoned in a panopticon and cannot do anything without being watched. He tries telling himself that it will all be okay and to stop imagining the worst. However, he is unable to banish the weight of troubling thoughts of the night's events as he fiddles with his breakfast. At least, he thinks, daylight makes a difference; it is not as terrifying as the darkness of the night.

Shortly after breakfast he is recalled to the Major's office.

'Good morning Reverend. I hope you slept well?'

'What was that screaming in the night?' he replies rather sullenly as he stiffly moves towards his chair.

'Screaming?' Beukes queries, frowning as if taken aback. 'I didn't hear any screaming. It must be your imagination or, perhaps one of our other guests was having a nightmare. I am sorry if you were disturbed in the night. But please sit down.'

Richard sits down on the edge of the chair with his chin in his hands, feeling absolutely miserable. He thinks Beukes is looking down on him with mock concern.

The Major says, 'I am sorry you are looking so down in the dumps this morning,' then adds rather blithely, 'but I'm afraid we must carry on with our conversation. Have you any further thoughts about the little talk we had yesterday evening?'

Richard mumbles, 'No. It is blackmail, so if you must charge me then you must do so.'

'Oh dear, blackmail is a very serious accusation is it not?' He pauses and when Richard does not respond continues. 'You know Reverend Atwell; it seems that you haven't really thought about this. I do not want to have you charged under the Immorality Act. I can assure you a trial will be blazoned on the front pages of the newspapers. I can just see the headlines; *priest on immorality charge*. Of course, they will probably think up something a lot more salacious than my poor effort. And I can tell you the prosecution will put your wife on the stand to answer intimate questions about your sex life and whether she is satisfying you. Do you really want that? Remember, we have the hard evidence and there is evidence that we have that you don't even know about. We have someone who was a student with you, and at a multi-racial conference he saw you dancing very closely with a Bantu girl. Now I know that was some years ago, but he will give evidence that you already had predilections in that direction then. You see, we have been watching you for some time,' and he taps a fat file lying on the desk, 'and a search through here will no doubt reveal further evidence. I think there is a good chance that the verdict will probably go our way. But, even if some clever liberal lawyer gets you off, your name will be tarnished and your career as a minister will be in smithereens. The strain on your marriage will be immense and you will be an outcast in our society. People will always regard you with suspicion. You know how they say,' and he enunciates the words one by one and with emphasis. 'Where there is smoke, there is fire.' He pauses for a moment. Richard is sitting hunched-up, looking at the floor. 'Now, you may not believe it, but I've grown to like you, so I don't want all this to happen to you. Go back to your room, and I urge you to think very carefully about the danger you are in that could wreck your career and your marriage. Perhaps it will help you decide to tell me what you heard in that bakkie and then all this can be cleared up to everyone's satisfaction. So, I'll see you again in about an hour's time.'

Immediately the door opens, and an officer escorts him back to his room.

Being alone again, Richard is able to think a little more clearly. Strangely, he begins to feel more positive than earlier. He thinks that Beukes has overplayed his hand. He feels sure Noelene would stand by him and so, he believes, would the Bishop. He recalls the student conference, that it was a long time ago and in fact he only had a couple of dances with a black girl. All the other dances were with whites. He also reasons that whilst he might be unable to continue as Rector of Pemberton, and that's not certain as a substantial minority of his parishioners would probably support him; the Bishop could give him a chaplaincy job in a hospital or the university. He would not mind that at all. In any case, the immorality charge is only one of intent, not commission. Then thinking about his friendship with Simon, he decides he really cannot betray his friend and so he determines again to remain silent about what he was told in confidence.

He feels a bit disconcerted in trying to identify the student who is Beukes' informant. But remembering the thick file on Beukes' desk he becomes aware of feeling some pride in it. For the first time since he awoke, he sits up straight and throws his shoulders back. He thinks he must be quite important, on a par with Patrick Duncan or even Alan Paton for the SB to take so much notice of him. *Yes*, he says to himself; *I am a force to be reckoned with*. He feels a bit manic and light-headed as he gets up and strides around the room waiting for the Major's summons. He even mutters to himself; *I can still hold my position and put one over that bloody Beukes.*

When recalled, he enters the Major's office with an assumed air of confidence and, without being asked, sits down and leans back nonchalantly in the chair. He looks at the Major as though to say, I am ready for you.

Beukes mocks Richard's performance by clapping his hands and exclaiming:

'Ah, well done!' He pauses. 'I'm glad you are looking a lot more cheerful. I hope the change means you have something to tell me?'

Leaning slightly forward, Richard responds very deliberately:

'I want to repeat, I had no intention of having sex with the young lady, Nosipho. I was merely giving her a lift home from a meeting at the cathedral and there are reputable people who will be able to corroborate my story. I believe someone stole condoms from my home, and it is those that you now have. Furthermore, I do not believe Nosipho is the sort of person who would deliberately tell lies. I am very suspicious as to how that statement you claim she made came about. That is all I have to say,' and he sits back with his arms folded.

The Major leans forward with his elbows on the desk and the tips of his fingers touching. With a slight smirk Richard meets his gaze and imagines Beukes is impressed at the way he has come back at him with all guns blazing. He thinks; *this is what I must do. He will respect me if I stand up to him.*

'Okay,' the Major says nonchalantly. Then his manner changes. With a frown he looks directly at Richard and speaking more urgently with a seriousness in his voice says, 'Look, I'm dealing here with something a lot more important than whether you were or were not foolish enough to go off with a Bantu girl. What I am dealing with are terrorists, matters of life and death.' He pauses and picks up a silver paper knife. 'What I'm talking about are serious acts of murder and terrorism. Our work here in this place saves the lives of thousands upon thousands of people and secures your future and my future and the future of coming generations in this country. Now, you have tried my patience too far, so I am going to be blunt with you. I believe, no, I am convinced, you know more than you are telling me about Bantu Ndlovu. I also know you are keeping this information from me out of a misguided sense of loyalty to this Bantu minister. But eventually you will have to come clean with me. We are currently holding you under the 1963 *General Law Amendment Act* which allows me to detain you for questioning for 90 days,' and noticing the look of confidence vanishing from Richard's face he emphasises, 'yes, I said 90 days. And if after that I am still not satisfied, I can easily use the *Terrorism Act* that was passed last year which provides for me to hold a person indefinitely, who I believe has information about terrorism. That person is you,' and he points the knife at Richard. 'So, unless something makes you change your mind, you can be preparing for an awfully long stay here.' He pauses a moment and then adds darkly, 'And it is just possible you might also start to have nightmares. Now, I have no further plans to talk to you, but if you have something new to tell me, then all you must do is tell the officer who brings your meals. And, by the way, I think we will have to move you to less comfortable accommodation.'

Richard is white as a sheet and feels weak at the knees as he follows the officer back to the room. The confidence that was coursing through him a moment ago has dissolved into nothing, and he feels quite dizzy as though he is standing on the edge of an abyss.

*I cannot endure another night like last night. Will I now be tortured?* These are the thoughts that rush into his mind. Those horrendous scenarios that he has previously read about begin to haunt him. How a prisoner's head is held under water until on the verge of drowning. How electrodes are attached to a man's genitals and then the current is turned on. And that is besides the beatings. He shudders and sits down on the bed in shock. Suddenly he cries out:

'God, oh my God, where are you? How can you let such awful things happen?' He falls at the bedside muttering, 'I must pray, I must pray.' He does not know what to pray. He resorts to the first Biblical quotation that comes to mind and in desperation he begs; 'Out of the depths have I cried unto Thee, O Lord. Lord, hear my voice. Oh please, please hear me.' He pounds the bed with his fists and rambles on for some time in this vein like a madman, and then buries his head in the bedclothes, sobbing.

Eventually his sobbing subsides from exhaustion and then suddenly the Biblical exhortation 'not to think of yourself more highly than you aught to think' comes into his mind. With a deep sigh he reflects on whether he has been wrong all the time and perhaps trying to be some sort of martyr. That was what the Bishop warned him against. He had thought he could out-manoeuvre Beukes. Wasn't that the sin of pride? A feeling of guilt begins to seep into him. His thoughts run on and he begins to wonder whether he is really being loyal to Simon by his silence? After all, Simon was just doing his job as a minister, he was not a member of *Umkhonto*. If he told them what he knew he could be preventing Simon from getting into trouble. On the other hand, by denying that he knows anything he is possibly putting himself and Simon in danger. The horrific thought occurs to him that Beukes might think they are both involved in *Umkhonto*. For a moment his mind goes blank with terror. Then he says to himself, *I should tell them what I know. Of course, maybe they have already detained Simon. By telling what I know I could be enabling the release of both of us.*

He stands up and his eyes light on his pullover, lying over the back of a chair. Noelene knitted that for him shortly after they were married. Thinking of her he continues arguing with himself while nervously pacing around the room, his head bowed, looking at the floor. Thoughts of how worried Noelene must be enter his head. He thinks that the longer he prolongs his detention, the more he will be prolonging her anxiety, which is not fair on her.

Even though he has had little to do with his parents since the search, he still has a high regard for them. He often has imaginary arguments with his father. In his head he now hears his father reciting, 'Never think you know it all. Pride comes before a fall.' *Isn't that it*, he says to himself, as though he has suddenly had a revelation. *Am I being arrogant in thinking I am right and that others are wrong?*

*And of course, it is never as clear cut as that. I might not agree with Beukes, but he doesn't strike me as a totally evil man. Perhaps I'm failing in Christian charity towards him. Perhaps I need to be more understanding of him and the difficult job he has. As he said he has responsibility over matters of life and death. National security is a huge responsibility. After all, as much as I think apartheid is evil, he believes it is a serious attempt to cope with the country's problems. He also wants what is best for our country. But if I claim that I am right and he is wrong, surely I am being very arrogant. Perhaps he is right that Africans aren't at the same stage as we are. Of course, Simon is an exception. Isn't that it?* These questions nag at him until he eventually says to himself, *I must have been mad to resist all this time. In any case, what I know is not all that important. It is not as though I know where caches of arms or explosives are hidden. I could tell Beukes what I know.* Then, after a bit of reflection, *but perhaps I'll try not to tell him that the man was a member of MK? That would be a betrayal of the trust which that man had in Simon, and his telling it to me in confidence? I could say he was just thinking about what MK does, and asking Simon if it was compatible with Christianity. That sounds reasonable enough.*

Just then there is a knock; the door opens, and his lunch is brought in. He decides to grab the moment.

'Would you please tell the Major I would like to talk to him?'

'He said you are only to talk to him if you have some new informations. He doesn't want you to be wasting his time,' is the gruff reply.

'Yes, I have new information to give him,' Richard replies in a subdued voice.

'I'll tell him.' The officer leaves the room.

Richard thinks that this must be for the best. It is surely presumptuous trying to be a brave martyr and, in a way, is perhaps being a little self-indulgent.

Throughout the afternoon Richard waits to be summoned. Questions as to whether he is doing the right thing continue to nag at him, but his thoughts of getting away from this horrendous place of detention outweigh his doubts. He cannot wait to get home, and as he waits the minutes seem to drag. Each time he looks at his watch the hands have hardly moved. Eventually at four o'clock he is brought a cup of tea. Again, he tells the officer he wishes to speak to the Major. He receives a curt reply.

'He will see you when he is ready.'

The afternoon wears on. Richard tries to pass the time by alternately reading the Bible, pacing around, and from time to time glancing out of the window where outside nothing disturbs the barren scene. Even the Jackie Hangman isn't on his usual perch. But then Richard spots the bird in the shadow of the fence pecking at something on the ground.

Gradually the light fades and gloom seeps into the room. At first, he is unaware of how dark the room has become until he returns to the Bible and realises it is too dark to read. He turns on the light and shortly after that his evening meal is brought in.

After he has eaten and the officer returns to take his tray, Richard tentatively repeats his request:

'I don't intend to be rude, but at lunch time I asked to speak to the Major. I had hoped we might clear this matter up today so that I may go home. Tomorrow is Saturday and on Sunday I have services to conduct so I would appreciate it if the Major is able to see me this evening.'

'The Major is busy with important business. He will see you when he is ready.' With that, the officer leaves the room.

Richard spends the evening waiting. Each time he hears footsteps he hopes they have come to call him. It reminds him of how as a child he would wait for his parents to return home when they had gone to an evening cocktail party. He would wait at a window and each time he saw the headlights of a car he would hope it was them. He fantasises that Beukes is at a cocktail party. He hears people passing his room, but no one stops at his door. Nothing happens except that in the distance he hears a rumble of thunder. Soon Richard is struggling to keep awake, as he sits nodding at the table.

When the hands of his watch have finally crawled round to nine o'clock, he decides he will give it until half past nine and will then go and have his shower. The threatening storm appears to have passed. A deathly silence prevails, and it is now a long time since he heard footsteps pass his room. Even at nine-thirty, he still desperately hopes to be called and extends his time limit to ten. He grumbles to himself; *why now that I am willing to talk to them will they not see me? I suppose this is a way of punishing me.* Eventually, well after ten o'clock has passed, he drags himself up and goes to have a shower but leaves the door slightly ajar in case someone comes so that he can quickly get ready to see them. Still no one comes. He feels as though he has been forgotten, and eventually, dejectedly, he goes to bed.

# Chapter 20

(Saturday 13th January 1968)

Richard is in a troubled sleep when the door opens, and the light is switched on. In a fright he throws the bedclothes back and sits up. His eyes take a moment to adjust to the light and then he sees an officer he has not seen before who is standing in the doorway.

'Come with me,' the officer commands curtly.

'But er... I'm in my pyjamas. I'll quickly change into some clothes?'

'I said come, and you will come as you are.'

Padding along in his bare feet, his pyjamas flapping loosely on him, he follows the officer out the door, still in a bit of a daze. He becomes very apprehensive when he notices he is being led down the corridor in the opposite direction to the Major's office. He realises that he is in a much bigger house than he had thought. At the end of the corridor he is led into a room that is bare except for a table and two upright chairs. There are no windows, and a single light bulb hangs down from the ceiling. There is not even a mat on the concrete floor that feels cold and damp to his bare feet. A slim athletic-looking man in khaki trousers and a white open-neck shirt is sitting at the table reading through a file of papers. A black leather-covered cane lies on the table. He does not look up as Richard and the guard enter.

The escort indicates to Richard that he must sit down on the spare chair, and he closes the door; but, unlike, in interviews with the Major, the escort remains in the room. The man at the table continues to ignore Richard. He is much younger than Beukes, has a lean face with a small dark moustache, and black greasy-looking hair. Richard is confused and nervously fidgets on his chair. He now remembers his spectacles are still in his room; and being without them makes him feel more vulnerable. Then fear kicks in, and he finds his hands are shaking.

After some minutes the man grunts, shuffles the papers together, puts them down and looking up at Richard with a menacing frown demands:

'Well?'

Richard says the first thing that comes into his mind.

'I was expecting to see Major Beukes.'

'Oh, were you now!' Richard twitches with fright as the man suddenly stands up, leans forward resting his clenched fists on the table and shouts in Richard's face. 'Well you've got me.' He is a tall man, and towers over Richard. He picks up the cane and starts slowly and deliberately pacing around the room like a leopard quartering its prey. He spits out his words.

'So, what have you got to tell us?' He spins round to face Richard and shouts, pointing at him with his cane, 'and it had better be good.'

In his terror with his heart pounding Richard struggles to remember what he wanted to say.

'I er... I want to apologise to Major Beukes—'

The man interrupts screaming at Richard:

'I'm not Major Beukes.' Then, lowering his voice to a sinister whisper and leaning towards Richard, 'I am Sergeant Wilkinson, but here I am known as *die Draak*.' He cracks the cane down on the table like a rifle shot, and, jerking back with fright, Richard nearly falls off his chair. Standing erect again, the sergeant continues, 'I'm also of English stock you know, but people like you make me ashamed. Now, do you know what a *draak* is?'

Richard thinks he knows but hesitates, being too terrified to get it wrong.

'So, you don't know, you stupid fool. Why haven't you bothered to learn the language of this country? Well I'll tell you. A *draak* is a dragon.' Then placing his hands on the table and leaning over him he hisses into Richard's face. 'I'm called the dragon because I spit fire to burn away all the lies people like you tell me. So, you had better watch what you say.'

In terror Richard stutters, 'I-I-I wanted to s-say I'm sorry... I didn't tell Major Beukes all I knew and I'm now ready to talk.' There is a pause before the interrogator shouts:

'Well, talk then you bloody fool or I shall lose my temper.'

'I don't know if I can remember everything that was said that day—'

He prods Richard painfully in the chest with his cane.

'You had better bloody remember.'

Trembling, Richard feels faint, his vision is blurred and holding onto the table he answers in a pleading voice:

'The Reverend Ndlovu was asking my advice.' He pauses in an attempt to clear his head and feels Wilkinson glaring at him. 'He is not a member of *Umkhonto we Sizwe*, I promise you. Someone had asked him whether, as a Christian, one could belong to *Umkhonto* if it committed acts of violence.' He wipes his eyes with the sleeve of his pyjamas.

The sergeant throws his arms aloft.

'Oh God help us; we've got a bloody cry baby here.' Turning to Richard he yells, 'Come on, come on, snivelling won't help you. I need to know everything that was said.'

'I advised Simon, that is Reverend Ndlovu, that this was a very dangerous subject, and he should have nothing to do with *Umkhonto*.' He pauses while the interrogator scowls at him. 'That was the gist of our conversation.'

'Do you expect me to believe that was all?' He shouts, 'You must do better than that – or else.'

'Honestly, that is all I know. I can't think of anything else.'

'For a start, who is this man? Come on, I want names.'

'He is the Reverend Simon Ndlovu of KwaBopela Methodist—'

'No!' he shouts. 'I know that, you idiot. Who is the man who is involved with *Umkhonto*?'

'I don't know. He didn't tell me his name.'

'Is he a member of the Bantu minister's church?'

Even though terrified, Richard does not want to implicate Simon.

'I don't know.'

The sergeant turns his back on Richard and again throws his arms in the air in frustration as he resumes pacing around the room.

'You don't know! Oh God, give me strength.' He then adopts a sarcastic tone while jauntily sauntering up and down the room twirling his cane. 'So, one day, somebody, we don't know who, is just walking past the church and decides he'll go in and ask the minister a question just for the fun of it!'

'It is possible. Sometimes people do that.'

He stops and stares at Richard.

'Do you mean to tell me that this was just a theoretical question? That this Bantu came to see this minister just to settle a question of debate? And then the minister goes to the trouble of raising the question with another minister, you. And you then advise him that he should not have anything to do with such discussions because, in your own words, it is a very dangerous subject.' Then at the top of his voice, 'Since when is a purely theoretical question so dangerous?'

Richard answers miserably, 'I don't know.' He feels trapped.

Wilkinson bends over the table, and shouts in Richard's face, 'You liar.'

He is so close Richard feels a spray of spittle on his cheek and he tries to shield his face by turning aside. At the same time, he grabs the edge of the table to steady himself.

'You are bloody well not telling me everything.' The sergeant slams his cane down on Richard's knuckles.

With a yelp he implores, 'Please, please don't hurt me.'

The interrogator ignores him and continues shouting:

'You know the man is a member of *Umkhonto*, and they were planning terrorism. That is why you said it was a dangerous subject and that is what you are not admitting to me, and your lies are making me want to beat the shit out of you.'

Like a little child Richard cries, 'Please Sir, they were not planning anything. The minister is—'

'Did he mention anything to you about bombs?'

Richard hesitates, remembering that a bomb at Hopedale station was mentioned, but he is too terrified to say anything.

The interrogator notices Richard's hesitation.

'Ah!' he shouts triumphantly. 'So, a bomb was mentioned, and you are now trying to think how you can cover it up. Well, it won't work with me. Where was this bomb going to be planted?'

For a second Richard is distracted by a bright red droplet of blood that has appeared on his swelling hand. He notices the light reflecting from that tiny red bead. He gently caresses his painful hand, smudging the blood over his fingers.

Despite his terror he summons up all his reserves of strength and stammers:

'I n-n-never said they were talking about p-planting bombs. Please believe me. The Reverend Ndlovu and the man were not planning t-terrorism. The man knew *Umkhonto* was involved in using bombs and… and he wanted to know if as a Christian he could belong to that organisation.'

'And where were they going to plant this bomb?'

'He didn't talk about any plans to plant a bomb.'

'You liar,' he yells. 'We have already established that he talked about a bomb. People don't talk about bombs unless they are going to use them. So where was it going to be placed?'

Richard hesitates.

The sergeant slams his cane on the table again.

'Come on, come on. I haven't got all night. I want to know.'

'Well, it was only in general terms as an example of what *Umkhonto* has been involved in. The man didn't talk about any definite plans.'

'Okay, so we now know this man is a member of *Umkhonto*.'

'I suppose he could be, or he might have just been thinking about joining.'

'He is a member, and you know he is. And he did not just turn up at the church for the fun of it. He came because this was a meeting of *Umkhonto* comrades and we all know their business is to plant bombs to murder innocent women and children. That is the truth, isn't it?'

'No. Reverend Ndlovu is not a member of *Umkhonto*.'

Wilkinson shouts, 'Yes he is.'

'No, I said no.'

'Yes he is.'

'No, I'm sorry, but I think you're mistaken.'

'Why is he then sympathetic towards *Umkhonto* and allows their members to meet there?'

'I don't think he does.'

'So, you don't *think* he does, or is that something else you are not telling me?'

'I'm trying to tell you everything I know.'

'Umm…' He pauses for a moment and resumes his pacing. 'You know this bantu Ndlovu very well. What can you tell me about him?'

'He is a friend of mine—'

Wilkinson interrupts and says with heavy sarcasm, 'A friend of yours, is he?' He turns to the officer at the door. 'Did you hear that? The Reverend here is friends with a bloody black communist who masquerades under the cloak of religion.'

'He is not a communist.'

He spins back to face Richard and bellows:

'I wasn't speaking to you. Okay, if you're so keen to talk – tell me, why does this minister run a shop in his church? I thought churches are for God and prayer. The Bible tells us Jesus chased the traders out of the temple. So, what is this shop doing there? And why does Ndlovu tell people from the pulpit that one day they will be free? Isn't that stirring up the people to commit violence? And that is what the communists and *Umkhonto* do.'

'Reverend Ndlovu is against violence, he—'

'You're a liar,' he shouts.

Richard begs him, 'Please, I'm trying to tell you. I am not telling lies. I promise you, Reverend Ndlovu is against violence.'

'Why then does he let his church be used by *Umkhonto*, an organisation committed to violence?'

'I don't believe he does.'

'Why then are there *Umkhonto* members in his congregation?'

'I don't know if there are.' Richard looks up and sees the sergeant staring him down so he adds, 'I suppose there might be.'

'You suppose there might be! And if there are, then it follows that Ndlovu, who must know his congregation, will know who these members are and is shielding them.'

He slaps his cane down on the table, sits down, picks up a pen and starts to write on a pad.

Richard is sitting bolt upright, trembling with fear. He takes a tissue from his pyjama pocket to wipe his face and to dry his eyes.

After writing a few sentences, the interrogator turns to the other officer:

'I have recorded here that Reverend Atwell accidently closed a door on his hand thus sustaining a slight injury and you are a witness to that.'

'Yes Sir…'

There is a pause. Then looking exceedingly pleased with himself the officer adds, 'Of course, he wasn't properly awake and didn't know what he was doing.'

'That is right, thank you.' Wilkinson writes some more. Then taking his cane he stands up and resumes his harsh loud tone.

'There is one thing you are still lying to me about. This man who came to see the minister. He is a member of *Umkhonto*, and he knew about plans to plant a bomb in Hopedale. That's right isn't it?'

Before he can stop himself, Richard answers. 'Hopedale station was mentioned.' Then he quickly adds, 'But it was only as an example of what *Umkhonto* might do. He might have said the town hall or anywhere else. It was just a theoretical example.' There is silence while he feels the sergeant's glare burning down on him. Richard looks up in supplication, 'Please Sir, believe me. That is the truth.'

'So, a bomb was to be planted at Hopedale station and the town hall was also a possibility.'

'No, no. That's not right.'

'But that's what you've just said. Now you're trying to wriggle out of it.'

'I'm sorry, I'm not explaining this very well. There were no plans to plant any bombs.'

With the back of his hand the sergeant gives Richard a vicious clout across the face sending him tumbling to the floor. He stands over Richard and yells at him.

'Stop telling me bloody lies. We all know *Umkhonto* has bomb plots and you're trying to tell me I've got it wrong.' He walks away from Richard and resumes pacing from one side of the room to the other.

'Please Sir, may I sit down again?'

When he does not get an answer, he looks towards the officer at the door who looks away. Richard lifts himself and, half crawling, slinks back to the chair. His head is beginning to throb, his cheek is stinging, and his nose is bleeding slightly. He pleads, 'Please don't get cross with me. I'm trying to tell you all that was said in the bakkie.'

The sergeant stops in his tracks and shaking his cane at Richard growls:

'Why didn't you tell us this when you first arrived here? Why did you waste our time by telling lies and saying you knew nothing? That's why I think you are still hiding things from us.'

Richard does not answer. He looks down at the floor and retrieving his tissue dabs his nose.

'Come on, tell me! Do you realise it is an offence to tell lies to a police officer? Do you realise we are at war with terrorists, and people can be dying while you waste our time hiding information?'

With his head bowed Richard whimpers, 'I've now told you everything I know.'

Speaking very deliberately the sergeant sneers:

'You are a bloody sissy. A pinky liberal who says one thing one day and something else the next, and you are too bloody stupid to see the evil these people are up to. You call yourself a minister and you tell lies and are willing to stand by and see people being killed,' and his voice rises to a crescendo as he shouts, 'because you haven't got the guts to stand up for your own people. People like you are repulsive and make me sick.' He spins round with his back towards Richard. 'Get him out of my sight. I've had enough of him.'

The officer at the door commands, 'Come!'

Richard is so terrorised he can hardly stand up. He feels as though his legs are going to give way. He reaches out to the sides of the door to steady himself as he stumbles out of the room. He is terrified he is being taken to be tortured. However, he is returned to his room. Once there he staggers to the bathroom where he retches and retches but little comes up. He feels hysterical. With shaking hands, he tenderly splashes some water over his face. The cold water stings his swollen hand where the skin has been broken. Clutching the wash basin with his good hand, he stares at his face in the mirror as though he does not recognise the image. There is a red streak across the side of his face which looks puffy, and a bruise is already appearing under his eye. But his nose has stopped bleeding.

After a while he shuffles back into the room. He collapses on the bed weeping. There are tight cramps in his stomach. Thoughts of torture and extreme pain flit haphazardly through his mind. He moans; *how have I got myself into this mess*? He is shivering as he lies curled up on the bed. He lies there in that catatonic state for what to him seems like hours until, mercifully, he eventually falls into a deep sleep.

# Chapter 21

(Saturday 13th January 1968)

It is daylight when Richard begins to wake up. Although he has slept soundly, he feels desperately tired. In his half-awake state he is aware of a throbbing headache, there are pains in his stomach, and, stretching himself, his joints feel sore. The fingers of his bruised hand are stiff and painful as he tries to flex them. That brings the horror of the night's interrogation back to him. With a jolt he is fully awake and staring through one eye at the ceiling. His other eye is gummed up. He wishes he could just go back to sleep to blot it all out. He feels helpless. Recollections of the sergeant's questions and aggressively violent behaviour whirl around his head. Painfully he manoeuvres himself until he is sitting on the edge of the bed. He puts his head in his hands and feels the tenderness of his cheek. He goes to the bathroom and to his horror sees he has a half-closed black eye. He gently bathes his face in cold water. After that he returns to sit on his bed. He looks at his watch. It is just past six o'clock. *Pray, pray*, he says to himself. He gets up from the bed and kneels, praying desperately for help. His prayers are random pleas to get him away from this place. He then tries to say Mattins, but his mind is too distracted by the night's ordeal. After struggling at his prayers for some time he gives up. He feels weak and useless and slowly and with some effort gets himself dressed.

When his breakfast is brought in, Richard is relieved to see it is not the officer of the previous night, but the same one who had attended him the day before. He is as taciturn as ever and does not return Richard's subdued greeting.

He tries to eat his porridge but finds it difficult to swallow and he feels sick. He pushes the food aside and sits at the table with his head in his hands.

It is still early in the day when the officer returns.

'The Major wants to see you.'

Just then Richard feels a desperate need to go to the toilet.

'Please, excuse me a moment so I can go to the lavatory.'

'Okay but hurry up. The Major doesn't like being kept waiting.'

He feels a need to pee but is so tense he barely manages to force out a dribble, and feeling totally miserable he zips up his fly and returns to the officer.

In the office Beukes is reading a typed sheet of paper, and with a casual wave of his hand he indicates to Richard to sit down. Richard is trembling with nerves as he waits. After a moment, the Major puts the paper down, removes his glasses and looking up with a smile says:

'Ag man, I am sorry. I was busy yesterday... my goodness! I was told you had an accident in the night, but you look as though you've done a few rounds with a heavyweight champion. Anyhow it will clear up in a few days. So, as I was saying; I was busy yesterday and had to ask Sergeant Wilkinson to take your statement. He comes on for the night shift as it were. He's a bit of a rough diamond, but in fact an exceptionally good man. He's an old-fashioned family man you know. He dotes on his two little girls and is so proud of them and I think he is a deacon in his church. He is also one of my most trusted men and committed one hundred per cent in the fight against communism and the destructive forces in our land. Now, he has given me this statement from your discussion with him.' He picks up the sheet of paper. 'I'd like you to read it and then sign at the bottom. Once signed, you will be free, and I will arrange for you to be returned to Hopedale where you may collect your car.'

The thought of this nightmare coming to an end is like a burst of light. With considerable relief, and feeling light-headed, Richard takes the paper and reads it.

*'Statement made by the Reverend Richard Atwell on 13th January 1968.*

*On the 9th January 1968 I was taking Reverend Ndlovu in a pickup truck to KwaBophela. While we were driving along Reverend Ndlovu asked my advice. He said that a member of the Methodist Mission in KwaBophela, a man (he did not tell me his name) belonging to the terrorist organisation Umkhonto we Sizwe had come to Reverend Ndlovu and had spoken to him about Umkhonto. They were talking about acts of terrorism and people being killed and a possible bomb at Hopedale station was mentioned. He had come to speak to the Bantu minister because he knew he sympathized with the aims of Umkhonto and had Umkhonto members in his congregation. I advised Reverend Ndlovu to have nothing to do with this dangerous organisation. That was the end of our conversation.'* At the bottom of the page is a dotted line for a signature and the date.

Richard's elation at the prospect of going home is replaced by utter dismay. To make sure he read it correctly he reads the statement for a second time while Beukes lights and smokes a cigarette. He thinks; *perhaps I must sign so I can get away from here.* After some reflection, however, he realizes that signing would be to betray Simon. In any case he knows the statement is not true. In some distress he responds:

'I don't know what to say.'

'Why? Is there something else you have not yet told us?'

'No, it's not that.'

'Well then, if there is nothing further you want to add, all you have to do is to sign the statement and you will be free.'

Again, Richard wonders what he should do, but finally says with anguish, 'I can't do it.'

The Major looks at him with a surprised expression.

'Why ever not?'

'Some of this statement is true, but there are parts that I never said.'

'Oh! Well I never! You know, Sergeant Wilkinson is scrupulous in making sure that statements are correct. I'll have to send you back to him, but before I do, what specifically do you think is not right about the statement?'

The sheet of paper is shaking in Richard's hand, but he manages to point to the relevant sentence.

'Here, this bit about terrorism and bombs. The statement reads as though they were planning some military action. Reverend Ndlovu never said anything like that. They were only using those words in a general sense as an example of what *Umkhonto* might be involved in, and the man was wondering if, as a Christian, he could belong to an organisation that was involved in those acts.'

Beukes looks at Richard through lowered eyelids while he blows out a cloud of smoke. Then he holds out his hand.

'Here, let me see it.' He replaces his spectacles and looks at the paper. 'No man. This *is* a general statement and does not imply what you are suggesting.'

'But because it is not specific, I am worried it could suggest that they were actually planning something, whereas what they were discussing was whether acts of violence were compatible with the Christian religion.'

The Major leans back in his chair with a loud sigh and then staring at Richard over the top of his glasses says:

'You know, Reverend, yesterday you told me you couldn't remember what transpired in that conversation. Now suddenly you seem to have a noticeably clear recollection. So, what am I to believe?'

Richard feels guilty and now wishes he had told Beukes the truth from the start. He clutches his hands between his knees not knowing what to say.

Beukes sits forward and looks again at the statement.

'Is there anything else you don't agree with?'

'Please believe me. I'm deeply sorry I wasn't straight with you from the start, but I have had time to reconsider and I now know I must be honest with you.' He looks up at Beukes who does not respond. 'I really am sorry, and I feel ashamed of my behaviour.'

Now the Major responds sternly, 'And you should be. But are you telling me there are still mistakes in this statement?'

'Um, yes.' He clears his throat. 'Forgive me, but I never said Reverend Ndlovu sympathised with the aims of *Umkhonto* and that he knew members of *Umkhonto* in his congregation. In fact, I have told you that Reverend Ndlovu is opposed to violence and to this organisation.'

After a pause while he stubs out his cigarette and looking at the statement, the Major replies:

'Ja, you did say that. Just to show you I am a reasonable man I'll delete that bit.' With a ruler he draws a black line through some of the words. 'In any case,' he adds shaking his head, 'that is not important.' Taking off his glasses and putting them into his breast pocket he pushes the paper back towards Richard. 'There, you can sign it now.'

Richard looks at it and notices only half the sentence has been deleted and taking some courage from the Major's concession says:

'If you don't mind there is also this bit. I never said the man was a member of *Umkhonto*, or that Reverend Ndlovu had *Umkhonto* members in his congregation.'

'No!' the Major answers severely. 'I do mind. Look here Reverend, I have tried to meet you halfway and you are still not satisfied. Sergeant Wilkinson specifically told me you had said the man was a member of *Umkhonto* and only a moment ago you said to me that the Bantu man was wondering if as a Christian he could belong to *Umkhonto*. You admitted it right here to me. But if you won't sign then you must go back and tell the sergeant what he got wrong.'

The door opens with the usual command from the officer at the door.

'Come!'

Richard cannot bear having to confront Wilkinson again and, in a panic, he interrupts, 'No, wait a bit. Yes, I'll sign it.'

'Are you sure now?'

'Yes, yes. Um... he must have been,' he says with a sigh.

The Major waves the officer at the door away and slides a pen across the desk.

Richard's hand is shaking so much he has trouble signing, and what he writes is barely recognisable as his name. His hand trembles as he passes the sheet back to the Major who holds it up and looks at it with a scowl. Then he hands it back.

'Would you please print your name underneath the signature?'

Richard does so with a little more success and shakily returns the page to the Major who glances at it.

'Well then, that concludes our business. You will now be returned to the main charge office and you are then free to go. I must warn you however, that withholding information about a terrorist organisation is a serious offence. We are letting you off this time, but in future you must call your police station straight away if you pick up any information. So, I hope I will be hearing from you again without the need to detain you. Furthermore, as these are matters of state security, you are not to talk to the press about your time with us. Of course, if you do, I will have to resort to charging you for withholding information. I could also put a banning order on you and then you will not be able to talk to the press, but I really don't want to do that. After all, if you are banned you will not be able to go to KwaBophela and that would restrict you in getting further information for us. You can now collect your belongings. Someone will be ready to take you in a few minutes.'

Richard stands up and with a clammy hand reaches out to shake the Major's hand. However, Beukes ignores him because he is scrabbling around in one of his desk drawers. There is an officer waiting at the door, so Richard turns to go.

'Thank you Major.'

'Wait a moment. You might like to take this.' He holds out the packet of condoms. 'We won't need these anymore.'

'Oh! Thank you.' Richard hesitates. 'So, what will happen about the Immorality charge?'

'Luckily for you, that has been withdrawn.'

He feels grateful and in awe of Beukes who has now turned his back on Richard.

'Well, thanks again Major. I'll say goodbye then.'

'Ja, okay. Goodbye,' he says dismissively over his shoulder.

Richard is led back to his room as if in a trance. There does not appear to be any rush to take him back and he waits anxiously, worrying that Beukes has changed his mind and is going to keep him there. At last after about an hour an officer comes to fetch him. Gratefully Richard follows, clutching his parcel of clothing under his arm. He is again taken in the back of a police van, but as he is going home, he does not mind. To Richard the journey appears to take much longer this time and he cannot wait to get there. Sitting in the van his only thought is the hope there will be no hitches and that nothing further will prevent his release.

At last he is in his own car. The black officer at the gate salutes him as he drives out of the police station yard, and he is on his way. He still feels very shaky and as soon as he reaches the Pemberton Road outside the city he pulls over to the side and stops. Resting his head in his arms on the steering wheel he gives way to sobs of relief. The sense of being free and away from the nightmare he has been through is more than he is able to contain. He feels as though he is still in a dream-like state. Presently he reaches into the glove compartment for some tissues. It feels so good to be in his car, knowing where things are and being in control again. Then he gets out of the car, stretches himself and starts running to and fro along the road swinging his arms in the air like a dervish. Finally, he feels ready to resume his journey. Looking at his watch he sees it is already three o'clock in the afternoon. He has missed lunch without even noticing it. As it is Saturday, Noelene should be at home, and he wonders if she knows of his release.

# Chapter 22

(Saturday 13th January 1968)

When Richard turns into the Rectory drive, Noelene comes rushing out the house to greet him. Although she did not know he was coming she had spotted the car through a window. The two of them stand by the car sobbing and clinging to each other as though some unseen force is trying to pull them apart.

Eventually Richard whispers, 'Come on darling. Let's go in. I must sit down, or I think I'll collapse.'

It is then that she sees his eye.

'Whatever did they do to you? Are you okay?'

'Yes, I'm very shaken and tired, but just so glad to be free. Let's go in and I'll tell you everything.'

Sitting around their kitchen table drinking coffee he tells Noelene all that happened. It comes pouring out in a disjointed way, and although she tells him to slow down as she tries to piece it all together, he rattles on in a manic manner. Although feeling exhausted, he cannot seem to sit still and keeps standing up, walking around, and sitting down again while he recounts the events of the last two days. He starts with the terrifying midnight interrogation and then his shock at being held in the Hopedale police cells. He has just started telling her about Major Beukes when she stops him.

'Sorry to interrupt, love, but you know I've just remembered, I promised to let the Bishop know if I heard anything from you, so I think I must give him a call to tell him you're home. Then you can tell me the rest.'

'Okay, but I don't want to talk to him, so if he asks to speak to me, please make some excuse.'

She is fortunate to get through to the Bishop right away who says he will call in to see them early on Monday. He adds that the Archdeacon has already arranged for someone to take Richard's services the next day, so he must take the day off. She mentions to the Bishop that Richard had been advised not to talk to the press. In response the Bishop instructs her to refer any calls from news reporters to him.

After that interlude Richard continues by telling her about the blackmail attempt, the condoms and suddenly he adds, 'And I still don't know what happened to Nosipho.'

'Oh yes, Canon Wilson phoned yesterday to ask if there had been any news from you and to tell me, Nosipho had been released. Of course, the Bishop had told him about your arrest, and he found out about Nosipho by enquiring at Hopedale police station.'

'Well I'm relieved to hear that. You know they claimed she had signed a statement that I had made advances to her, but I can't believe she would have lied like that.'

They are still talking about Nosipho when there is a knock on the back door. Richard is feeling on edge, and at the sound of the knock he twitches as though he has received an electric shock. Noelene goes to the door. Standing at the door is Simon. Instead of his usual lovely smile he has a frowning and serious expression. He stretches his arms out to embrace her saying, 'I am so sorry to hear about Richard...' Then he sees him.

'Hau!' he exclaims loudly, and his brilliant smile appears. 'I had heard you had been detained.' Moving past Noelene, he embraces Richard. '*Hau Mfundisi*, but am I glad to see you man.' He stops and holding Richard at arm's length looks at him. 'Hey, did *they* beat you up like this?'

'Ja, but I'm okay.'

'Good Lord, you look as though they really knocked you around.'

'It was terrifying.'

'Oh man I'm sorry, but at least you're back home again.' He then turns to hug Noelene. 'Oh, this is great. I came here to sympathise, but now we can celebrate.'

Simon turns from Noelene and, dropping himself on a chair, asks, 'So, what happened? When did they let you go?'

Richard is feeling awfully guilty. He really did not want to see Simon so soon. He thinks he has betrayed his friend. He knows he must tell him about the statement he made and is wondering how he is going to do it. Nervously he mentions the tape recorder in the bakkie.

Simons jumps up with an anguished exclamation:

'*Hayibo*! The swines.' He stands there with his arms akimbo, looking furious.

Noelene is feeling very uneasy and now she interrupts, 'I think Richard has probably had enough. You must be exhausted, dear. Can't you two talk further another day?'

But Richard holds up an open palm to stop her.

'No, there is something I must tell Simon.'

At this Noelene whispers, pointing to the garden.

'Then I think it might be wise for us to talk outside.' She raises her eyes with a brief glance around the room. 'You know, walls might have ears.'

'Ja, of course,' says Simon still looking angry and worried, but he adds looking at Richard, 'Only if you feel up to it. You've obviously been through a bad time so I'm sure you need to rest.'

'No, I must speak to you.'

Noelene suggests, 'I think the back garden is the most secluded place. Let's get some chairs from the veranda.'

Next to the khaya at the back there is a patch of grass shaded by a flame tree, with frangipane trees shielding the area from the road. Noelene brings out some cold drinks, and once they are settled there, Richard briefly outlines what happened and then says:

'I don't know how to say this, but I think Simon, I have let you down very badly. They were questioning me and questioning me, and it was all about you and that man from *MK* that came to see you. Eventually under a lot of pressure and threats and...' At this point Richard chokes back sobs. Noelene reaches over and takes his hand. Tears are also welling up in her eyes.

'Come on dear, you did your best. What else could you have done?' Then turning to Simon who is looking mystified, she adds, 'They forced him to sign a statement.'

Richard interrupts and says desperately, 'I kept telling them you were against violence and that you were not a member of *Umkhonto*.'

With urgency Simon asks, 'So, what's in this statement? Have you got a copy?'

'Damn! No.' He adds lamely, 'I should have asked for a copy.'

Simon punches the air in anger.

'The bastards. That is what they do. Then they can change the statement to suit themselves. Anyhow, what was in the statement?'

'I told them you had nothing to do with *Umkhonto* and I got them to delete that from the statement.'

Simon throws up his arms in horror.

'You got them to delete that I had nothing to do with *Umkhonto*?'

'No, I'm sorry. I am getting in a muddle. I told them you had nothing to do with *Umkhonto*, but they had written that you were sympathetic to the aims of *Umkhonto* and that second bit is what I got them to delete.'

'And they did delete that?'

'Yes.'

'So, how did you let me down then? What else did the statement say?'

'There was a bit about the man who came to see you. The statement said he was a member of *Umkhonto* and I asked them to delete that as well, but they would not. They said they would keep me there until I agree to sign. But that wasn't all. The statement said we talked about sabotage and a bomb at Hopedale station...'

Simon jumps up again and prowls around exclaiming, '*Hau*! The slimy snakes.'

'Yes, I tried to get them to remove that as well, because I said it could be understood as though *you* were planning sabotage. I said sabotage and bombs were only mentioned as some of the acts *MK* are involved in and that the discussion was about whether a Christian could belong to an organisation that was involved in violence. But he would not remove it, as he said it was only a general statement, but I'm afraid they will use it against you, as if *you* were planning violence. And then, the coward that I am, I signed the bloody thing,' and he looks at the ground trying to stifle the emotions welling up in him.

Simon crouches down and kneels on the grass by Richard's chair and puts a hand on his shoulder.

'Hey, hey, hey man. Don't upset yourself. It sounds like you only told the truth, and you tried your best to protect me despite their pressure.'

In an aside to Simon, Noelene says, 'It seems there was a clear threat of torture and they did hit him as you can see.'

With tears in his eyes, Richard says, 'Yes, but I should have been braver and not told them anything. And now they are sure to come for you to find out who the man was from *Umkhonto* and they probably think you are in league with them. In fact, the sergeant said your church was an *MK* meeting place, although I said that was not true.'

Simon shrugs.

'Well if they come for me, they come for me, and in any case, I have known for a long time that would happen sooner or later. Now I am at least forewarned. So come on man, you must not blame yourself. All this is part of the struggle. As you know, God never promised us an easy life. Look what happened to Jesus.' Then with a huge grin and in a mocking whisper, 'Do you think I should go and hide the dynamite under the pulpit?'

A slight smile appears on Richard's tear-stained face.

'Come on, that's the spirit,' says Noelene. 'Simon is right. We have to expect trouble and the fact that it has come our way shows you are doing something right.'

'*Yebo* man. You must listen to your wife. Men like you can stand tall. Hey, and remember in a few months it will be Easter and God's victory. Come on, you know how the hymn goes,' and he starts to sing, raising his voice as though he doesn't care who hears. 'The strife is o'er, the ba-attle done. Now is the Vic-tor's tri-i-umph won.' Then dropping his voice and shaking his right fist in the air. '*Yebo* man, we will be free.'

Richard dries his tears and Simon stands up. The sun has by now disappeared behind the trees towards setting and long shadows cover the garden.

Simon looks at his watch.

'Hey man, I should be on my way home.'

Richard stands up.

'Let me take you in the car.'

'No. You have only just come home so your place is now here with Noelene. And don't worry; there are plenty of buses at this time of day. Everyone is going home from work now. You have had quite enough for one day. In any case, have you looked in your car to see if there is a tape recorder planted there? Remember, your car has been at the police station and you don't know what they could have done to it.'

'Good Lord, you're right. I hadn't thought about that.'

'But I must go now. *Sala kahle* my friend and remember you have been very brave. There is nothing more you could have done.'

Richard embraces Simon.

'Thank you, thank you, you know I can't thank you enough. Yes, *hamba kahle* and may God go with you.'

# Chapter 23

(Week beginning 15th January 1968)

At seven thirty on Monday morning, Noelene is up and dressed for work. Richard, unshaven, is still in pyjamas and dressing gown and they are eating breakfast when there is a knock on the front door. Simultaneously the door opens, and a voice calls out, 'Hello! It's only your Bishop.'

He comes through to the kitchen.

'I'm sorry to be interrupting your breakfast. You know I like to get started early. As they say, the early bird catches the worm.'

Richard feels the comment is directed at him as he is not yet dressed and that he has been caught out as the worm. Noelene apologises for him.

'Normally Richard is up, but I thought he deserved a bit of a lie-in today.'

The Bishop sits down at the table saying:

'Ah Noelene, I wouldn't mind a cup of coffee and while you're making it, Richard and I will get down to business.' Turning to Richard and talking rapidly he continues, 'As soon as Noelene told me you had been detained, I phoned Brigadier Bezuidenhout. He promised to make enquiries, and, in the meantime, I sent a letter to the Minister for Law and Order in Cape Town. When Dolfie – that's Bezuidenhout's Christian name – when he phoned back he assured me you were being well treated, but that they needed to question you as they believed you, probably without realising it, had vital information about a terrorist cell. So please tell me what is going on? Oh, and by the way, there is a small piece in today's paper just saying you had been questioned by the police, that you had been co-operative and had now been released without any charge. Although the paper called me, I only told them you had been released. I think they got the rest from the police.'

Richard does not know how to respond as he tries to assimilate what the Bishop is telling him. He is particularly disturbed, hearing about the newspaper report as he's worried that it could be understood as collaborating with the police. However, he starts by saying:

'Well, I was certainly *not* well treated, but perhaps I should start at the beginning.' He tells the Bishop about the tape recorder in the bakkie, what Simon had said, how he was arrested with Nosipho, and all the subsequent events, until finally his interrogation by Wilkinson. While he is speaking, he notices that the Bishop looks distracted and from time to time fiddles with his diary, paging around in it. All Richard gets from him are a few impatient-sounding grunts, and the occasional terse, 'Okay, go on.'

When he is finished the Bishop exclaims:

'Wow, you are getting yourself into deep water. You remember, I warned you after the search to lie low for a bit. But let's forget that for the moment. You are back here now, and you have been cleared of any charges. Also, from what you have told me, although it was stressful and they were a bit rough with you, you haven't suffered any serious harm, so I hope you can now put it all behind you.'

Richard is dismayed.

'But surely, I was there under duress as a prisoner. They were going to keep me there until I said what they wanted. And that sergeant assaulted me, giving me a black eye. The bruising might now have partially disappeared but look…' and he holds up his scab-encrusted blue swollen hand for the Bishop to see. 'He also did that. And that is not all – there was the threat of torture if I did not sign that statement. As the Major put it, I might start to have nightmares. And they clearly see Simon in KwaBophela as a threat and are—'

The Bishop interrupts, 'Hey, hold on a minute. I'm Bishop to the Anglicans not all the other denominations as well. Of course, I have every admiration for what the Methodists are doing in this area, but there is a limit to what I can be concerned with.'

Richard is running his fingers through his hair looking distraught.

'I don't know what to say Bishop. I don't think you appreciate what I've been through. This country is supposed to be a civilised Christian democracy and—'

The Bishop stops him again.

'Okay, okay Richard, I'll have another word with the Brigadier, but are you sure it was as bad as you make out? By your own admission you were terrified, so you could have imagined all sorts of things. I know enough psychology to know that the mind can play some incredible tricks, especially if you are under stress in a strange environment in the dark hours of the night.' He reaches over and puts his hand on Richard's shoulder. 'Look, I won't deny you've had a tough time buddy, but these are difficult days and whilst our government does a lot of things you and I would disapprove of, there is the terrorist threat you know. You should hear some of the stories I hear from chaplains with our forces on the border. But look, I want to help you. I'll tell you what – I know a good psychotherapist in Hopedale. I will arrange for you to go for counselling and for the bill to be sent to me. That will enable you to work all of this out of your system. And, as I said, I have written to the Minister and I will let you know when I get his reply. In the meantime, I think it would be very unwise of you to have anything further to do with that minister in KwaBophela. You weren't ordained to cart fridges around you know.' With that, he stands up looking at his watch. 'I'm sorry, I have to rush now, so if you bow your heads, I'll give you a blessing.'

Richard is seething and does not take in the words of the Bishop's blessing. He remains stubbornly seated when the Bishop leaves, so Noelene sees him to the door.

At the door she says plaintively, 'Simon from KwaBophela is a close friend of ours. I don't think it would be right for us to just drop him like that.'

'Some friendships are good for us and some aren't. Look, I trust your judgement Noelene. Richard has clearly got himself into deep and dangerous waters and he now needs to spend a bit of time in the shallows. What that will mean in practice, I'll leave for you and him to decide. But Richard is clearly distressed, so please see that he doesn't overdo things for the next few days, and that he goes to talk to the counsellor. And do let me know if there is anything else, I can do for you. Now I must run – bye.' He sprints down the veranda steps two at a time, and with a wave to Noelene, jumps into his car.

In the week following his interrogation, Richard experiences several ups and downs. Like a firework, he burns brightly for a short time working with frenetic energy. Those times are, however, followed by long dark periods of desolation and deep depression when he sits in his study doing nothing. He reluctantly keeps the appointment the Bishop makes and after the initial counselling session he does feel a little more hopeful, but that also does not last. *In any case*, he reasons to himself, *I have more experience of listening to people's problems than this young psychotherapist. She looks like she is just out of university. There is not much she can teach me.*

At the end of the week he receives a copy of the Minister's reply to the Bishop's letter. It simply states that he was well treated while in detention, despite his provocative behaviour, by initially deliberately withholding information pertinent to an investigation into terrorism. There is no additional comment from the Bishop, which Richard takes as an Episcopal acceptance of the Minister's statement. He feels terribly let down. He has had a few phone calls and messages of support, but not nearly as many as when the Rectory was searched. Because of the muted press coverage, many who might have supported him did not even know he had been detained.

He desperately wants to talk to Simon again and wonders if the police have yet been on to him. Each day he intends to drive out to KwaBophela, but somehow, he has not yet managed to do so. The longer he leaves it, the more it adds to his depression.

# Chapter 24

(Saturday 20th January 1968)

It is Saturday afternoon, exactly a week after Richard's release, and he is feeling a little more positive. He has managed to complete preparations for his Sunday services. Despite all the mixed feelings that still whirl about inside him he has managed to write a sermon without experiencing too many inner distractions. With his work done he wanders lazily into the lounge, stretches out in his favourite chair and picks up the daily paper. He skims through the front-page news and then turns over. His eye catches a small headline in the bottom corner of page two. It reads: 'African Minister dies in custody.' It is as though time has stopped and his eyes are glued on the text as he reads, 'The police have reported that on Thursday night a Bantu male being held for questioning under the Terrorism Act of 1967, slipped in the prison shower and died as a result of head injuries. He was named as the Reverend Simon Ndlovu of the KwaBophela...' Richard can't read any further. He blinks, his hands tremble, then his eyes cease to focus, and he slumps back in the chair, the pages of the paper falling at his feet.

Noelene is sitting on the veranda knitting and listening to her portable radio. She likes it when Richard is home. In their busy lives they have little time to relax and although they are not doing something together, she knows he is just a few yards away, and that gives her a feeling of contentment. The three days when he was detained were an absolute nightmare. The week following has also been really difficult as the effects of that harrowing experience has plagued them both. Some nights Richard has been screaming in his sleep and Noelene has had to shake him awake and comfort him. She has also found it difficult to cope with his bouts of depression when he has hardly said a word to her the whole day. She found it quite frightening when she would try talking to him and all she would get in response was a blank look. However, today has been a better day. They had a good lie-in and had made love. Richard seemed more at ease and she was now hoping that perhaps they were beginning to put the horror of his detention behind them. She was looking forward to the evening when they were planning to take a picnic supper to the Drive-In Cinema at Hopedale to see the film *Jonathan Livingstone Seagull*. She had read the little book and had been wondering what the film would make of it. She is just thinking of going to the kitchen to start grilling the hamburgers for their picnic when she hears a moaning sound from Richard in the lounge that puts her on alert. She calls out, 'Richard! Are you okay?' When she gets no reply, she lays aside her knitting, gets up and walks into the lounge. She gasps seeing Richard slumped over the side of the chair in a faint. She rushes over to him, grabs his shoulder and shakes him.

'Richard, are you alright?' He gives a slight groan as his head flops over to the other side. He is as white as a sheet. She pushes him into an upright sitting position and shakes him again.

'Come on Richard, wake up, please, wake up.'

He blinks his eyes.

'Richard, Richard, what's the matter?'

'Ooh, what happened?' He moves his arms as if pushing away something covering him.

'I don't know what happened. You seem to have fainted. Should I get you some water?' He shakes his head as if trying to clear it.

'I feel so muzzy. What happened?'

'I thought I heard something and came through and found you lying here.'

Then Richard sees the newspaper lying on the floor.

'Oh no,' and he slumps down again.

'What's the matter? Should I call Doctor Ruben?'

'No.' He sits forward as if in pain and points to the paper. 'Just read that.'

She gathers the sheets of paper that have fallen apart and glances over the front page.

'Read what?' she says.

With a lot of effort, he slowly replies:

'No, give it here. I'll show you.' He takes the paper from her and turns the page. 'Oh, I hope with all my heart that I'm wrong and that I've just been dreaming.' He fumbles with the paper. 'Oh God, no. There it is,' and he points to the item.

Noelene takes the page and reads. She gasps, 'Oh, my Lord!'

Richard breaks into loud sobs, 'It's all my fault. It is my fault. I betrayed my friend. I'm no better than a bloody Judas.'

Noelene is also in tears and kneeling at the side of the chair she cuddles him, with her head on his lap. They remain like that for some moments. Then Noelene straightens up and wipes away her tears. She says with angry emphasis, 'It's not your fault. You did everything you could to protect him. The bloody Special Branch has done this. They killed him.'

Richard puts a finger to his lips, 'Sh, sh, they might hear you.' There is a pause and then grabbing the arms of the chair he screams, 'What the hell! They might as well kill me as well,' and he snatches the paper from Noelene and throws it into the air. The pages flutter apart and scatter on the floor.

She jumps up in shock and shouts back:

'No, don't talk like that.' Then attempting to be reasonable she adds, 'We've got to be brave,' and she tries to hug him, but he pushes her away.

'Don't touch me,' he shouts angrily. He folds his arms over his head as he crouches down in his chair. Noelene hangs on to one arm which makes him shrink away from her. After a while she lets go and, again wiping tears from her eyes, stands up and wringing her hands says:

'Why, why? Simon was such a good man. Why did they do this to him? And oh! what of Florence and the children?'

She gets no response from Richard for a while. Then he mutters quietly, 'It's me. I did not even go and see him. I did not even know he had been arrested. I am no better than a murderer. It's my fault he is dead.'

'Don't talk like that. You know it is not true. It's these bloody police. Now come on,' and again she tries to take his hand, but he swats her away and buries his head in his arms. She stands back feeling helpless. In desperation she says, 'Come on, I'll go and make us some tea.' She turns to go to the kitchen but stops as she sees some movement from him. He has his hands over his face and is peering insanely at her through parted fingers. She sees eyes that are pleading for something – she doesn't know what. Then suddenly it happens. He jumps up, startling her, and rushes to the wall pressing his hands against it as if trying to push it over and screams.

'Get out, get out quick before it falls.'

She quickly grabs him trying to pull him away from the wall.

'Don't be silly. Of course it won't. Come and sit down.'

He violently shrugs her off sending her sprawling to the floor and again pushes the wall, shouting, 'I tell you, get out, get out.'

'Okay, okay, I'm going.' Terrified she gets up from the floor and runs to the study, where she frantically pages through their book of phone numbers for their local GP. She dials the number, praying that Doctor Ruben will be in, remembering that the chances are not good as it is Saturday. While she is waiting for the phone to be answered she hears a thud in the lounge. Holding on to the phone she peers around the door and sees that Richard has collapsed in a heap next to the wall.

# Chapter 25

(The next two days)

It is Sunday afternoon and Noelene is sitting at the side of Richard's bed in a private ward in Hopedale's Manor Hospital. He has been asleep the whole time she has been there. The ward sister has told her he is sedated. She said he must be kept calm for a few days, and then hopefully he will be okay.

Sitting beside him, Noelene is knitting to pass the time and becomes aware that she has adjusted the rhythm of her knitting to Richard's loud breathing. The regular beat gives her some assurance. Through the open window she can hear the hum of the city's traffic. A pleasant soft cool breeze plays with the curtains at her back. She is glad of the fresh air as she hates the antiseptic smell of the hospital. She hears a trolley with a squeaky wheel being pushed down the corridor, and the rattle of crockery. There is a knock on the door and a black ward orderly in a green overall comes in, pushing a tea trolley. She greets Noelene:

'*Sawubona*, I see the baas is asleep. Would Madam like some tea?'

Noelene is grateful for the tea and the break in the monotony of her visit.

After an hour she begins to think about going home. Being at Richard's bedside has been reassuring, but she is feeling very tired. The emotional upheaval of the last twenty-four hours has been exhausting, and the uncertainty of how he will come through this is taking its toll. She has just put her knitting down when she notices he is stirring. He turns his head towards her, blinks and pulls back the sheet to free an arm.

'What… where…' he mumbles.

She leans forward placing her hand on his arm.

'It's okay dear. You're in hospital.'

He props himself up on his elbows in a half-sitting position. He registers that it is Noelene at his side.

'Darling! What's happened?'

'Relax. Lie down. You have to rest.'

A look of panic appears on his face.

'But… why am I here? What's happened?'

'Come on. Take it easy and lie down and I'll tell you.'

'No. We have to go home.' He sits up as if he is going to get out of bed. 'I still need to read through my sermon for tomorrow.'

She takes a firm hold on his arm.

'No. There are no services tomorrow, and you must rest.'

He makes a weak attempt to shake her off. He looks down his chest at his pyjamas and exclaims, 'What the hell... what is all this and... and, why am I in bed?' he mutters angrily.

Noelene reaches over and presses a button on the end of a lead. Almost immediately a nurse in a smart white uniform with a starched origami-like cap comes in, shortly followed by another nurse.

The first nurse says firmly, 'No, Reverend Atwell! You mustn't get up.' They each take an arm in a firm hold, and with a puzzled look he allows them to ease him back onto the pillows. The nurse continues in a stern voice. 'You must rest, or you won't get better.'

He gives the nurses a bemused look and then, turning to Noelene, attempts to sit up again. She puts a soothing hand on his arm.

'They are right, dear. You are not at all well and you must try to relax. Lie down and I'll tell you what happened.' In an aside to the nurses, 'He's only just woken up.'

With a huge sigh he falls back on the pillows. The nurses pull the sheet up and tuck it tightly in at the sides so that it looks as if he is bound to the bed. One of nurses says to Noelene, 'Please ring if you need us.' She then turns to Richard. 'Now, no more trying to get out of bed. You are in the best place here and if you rest, we will soon have you well again.' She smiles at Noelene and leaves the room while the other nurse looks at a clipboard at the foot of the bed, glances at her lapel watch, hooks the clipboard back and also leaves, closing the door behind her.

Looking at Noelene and shaking his head, Richard pleads:

'So, what's happened? Please tell me.'

Patting his shoulder, she says:

'Love, you've had a minor breakdown. It happened yesterday and the doctor thought it best if you were admitted to hospital. You are in the Manor Hospital and they have kept you sedated since you came in. It is now Sunday afternoon.'

He looks at her in disbelief.

'Sunday afternoon!' he exclaims frowning in puzzlement. There is a pause as he struggles to make sense of it all. 'But what then happened to my services?'

'You don't need to worry about the church. Everything has been taken care of by the Archdeacon. He arranged for old Tommy Tompkins to come and take the services and Stan was on hand to help him. Everyone at church sends their best wishes and will remember you in their prayers.'

He does not appear to take in a word she is saying as he pulls the bedclothes off and stands up next to the bed.

'We must try to get out of here.' He points at the door. 'I suppose that door is still locked. We must get out of here or Wilkinson will come for me again.' Then pleading he adds, 'Please tell them, I've told them everything I know.'

'No, Richard, you must stay in bed. Please listen to me.' She desperately presses the bell.

He looks at Noelene.

'So, they have got you here now as well.' In a half whisper he adds, 'they torture people here you know.' Something then appears to make him pause and he sits down on the bed with his legs hanging over the side scratching his head. A posse of three nurses enter.

'No, get away, please, don't hurt me,' he cries, shielding his face with his hands. However, the nurses' reassurances seem to penetrate his muddled thoughts and with a little resistance he is soon flat on his back in bed. They remain with him and after a short while a man in a white coat appears, with a stethoscope round his neck. Noelene is asked to leave the room for a moment. She waits outside the closed door. When the door opens the doctor comes out and explains to her:

'We have given him another sedative. He is still quite disturbed, but we are hopeful he will make a complete recovery. We will probably keep him here three or four days to see how things go.'

Returning to his room, Noelene is told that a nurse will remain with Richard until he falls asleep. He is still very confused but is more compliant, and so Noelene decides to take her leave.

Richard does not wake up again until the early hours of the next morning. His room is in semi-darkness. He lies there staring at the ceiling. His neck is stiff and painful, so he turns his head slowly from side to side. Now he can see a window and registers that it is dark outside. He feels very tired and gradually drifts off to sleep again… *He dreams that he is lying on his stomach, naked, on something like an operating table. Sergeant Wilkinson is shouting at him:*

*'This will make you talk, you bloody Commy Liberal.' He shoves a hosepipe nozzle into his anus and calls out, 'Okay, turn on the tap.'*

*Richard kicks his legs and twitches his body crying out, 'No, no, no, please no. I'll tell you…'*

A nurse passing his door hears his muffled shouts and goes in to check up on him. She shakes his shoulder,

'It's okay, calm down, you're having a nightmare. It's only a dream.'

'No, no,' he mumbles thickly as the terror slowly ebbs away.

'There you are. Just relax. Everything is okay and I'll stay here with you.'

His mind slowly starts to sort things out. He remembers that he is in hospital. Then he dozes off again… *This time he dreams he is talking to Brigadier Bezuidenhout. The Brigadier is assuring Richard that Simon will not be arrested. Then the scene switches and now Richard and Simon are standing on opposite sides of a chasm. A huge ball is suspended from the sky like a gigantic pendulum. The two men are laughing as each catch hold of the ball and then gives it a push so that it swings over for the other to do likewise. Suddenly Richard sees a squad of policemen rushing into view on Simon's side. They grab Simon, preventing him from pushing the ball with the result that its momentum is not strong enough to reach Richard as it swings back. It finally comes to rest in the middle of the chasm where no one can reach it. He is distraught as he watches the men manacle Simon, who turns to smile at his friend. He can hear the chains clanking, as the prisoner is led away…* He wakes in a cold sweat. Gradually he realises that the clanking is actually coming from the hospital corridor where an orderly is collecting up metal bedpans.

A nurse is taking his pulse.

'Ah, you have woken up.'

'Er… what?' He shakes his head slightly.

She continues, 'It's okay. You've been sleeping and it seems you've had some bad dreams, but everything is okay.' After standing at the bedside for a while she sits down at a table nearby and writes on a pad. When finished she turns to Richard and sees he is still awake. 'I'm right here if you want anything.'

He notices it is now daylight. He asks, 'I've lost track of time. How long have I been here?'

The nurse goes to the foot of the bed and unhooks the clipboard.

'Um, it looks like... yes, a couple of days, that's all. But don't worry about anything. The doctors say you are going to be fine once you've had a good rest.'

Richard finds her words reassuring, and lies back, relaxing for a moment. Then gradually anxiety begins to creep into him as he remembers the news of Simon's death. At first, he is not sure if that is also a bad dream. He feels his limbs tensing. He remembers his detention and wonders if Simon was taken to that house where Major... um... he cannot remember his name. His thoughts are all in a jumble and he feels like he is trying to find his way through a thick mist where everything remains ill defined. As soon as he gets hold of a thought it seems to disappear and it all becomes a muddle of whirling images as he struggles to remember what he had in mind a moment before.

He remains in this turmoil for much of the morning, dozing off intermittently. Each time he wakes he feels his head is a little clearer. He is beginning to remember how Major Beukes – *ah*, he exclaims to himself, *I have remembered his name*. He remembers how Major Beukes threatened him into making a statement, but he still cannot remember exactly what was in it. He wonders if he said that Simon knew that the man who came to him for advice was a member of *Umkhonto*. If he did then the police would have certainly used that in interrogating Simon. The thought occurs to Richard that he would really like to talk to someone. A faint hope keeps coming back to him that perhaps Simon's death is one of his bad dreams. It is all such a muddle. He must ask Noelene if Simon is really dead.

He can't remember much of what led to his hospital admission and she would be able to tell him. He realises that whatever happened it must have been a shock to her as well. But there are other things he would like to talk over, and he does not want to overburden her. He wonders who else he might talk to. There is the hospital chaplain, whom he remembers a nurse saying had been to visit him. He dismisses that option, because he does not want to talk to another priest, particularly one who knows him. He has quite a strong sense of professional rivalry and doesn't want to expose his vulnerabilities to another priest. There is the counsellor the Bishop referred him to, but she was too formal. He wants just an ordinary down-to-earth person. Then he remembers the nurse had said if he wanted anything he should ask, so what about one of the nurses? The nurse that had been at his bedside when he woke up seemed genuinely sympathetic and understanding. However, she is not in the room just now, but he hopes she will soon look in on him.

He doesn't find an appropriate opportunity however, because his lunch is brought in; his first proper meal in hospital. Shortly after lunch the nurses change shifts and then Noelene arrives to visit.

She is pleased to see he is awake, reasonably rational and calm. This is a great relief for her as she didn't know what to expect when she walked in. She has brought with her some 'get well' cards from parishioners. She knows they must take things slowly and thinks that reading the messages, which she found encouraging, would also be a comfort for Richard. He does take an interest in the cards but then suddenly asks, 'Is it really true that Simon is dead?'

Taken aback at first, she does not know how to answer. She looks up at him and finds he is steadily looking her full in the face. Reaching out and taking his hand she quietly says, 'Yes, I'm afraid he is, but let's not talk about it now.'

After a long silence he changes the subject and asks about some of the people she had seen in church the previous day. She is grateful that he does not again refer to Simon nor does he mention the events of Saturday. His psychotic breakdown frightened her very much and that is the last thing she wants to talk about now. She is also encouraged when he asks her to bring him some writing paper and the books at home that he had been reading. These are surely positive signs of his recovery and, staying later than usual, she only leaves when his dinner is brought in.

Shortly after dinner the Archdeacon arrives, dressed in a sombre black suit. He speaks in an affected tone of voice that Richard has always found irritating and patronising. He tells Richard he has temporarily taken over the running of Pemberton parish, so everything has been taken care of, and there is nothing for Richard to worry about.

With some effort, Richard tries to be as polite as possible.

'Thank you, Archdeacon.' Then he adds, 'If you don't mind, I'm feeling very tired and I have to rest, so I would be grateful if you would leave me now.'

However, to Richard's further annoyance, he does not leave, but instead suggests, 'Don't mind me.' Getting out his prayer book he adds, 'You rest, and I'll just sit here and quietly say Evensong for both of us and if you wish to join in please do. But don't worry and if you fall asleep, that is okay as well.'

Richard thinks; *trust him to bloody well think of saying Evensong*. He pretends to fall asleep while the Archdeacon drones softly on. Richard keeps up the pretence until he hears the Archdeacon leave. By then it is quite late, the nurses are changing shifts and the night sister comes in to give him his medication. She is an older rather plump woman, and looks a motherly sort which encourages Richard to ask, 'I'd like to talk to you if you've got the time?'

'Certainly,' she replies. 'I'll tell you what, I'll see to the rest of the patients and then I'll do you last so that before you take your medicine, we can have a little chat. In any case, you are on the mend, so hopefully you soon won't need any drugs.'

It is about a half hour before she gets back. During that time, he is feeling rather pleasantly relaxed, thinking that there is a chance this older woman would understand him and be someone with whom he might share his burden. So, when she is sitting at his bedside he asks:

'By the way, may I ask, what is your name?'

'I'm Sister du Plessis. You may call me Sister. Some of the girls here call me Dup, but I don't really like that,' she says smiling.

'Okay, thank you Sister. I want to tell you something that is weighing heavily on my mind. It's like this – I suppose it's something like a confession. By the way, I hope I won't shock you.'

'Ag, being a sister in hospital I have seen and heard all sorts of things. I don't think there is much that will shock me.'

'Okay. You see, I think I caused the death of a man who was a particularly good friend to me...' Richard pauses to see her reaction.

Her smile is replaced by a frown.

'Um, ye...s! When did this happen and who was this friend of yours?'

He begins to feel he is making a mistake in talking to her, but having started he plunges on.

'His name was Simon Ndlovu, and it happened about a week ago.'

Her frown darkens,

'But that's a Bantu name! Come on Reverend Atwell, aren't you imagining it?'

'No, seriously. I know it may seem strange that I had a black man for a friend, but really, he was a very good friend and a colleague. You see, because Simon was black, that was what caused all the trouble, I was detained by the police... Didn't you see it in the papers?'

Sister Du Plessis has often heard patients coming out with exaggerated ideas of guilt and or grandiose ideas of their fame or notoriety, so she interrupts and says forcefully:

'No no no! I do not want to hear any more of this. Listen carefully to what I have to say. You are a minister, not a criminal. You must stop having these funny ideas. It's all in your imagination. If you have done anything seriously wrong, there would be a policeman guarding you. I don't see any guard here, do you?' She pauses for a moment, but Richard does not respond. So, she continues, 'What has happened to you is that you are suffering from stress. It happens to ministers sometimes, because of their work. Now listen, you are a good man doing a good job and as soon as we can get rid of these strange ideas, the sooner you will be able to go home and get back to doing God's work. Now, I'll give you your medicine and perhaps tomorrow these funny ideas will have gone away.'

Richard feels he is up against a brick wall and that he has little choice but to do as he is told. Once Sister du Plessis is out of the room he lies back, feeling utter despair. *What a disaster*, he mutters to himself.

# Chapter 26

(End of January early February, 1968)

On the Saturday after his return home from hospital, Richard and Noelene are having a lie-in. They also take the opportunity to make love. As usual he rolls over to her side of the bed and they start to cuddle. After a while he pulls his pyjamas off, she slips out of her nightie and they are clasped in a passionate embrace. Normally by now Richard would have a hard erection, but today he is horrified to discover that little is happening. He quietly suggests to Noelene:

'Darling, Mr P doesn't seem to be properly awake. Do you think you could rouse him?'

She runs her hand down his stomach to his groin and strokes his penis.

'Ooh, he is rather flabby. We will have to see what we can do about that,' and she continues to gently caress it.

There is a slight stirring, but whilst it is partly swollen it is certainly not firm. He suggests, 'Perhaps if we have a go it will stiffen up.' He reaches for the condom he had placed at the side of the bed and tries to put it on, but it only fits loosely over his drooping member. This has never happened to him before. After an abortive attempt at trying to stimulate himself he angrily tosses the Durex aside and rolls away from Noelene feeling dreadful.

'It's no good. I just can't manage it.'

'But what's the matter?'

He heaves a huge sigh of despair and mumbles, 'I don't know.'

'Never mind.' Stroking his arm, she continues, 'You have been under a lot of strain and maybe it's a side effect of the pills you are taking.'

For a while he does not say anything. Eventually he mutters:

'Well it may be the pills, but I just feel I'm useless.'

'That's not true,' she says soothingly while Richard struggles to stifle the angry sobs that are rising within him.

Since being discharged from hospital, Richard is on sick leave, the Bishop having barred him from doing any parish work. The Bishop has also arranged for him to go on a retreat at the Blessed Sacrament Convent near Hopedale. Richard thinks it will be a waste of time. He has been there on previous retreats and does not believe that the dear old nuns will be able to cope if he unburdens himself to them. In any case, he decides that before he goes on retreat, he must visit Simon's widow and at least show some sympathy and possibly tell Florence about his part in the arrest. He wonders what is going to happen to her and their children and hopes to find a way to make some reparation and perhaps ease his conscience. He had missed the funeral, which according to Robin Farmer had taken place on the same weekend when Richard had had his breakdown.

Noelene is adamant that she does not want him going to KwaBophela.

'Seeing Florence and the children will just upset you, and we don't want you landing up in hospital again. Once you are properly over this and are stronger, there will be plenty of time to go and see her.'

For the next week, a thick fog of depression closes in over Richard. He seldom gets up before eleven in the morning and then all he does is to sit in a chair. There is a book at his side, but he doesn't get beyond a few pages before his mind drifts off. The spectre of Wilkinson looms up regularly like a monster and he goes over and over those events, imagining different responses he might have made. Although he wishes he could have acted more courageously, the reality of his weakness intrudes and he blames himself for being, in Wilkinson's words, a sissy. He tries to tell himself he must move on and think positively, but any such thoughts are quickly derailed, and he is back remembering his helpless quivering at Wilkinson's shouts and the crack of his cane.

Noelene tries to get him to talk to her, but he gets into a muddle knowing she does not like to hear him blaming himself, so he doesn't know what to say. She is barely able to disguise her irritation when day after day she comes home from work to find him still unshaven, in his pyjamas and having eaten nothing and done nothing. She begins to think he is consumed by self-pity and is not making any effort to get out of it. Each morning she suggests various things he might do. Before leaving home, she will put on some of his favourite LPs, but to him it is no more than background noise. He is vaguely aware that she is becoming exasperated with his low mood but feels there is nothing he can do about it. He feels he is a disgrace and through his cowardice has become irredeemable.

# Chapter 27

(February 1968)

After two weeks of sitting around and doing nothing, Richard decides he is not going to be able to move on until he has been to KwaBophela and faced Florence. He thinks he might see if he can do something for Simon's Co-op, and possibly raise some money for Florence and her children. That could give his life some purpose and, in any case, he feels he owes it to Simon's family. However, knowing Noelene will not be happy about him going, he does not tell her of his plans. Instead, on the evening before he intends to go, he mentions to her:

'If you don't mind, I'd like the car tomorrow. I think I might drive over to Hopedale to SPCK to see if there is a book I may buy with that gift voucher that I've had for some months now.' He does not like lying to Noelene, but reasons it is not really a lie, as he does plan to go to SPCK as well.

Noelene immediately agrees.

'That's an excellent idea. I do think you need to be getting off your backside, if you don't mind me saying so, and getting up in the mornings and doing things again. I am sure you will feel a lot better for it.'

So, the next day he drops Noelene off at school and once out of sight turns the car round towards KwaBophela. He has the car window down and a pleasant cool breeze ruffles his hair. Despite being aware that it will be a difficult visit, he is used to talking to bereaved people, and so for the first time since being in hospital he is feeling a little more at ease.

Driving along, suddenly one of his old fears returns and he glances in the rear-view mirror to see if anyone is following, but no traffic is to be seen and he is soon turning off the main road. Once on the gravel road he can keep his window down as the road is wet and the usual dust has been settled by a storm of the previous night. With mud splashing over the car he realises that unless he cleans the car when he gets home, he will not be able to keep his destination a secret from Noelene. There are no muddy roads on the way to SPCK. He decides he will tell her, although it will be after the event. Hopefully, he will be feeling so much better that she will realise that the visit has done him some good.

About a half a mile from KwaBophela a 'Road Closed' barrier comes into view. Stopping at the barrier he sees that a donga has been scoured out of the hillside cutting right across the road. He figures that it must be the result of last night's storm. A gang of African workmen are starting to repair the damage and one, who appears to be their foreman, comes over to the car. Richard explains that he is trying to get to the KwaBophela Methodist mission. The foreman replies:

'*Hau* baas, no motors going there today.'

'Well, may I leave my car here?'

'*Kulungile*[18],' says the foreman pleasantly. 'I pasop for baas,' and he directs Richard to a space at the roadside where it won't be in the way of the workmen.

Having parked, Richard sits in the car for a while having second thoughts. It is quite a long walk to the Mission and perhaps this is a sign that he should turn back. However, he notices that the foreman is organising some planks over the muddiest parts of the gully, clearly for Richard to use as a temporary bridge. With a sigh he decides that there is no turning back.

Thanking the foreman and the workmen, he carefully steps over the boards and sets off along the road dodging the puddles. He passes some women carrying bundles of brushwood on their heads. They turn and stare at him. He greets them in their language, and they make surprised responses. He knows it is very unusual for them to see a white man walking along a country road in a black area.

---

[18] Kulungile: Zulu – Okay.

Arriving at the Bantu Affairs office to obtain a permit he finds it is closed. Presumably the officials couldn't get to work because of the road being washed away. Again, he wonders if he should turn back. However, he owes it to Simon to visit his widow and he is determined to press on.

Nearing the Methodist Mission, he encounters a group of small children playing alongside one of the shacks. As he approaches, they stop their game and shyly move aside. One of them recognises him as the white minister, who occasionally visits and quietly greets him,

'*Sawubona Mfundisi.*'

The others chime in respectfully and he gets a chorus of greetings. He feels warm inside, pleased that one of them remembers him and he returns their greeting. A few steps further and the church building comes into view. He stops in his tracks with shock. In the yard at the side of the church lies the fridge, now smashed almost beyond recognition. For some moments he stands there frozen. Then he notices that several of the church windows are broken, and above them are streaks of black soot.

'What the hell?' he exclaims. With deep foreboding he continues towards the Manse. His knock on the open door is immediately answered by a woman he vaguely recognises as one of the church members. He greets her:

'Good morning,' but before he can ask for Florence she appears from another room. He steps towards her and takes her in a hug. 'I'm so sorry Florence.' He immediately becomes aware that she is not returning his hug. She feels stiff and emotionless. He thinks that perhaps it is the shock of her bereavement, and that her coldness is not personal. As he releases her she indicates a chair.

'You had better sit down.'

The other lady and Richard both sit down in well-worn easy chairs. Florence goes to an upright chair behind the dining table a little removed from them. A big oval framed picture of Simon in his clerical collar and gown looks down on them. Richard cannot remember that picture being there the last time he visited. While taking his seat he turns to Florence.

'I have been wanting for a long time to come and tell you how sorry I am about the tragedy that happened to Simon, but unfortunately I have not been well and have been in hospital. I was deeply shocked when I read about it in the paper.' Florence says nothing and only looks at the table in a distracted sort of way. He adds, 'I feel particularly bad because of my part in all this.'

Florence looks up and meets his gaze. She nods her head in a knowing manner before looking down again as though she is examining something on the surface of the table.

Richard is feeling nonplussed and does not know what to say. He is feeling terrible, as though he is intruding in an inappropriate way in her grief and is beginning to regret coming. However, he continues.

'Truly Florence, when I was detained, the police already had Simon's name. I tried to convince them that he was not connected in any way to Umkhonto. I told them he was against violence—'

The other woman interrupts angrily.

'That is not what they said to Reverend Ndlovu when they came to arrest him in the dark, long before the sun came up. The Mfundisi and his family were still asleep when they smashed the door down. The Mfundisi and Mother did not even have time to get out of bed. They said they had a statement from you that Reverend Ndlovu had information about terrorists that he was hiding from the police.'

Richard shakes his head vigorously declaring, 'No, no I never said anything of the sort.'

'They showed the Mfundisi a paper with your name. Now, who can we believe? Then they searched the Manse, turning everything upside down, and the children were crying, but the police didn't care. They took him away and we never saw him alive again.'

'That's terrible and I'm really sorry, but I can assure you that the statement I signed did not say anything like that.'

He turns towards Florence. 'I promise you Florence, I would never have wanted to get Simon into trouble. Please believe me,' he pleads.

She looks up and says slowly:

'It is not easy to talk about these things. My heart is hurting too much.' With a gesture towards the other woman she says, 'Sister Veronica will speak for me.'

Veronica immediately points a finger at Richard.

'So, you did sign a paper then.' And more vehemently, 'What did you tell the police?'

He feels his face going red, his body is tense, and his hands are sweating.

'I can't remember exactly, er...' he hesitates. Then he blurts out, 'I definitely told them that Simon wanted to have nothing to do with terrorism.' Veronica gives him a searching look and he feels she does not believe him. After a short pause he adds, 'The police twist people's words to suit themselves.'

Veronica continues glaring at him and an uncomfortable silence hangs in the air. Eventually she glances at Florence and then, turning back to Richard sighs:

'Well, I don't know. It might be as you say. But I tell you the people of KwaBophela think you are an informer.' Hearing the word 'informer', Richard feels a shudder of fear and dismay, but Veronica continues talking. 'Or that when they arrested you, you broke and told them what they wanted to know. They think that is why you were detained for only a few days. They say, when people who are against the government are arrested, they are kept in jail for a long, long time, sometimes many years, not just three days like the newspaper said. And the paper said you were *co-operating* with the police.'

Richard feels he is not convincing them, and his increasing feeling of guilt makes him extremely uncomfortable. Nonetheless he makes another desperate attempt to convince them.

'I can promise you; I'll even swear on the Bible, I am not an informer, and the police have twisted my words in that statement.'

Neither of the women responds to him and there is another uncomfortable silence. Sounds from outside of children shouting in their play, and chickens cackling waft into the room. Richard feels there is nothing more he can say. He asks:

'When I arrived, I saw some of the church windows are broken. What happened?'

'*Yebo*, that was the other thing,' Veronica says. 'The same night, while the police were searching the Manse, thugs came with hammers. We all know they were with the police. They smashed up everything in the church. They broke open the cupboards, slashed the bags of mealie-meal and sugar and poured it all out on the floor. It was a big mess. Every tin of food was broken, the fridge was smashed and the books that they didn't take away were piled up and burnt there inside the church. Now the walls and everything is black.' Then she looked menacingly at Richard. 'The people here think all of this happened because you betrayed us. I don't know if you have betrayed us, because I have heard it said the police will do anything. But I tell you, you must not come back here again, because I don't know what might happen to you.'

Richard shifts uneasily on his chair. He looks pleadingly at Florence. She still has her head down. He decides he must take the warning and go, but at the same time he does not want to leave the situation as it is. He feels a need to justify himself somehow. So, he says with a show of determination, which is not what he is feeling:

'Okay, I'll go now. But Florence, I want you to know, I tried my best not to say anything to the police that would endanger Simon. I am really distraught about what happened to him, and I promise I will pray for you and do all I can to help you and to get some justice for you and for Simon.' He stands to go, feeling his promise is really quite hollow, and that these two women must know there is little he can do. He continues to say the conventional words. 'For the moment, I wish you God's blessing and stay well.'

Florence does not look up and remains silent.

Walking to the door he says to Veronica, 'Stay well and God bless you also.'

She follows him and at the door, she insists again:

'Please, don't come back here. We don't want any more trouble.' She watches him from the doorway as he trudges heavily up the hill.

Previously he had never experienced any fear in being in KwaBophela, but now he looks around furtively. He realises he is extremely vulnerable and wonders if anyone could be hiding behind a hut ready to attack him. It is as though menace lurks around every corner. However, there are only the children playing and a few women doing chores outside their huts. Walking along the road he keeps glancing around and is wary of the few people he meets. He wonders if the workmen on the road are from KwaBophela and whether they might recognise him as the one believed to be Simon's betrayer. In any case, he thinks he should give them something for helping him across the gully and watching over his car. He looks in his wallet and sees he only has a twenty rand note. At the gully he gives the money to the headman asking him to share it with the others.

'*Hau*! Thank you baas.' He bows to Richard and then waves the note towards the other men who also give vent to exclamations and words of thanks. However, Richard feels no better and he drives away with a heavy heart.

Back at the Rectory he sinks into a chair and it is there that Noelene finds him at the end of the day.

'Richard, what's wrong? Didn't you go to SPCK?

'No.'

'Oh! Why not?' Then a thought occurs to her and she cottons on to his deception. She scowls, 'No, don't tell me – you went to see Florence?'

He sighs, 'Yes, I did.'

'And as I warned you it wasn't the right thing to do.'
'No, it wasn't.'
'So, what happened?'

He is reluctant to talk, but with a lot of questioning Noelene gradually gets to know the outline of the visit. She is shocked to hear that the church and the Co-op stores had been vandalised but is even more shocked and frightened to hear that Richard is being blamed for it. With a sinking heart and some anger, she exclaims:

'Well, you have got us into trouble on all sides. The whites are suspicious of us and now the blacks have turned against us as well. What are we going to do?'

That question was to hang over their heads for many more months.

# Chapter 28

(October 1968)

It is now eight months after Richard's breakdown and the church wardens have arranged a meeting with him. He assumes it has to do with preparations for the Christmas fete.

He meets them at the Rectory door and immediately senses that this is different from previous meetings. Stan is usually very chatty and always asks after Noelene. Today, he appears to be skulking behind his new colleague, Barry. Richard leads the way to the study. Church warden meetings always start with a drink, so Richard asks:

'Would you like a beer or something else?'

Barry responds in a serious tone:

'I think it might be better, on this occasion, if we do our business first, and then we might have a drink.'

Richard feels a bit put out by Barry's unusual approach and gives Stan a questioning look, hoping to get some support from him, but he agrees they leave the drinks until later.

When they are seated, Barry takes the initiative.

'Richard, we want to talk to you generally about the parish, because we can see things are not right. You had a very traumatic time earlier this year, but that is now many months ago and since then – and we think we are voicing the feelings of most parishioners – since then, our church has been going downhill. We, as church wardens, feel we must do something to turn things around, and we are here to offer you our help.'

Richard is immediately on the defensive.

'Well, I think you misled me. I thought you were coming to talk about the Christmas fete?'

The two wardens look at each other.

Barry says, frowning, 'In arranging this meeting, I never said anything about the fete, did you Stan?'

Stan shakes his head, so Richard continues:

'Okay, never mind that then. Well, we all know church life has its ups and downs. With Christmas and the fete coming, things will perk up again. But what do you mean by going downhill? All the services are still happening, and I haven't had any further sick leave or any leave for that matter since I was ill.'

Stan speaks up:

'Look Richard, please don't take this personally. After all, you and I have been friends for a long time. Now, I know money isn't everything, but the planned giving is well down on last year, and it's the same with church attendance.'

Barry chips in:

'Actually, over the last three months it has hit an all-time low. This isn't just a normal dip that's going to recover naturally. You see, Richard, to be honest, we feel you have not got the same zest that you used to have, and which drew people like me into the church. You know, Doris said to me last Sunday, "I don't know why I come to church to listen to sermons that I've heard before," and I think she was speaking on behalf of a lot of people.'

Richard answers belligerently:

'If you had to preach two, sometimes three sermons every week, I think you would also redo some old sermons; and in any case, I always try to update them.'

Barry continues:

'No, it's not just that, Richard. You have also been conducting worship in such an offhand manner, as though your mind is elsewhere, and you just want to get it over and done with.' He shakes his fist and says with emphasis, 'The passion you used to express is no longer there.'

'Okay, what do want? Do you want me to preach hell fire like Pastor Fred at the Full Gospel Church down the road?'

Stan answers:

'Well, he certainly brings in the crowds, but no. You know we don't want that. We want you to be your old self again and we want to see what we can do to help.'

'That's right,' says Barry. 'Because there are other things that have also been slipping, like the Olsen wedding when I had to come and call you from the Rectory, because you had forgotten all about it.' Richard fidgets in his chair with embarrassment at being reminded of this terrible lapse. Barry continues, 'Sheila was in tears being kept at the door waiting for you, and old man Olsen was furious. I can tell you; I spent a lot of time pacifying him. Now that was something really serious as I tried to impress upon you when we talked about it.'

'Oh, come on Barry, anyone can make a mistake.'

'Not over something as important as a wedding. You just cannot forget things like that, as I said to you at the time. But even if we grant you one serious mistake, it has not been the only one. The Bishop has passed this on to me,' and he takes a letter out of his pocket and hands it to Richard.

The letter is from the son of a lady whose funeral Richard conducted the previous week. He is shocked that a complaint has been made about him to the Bishop. His embarrassment is made more acute as he remembers how he got the name of the deceased wrong and one of the relatives had interrupted the service to correct him. The letter also reminds him, that in spite of the family specially requesting their mother's favourite hymn, he had forgotten that as well. He remembered it later when it was too late, but at the time it had completely slipped his mind. Reading the letter, he feels his face colouring.

'Well, I'm really sorry about this. If you leave the letter with me, I'll write to them this evening to apologise—'

Barry interrupts, 'That's no good now. The funeral was over a week ago. The Bishop phoned the family to apologise and wrote to them before handing the letter over to me to speak to you. And I can tell you his Lordship was not best pleased.'

Richard says sheepishly, 'I don't know how that happened. You know, I usually take a lot of care over funerals and I can't now remember why I slipped up with this one.'

Barry becomes more assertive.

'Well, it isn't just a slip-up. From my observation it is all part of a pattern...' He pauses for a moment and then continues. 'There is that new family, Hopkins, who recently moved here. They have been in church a couple of times. Have you been to visit them?'

'No, not yet, but I've got them in mind.'

'You see, that's what I mean, Richard. Having them in mind isn't good enough. When I arrived in Pemberton you were around like a shot, and I immediately got the impression that yours was a church that was alive and growing. Now it is the very opposite. And it all comes down to leadership. If the leader isn't on the ball the whole organisation falls apart.' He pauses, expecting Richard to respond. The minister however does not meet his gaze, feeling humiliated at being chastised by his church warden. Instead he takes refuge in opening his diary and jotting down the new family's name. Meanwhile Barry continues, 'We have people on our prayer list who are sick, some are in hospital. Have you been to visit any of them over the past two weeks?'

This is a bit too much for Richard. He glares at Barry, feeling he is being questioned like a naughty schoolboy. Angrily he comes to life.

'Hey! What is this? The blooming inquisition!'

Stan reaches across and pats him on the shoulder.

'No, no, no. Don't get cross Richard. We want to help you because things are just not right.'

Barry chips in:

'Look, we as church wardens have responsibilities, and I'm sorry but we must ask these questions, however unpalatable, because we are answerable to the Bishop.'

Richard's anger dissipates at the softer tone in Barry's voice. At the back of his mind he knows that what the wardens are saying is true and that he hasn't got a leg to stand on. Weakly he says:

'Okay, I'll visit everyone on the sick list and the Hopkins family as soon as possible.'

Barry emphasises:

'Let us set a target that that will happen over the next seven days?'

'Yes, okay. I'll do it by then unless something urgent crops up that takes up my time.'

'Right,' says Barry. 'Give me a call about this time next week to let me know how you got on and then I'll be able to report back to the Bishop.'

Stan adds, 'And to give you more time, we're going to take over chairing the fete committee – if that's okay with you. That is something we can do and there is no reason why you should be involved, except to be there on the day.'

Richard is quite relieved to hear this as he has always found the annual fete a tiresome chore.

'That will help,' he answers lamely. He feels wretched and a failure. He is also furious that the Bishop did not contact him directly but responded to the letter of complaint without his knowledge. However, he sees the sense in Barry's demands and determines to pull his socks up and to try to regain some of the motivation he felt in the past.

A few days later, however, Richard receives a phone call from the Bishop's secretary summoning him and Noelene to a meeting with the Bishop.

Richard and Noelene have no idea of the purpose of the meeting and both are feeling apprehensive as they drive over to the luxurious suburb of Upper Northwood in Hopedale on the day of their appointment. Richard is convinced that the meeting has something to do with the complaint but wonders why Noelene is involved. She is glad to have been included, being aware of rumblings in the parish, and she knows the Bishop sees her as an ally in relating to Richard.

They turn into the long drive through tall palm trees that takes them up to the palatial home that is the Bishop's House. At the door they are met by his secretary, and shown into the office, while she explains that the Bishop is on his way from the airport, having just got back from Johannesburg, and is late because his flight was delayed.

The office has open French doors leading onto a veranda overlooking the swimming pool. The office looks cluttered and untidy. The bookshelves are overflowing and there are piles of books on the floor. Propped up in the corner of the room is an Episcopal crook, and a richly embroidered cope hangs from the half-open door of a cupboard.

While chatting to Noelene and Richard, the secretary attempts to bring some order to the pile of papers on the desk. She comments:

'Bishop Andrew is really so busy you know. He just doesn't get time to look at a lot of this.' She holds up a pile of mail. 'I shall have to see if I can filter some of this out.' Just then a car is heard racing up the driveway. 'Ah, that must be him now. I'll disappear with this,' and she leaves the room carrying the pile of mail and some files.

Soon the door flies open and the Bishop sweeps in, dropping a fat briefcase next to the desk. Richard and Noelene stand to greet him.

'Richard, Noelene, thank you for coming. Please sit down.' He seats himself behind the desk and continues talking in a rapid, out-of-breath manner. 'Now I hope you are both well?' He does not wait for an answer and continues, 'I want to come straight to the point and be honest with you. You have been in Pemberton for nearly five years and during that time you have done some good work. But earlier this year you went through a difficult time that has, and is, evidently still taking its toll. What you now need is a change; the opportunity to put all that behind you and make a new start. I am therefore going to give you a new appointment. But as you know, I don't act dictatorially, and I do have an alternative suggestion – so you have a choice. The appointment I have in mind would involve you joining the Archdeacon in his parish as his assistant.' The Bishop notices the look of horror on Richard's face so he quickly adds, 'It will be a temporary appointment for about a year, just to give you time to get over the trauma the two of you have been through this year. When you and the Archdeacon feel you are ready to move on, then I will be willing to discuss another parish with you.'

Richard answers sullenly, 'In other words, I'll be his curate.'

'That's not the way I see it. As you know the Archdeacon must be away a lot, so much of the time you will oversee a very large parish. Your title will be Senior Assistant Priest and your stipend will reflect your responsibility and be that of a Rector, namely the same as you are getting now.'

In a grumpy tone, Richard mumbles, 'But in reality, I will be a glorified curate.'

Noelene interjects, 'Come on Richard, you know we can't go on like we are now. Perhaps taking a step back will be just what you need in order to go forward again.'

'Well, it strikes me more like punishment for that letter of complaint.'

At this the Bishop bridles:

'I don't like your tone, Richard.' He leans back in his chair. 'I'm trying to help you, and you should listen to Noelene.' He leans forward again and with emphasis says, 'You have to realise that you're in trouble. If you go on as you have been at Pemberton, it will not be long before I'll be asking for your resignation. It's that serious.'

Richard looks up, clearly struck by the Bishop's severity, and tries to be a bit more agreeable.

'Okay. Did you say you had an alternative?'

'Yes, this is a little more problematic. You got a First in Classics at university, didn't you? I guess you know Professor Newman. He worships at the cathedral and is a good Anglican. Now he has been expanding the Classics Department. He tells me he could take you on at the beginning of next year as a part-time junior lecturer, with the possibility of you going full-time if his plans continue to work out. I think it will be good for the diocese to have a priest on the university staff. You will be paid by the university, but the problem is, because you will be part-time, you would initially have to take a cut in salary. Maybe if you helped at the cathedral on Sundays, the diocese might be able to supplement your pay to some extent. In any case, I would want you to be attached to the cathedral to keep your hand in because you may, in the future, come back into full-time ministry.'

This is something that has not occurred to Richard, and the fact that the Bishop has been talking about him to others without his knowledge, does not immediately bother him. He recalls that when he had completed his Masters degree, the Classics staff had wanted him to stay on in a teaching and research capacity, but at that time he had felt he had had enough of academic work, and wanted to be involved in practical ministry. Now getting away from the hassle of parish life, and the kudos of being a university lecturer, has some appeal for him. At least, he thinks, it is by far preferable to being a lackey of the Archdeacon. He answers in a more conciliatory tone.

'That's something I hadn't thought of.' He turns to Noelene. 'There is a lot to consider here—'

The Bishop interrupts:

'That's right. Now you two go away and think about it. Go and see the Prof and the Archdeacon to get a fuller picture of what they would be expecting of you, and you could put your questions to them. You can then let me know what your decision is in say, ten days' time.' With that he presses a button and talks into an intercom. 'Sylvia, would you please show the Atwells out.'

Richard is feeling quite bemused by what has been put to him. He would like more time to take it all in. Everything is moving too fast. The Bishop is already standing up with hand outstretched to bid them farewell and his secretary is at the door. Noelene stands up, followed by an obviously reluctant Richard.

As he shakes the Bishop's hand he says:

'This has really been sprung on us and there is not just a lot to think about, but the parish will have to be prepared. Taking leave of people with whom we have built up some good relationships, will need to be handled sensitively and—'

The Bishop interrupts again:

'As I said, talk to the Archdeacon. Look, I'm sorry, but I'm already running late, and I have to see someone at the Diocesan office in ten minutes.' He picks up one of his phones. 'I must also make a couple of calls before I go. So please excuse me and I'll hear from you in a few days' time.' With that he starts dialling, and Richard and Noelene follow the secretary to the front door.

# Part 2 RICHARD AND MOSES

# Chapter 29

(March 1983)

Doctor Richard Atwell is wandering along the main path towards the Campbell lecture theatre for his last lecture of the week. It is a warm, sunny, Friday afternoon. Whenever he is outside, he hitches up his black academic gown, now going green with age, and holds the corners out with his arms like horns so that the gown makes an awning over his balding head to keep the hot sun off. He cuts a strange, hunched figure, but students passing him do not give him a second glance as they are used to seeing this idiosyncratic lecturer wandering about the campus looking like a giant bat with outstretched wings. He is in fact known to the students as Batty. Even if he is not blinkered by his gown, he would not notice the students as he appears preoccupied with his own thoughts.

It is now fourteen years since he left Pemberton, although he seldom thinks back to what he regards as a part of his life that he would like to forget. Since joining the university, he has immersed himself in research, gaining his doctoral degree with a thesis on Greek sepulchral monuments, with special reference to the Mausoleum of Halikarnassos. On the campus, he is something of a loner. He never attends university functions and the only people he ever talks to are the other three members of the Classics department and then it is usually about some classical point of debate or a work issue. He is now on his way to lecture on classical architecture to a second-year class and feeling a little annoyed with himself for having forgotten to bring with him the slides he had taken on his last trip to Greece and Italy.

Entering the theatre, he drops the corners of his gown so that it hangs on him normally. He notices that the janitor has set up the slide projector as he had requested. The room seats about eighty people and the ten second-year students are scattered among the front few rows. He gives them the classical Greek greeting and gets a mumbled response. He moves the projector to one side of the rostrum.

One of the students calls out:

'Sir, aren't you going to show us your slides?'

'Er, no. I forgot to bring them, but we can have them next time.'

A collective groan emanates from the students.

Doctor Atwell takes no notice and starts his lecture. He knows the subject so well he has no need of notes and resting his elbows on the lectern his voice drones on while he has a faraway look in his eyes. It isn't long before one of the students, in the stuffy warmth of the lecture room, has nodded off; another is doodling on her note pad; a couple are having a whispered conversation and a few conscientious students are attempting to take notes.

Five minutes before the lecture is due to end, the students begin to shift about in their seats and start to gather up their books and papers. As the last minutes tick by and Doctor Atwell continues his monotonous peroration, they become increasingly restless until finally their coughing and the clatter of their books breaks into his awareness and he emerges from the classical dream world in which he has lost himself.

'Oh, is it time to finish?'

'I think time is up,' says one of the students.

The lecturer fumbles with his gown and pulls back a sleeve to look at his watch.

'Good heavens, yes.' Then with a dreamy smile he says, 'I think I got carried away. Okay!' and lifting his gown over his head he ambles out of the lecture theatre.

Coming out the building he is stopped by a tall, slender, young black man dressed in tie, black blazer, and neatly-pressed grey flannels.

'Excuse me. Are you Doctor Atwell?'

Richard stops abruptly and he is vaguely aware of feeling a frisson of fear.

'Er, yes,' he says lowering his gown and pulling it down over his head like a nun's veil, clutching it at his throat.

'I'm very pleased to meet you. I am Moses Ndlovu, the son of the late Reverend Simon Ndlovu. That kind man over there,' and he points to a black gardener in brown overalls watering the flower beds a short distance away, 'told me this was the place to find you.'

'Moses Ndlovu... Simon... oh yes. That's a long time ago.' Nervously he adds, 'What can I do for you?'

'Please forgive me for delaying you here. I didn't know how else to meet you and I wanted to speak to you personally. It is a very great privilege for me to talk to such an important person as a university doctor and I'll try not to waste your time. You see, I knew you when I was still a small boy and I have recently learnt a lot more about you.' At this, a nervous shiver ripples down Richard's back. He wants to walk away but the young man is still talking rather urgently.

'The reason for me wanting to see you is that my mother has told me she did you a bad injustice. She wants me to apologise to you.'

Richard blinks looking puzzled. Moses continues:

'Many years after my father was late, my mother was living in Nongoma in Zululand. One day she moved the table my father used for writing his sermons, and one of the drawers fell out and broke. When she picked up the pieces, she found a book hidden under a plank at the bottom of the drawer. No one knew about the book and the police never found it when they searched our house in KwaBophela. My mother can't read, but she gave the book to me to read.'

From a bag he is carrying over his shoulder, Moses takes out a thick exercise book with a rather tattered black cardboard cover. He hands the book to Richard who receives it but keeps one hand holding his gown tightly under his chin.

Pointing to the book Moses says:

'This is that book. Every day, my father wrote down the things he had done that day in this book. When she found the book, she asked me to read it to her. Each evening I would read a few pages to her, which she found to be a great comfort. Then I came to the last writing of my father, the night the police broke into our house and took my father away. In his last words he wrote how he had gone to see Mrs Atwell and found you had been released by the police. He wrote how you told him the police had a secret tape recorder in the lorry on the day you fetched a fridge and how you were threatened by the police, but you still tried to protect my father. Then against your will they forced you to sign a paper saying that my father was helping a man from Umkhonto. My father wrote that what you had signed was actually true, but that you believed it would be used against my father and that you were very upset about that. When I read this to my mother she cried and cried. She cried because it was my father's last writing, but she cried also because she said she knew then that Mfundisi Richard – I beg your pardon for using your Christian name, but that is how she said it – had spoken the truth to her and that the police had made up the statement they showed to my father. She is deeply sorry and wants to apologise to you.'

'Oh, well, um... there is no need for an apology, but please thank your mother very much,' replies a stunned Richard, letting go of his gown to free his hand to turn a few pages of the book and read snatches of the contents. Having read a few lines he comments, 'By the way, this looks interesting. And he wrote it in English.'

'We would be honoured if you want to read it, and I could leave the book in your safe keeping and I shall come and receive it back from you on a day of your convenience.'

'I think the privilege will be all mine,' replies Richard.

'I thank you, Doctor,' and bowing slightly Moses turns to leave. 'I hope I have not seriously delayed you. So, as we say in our language, *Sala kahle*. I shall come again and find you here.'

Richard is feeling quite overwhelmed.

'Oh, yes…' He struggles for a moment to remember the appropriate response to the farewell but fails to get it. 'Yes, goodbye, and thank you again.'

Richard remains standing there, the late afternoon sun shining on him as he eagerly turns the pages of the book. He then thinks of other things he might have said to Moses and wants to call him back, but looking up he sees the young man is already at the campus gates, certainly out of earshot, and will soon be disappearing down the road. He exclaims aloud:

'Damn! I didn't even ask after the health of his mother or where she is now or what he is doing or the other members of the family.' Muttering to himself he makes his way to the main university block, then down a long corridor to a tiny room with the plaque 'Dr. R. Atwell' on the door. The walls of his office are lined with books and ring-files and his desk is cluttered with papers. The room is so cramped he has to manoeuvre his chair in order to close the door. He hangs his gown on a hook, shoves aside the pile on his desk to make a space for Simon's book and, sitting down, starts reading from the first page. As he reads, it is as though something frozen inside him is beginning to melt. Simon's writing is neat and easy to read, and Richard has learnt to read fast. However, he is still reading when he becomes aware that daylight is fading, and he is beginning to struggle to make out the grey pencil letters on the page. He leans back to reach a switch and the solitary light hanging over the desk comes on. He promises himself he will only read a few more pages before going home. Over an hour later he turns the last page. He reads the final entry that Moses had referred to and comes to the last few sentences.

*'I expect sooner or later the police will come for me. It will surely happen. It certainly is not Richard's fault. He has been a good friend.'* That is where the writing ends and all that is left are several blank pages.

Richard leans back in his chair, with his hands cradling the back of his head. He feels a deep sadness. But he also thinks that he has just received a wonderful compliment from the dead. He wonders if anyone could pay another person a greater compliment than to say of that person, 'he has been a good friend'. Together with the sadness, he also experiences a warm feeling, the feeling he used to get when embraced so spontaneously and in such an unrestrained manner by Simon. Then his eyes alight on the wall clock.

'My God, look at the time!' he exclaims. 'Noelene will be wondering what has happened to me.'

In fact, Noelene is waiting for him, with their dinner keeping warm in the oven. She has got used to his erratic and absent-minded behaviour. However, the moment he walks in the door she knows something has changed. She notices that, relative to his usual amble, he has walked in briskly and there is a sparkle in his eyes as he greets her.

'You will never believe who came to see me today.'

While she is dishing up their food, he tells her how he was stopped by Moses and how he came by the journal.

Normally they eat mostly in silence, but tonight he is animatedly telling her about what he has read in the diary. He finds the entry describing Simon's conversation with him in the bakkie and reads it to Noelene. He then turns the pages to that final entry and invites her to read it.

'Just look at this.' Choking with emotion he adds, 'That is what convinced Florence that I hadn't betrayed Simon.'

Noelene is amazed and pleased both by the discovery of the journal, but especially by the change in Richard. The only enthusiasm she has lately experienced in him is when he is talking about a trip to Greece or Italy and the archaeological sites he wants to visit, all of which she finds rather boring. She went with him on his first trip, but after a few days left him to his own devices and instead spent the time sunning herself on a beach and reading. After that he went without her. Whenever he has been tied up in his academic work, she has involved herself in her own interests and has often thought that their marriage had degenerated into being a marriage only in name. She has wondered about divorce but retains her Christian commitment to marriage and reasons that it would be silly to leave him when she is free to do most of the things she wants. But she misses the companionship of those earlier times in their marriage when they used to share an intellectual, emotional and physical intimacy.

Towards the end of the meal, Richard suddenly becomes quiet and Noelene realises that, like so often in the past fourteen years, he is preoccupied with something and cut off from her. She gets up from the table saying:

'I'll do the dishes and then I'm going to have my bath.' As she moves from the table, she hears him groan and mutter:

'I can't bluff myself. Florence might forgive me, but I did sign a statement that I knew would be used against Simon.'

Noelene stops and standing with a pile of plates and dishes in her hands, responds with exasperation:

'Oh, stop it Richard. She is not just forgiving; she is apologising to you. Yes, you signed it, but you signed it under duress in the most appalling circumstances. You weren't yourself. And in any case, we know that whatever you said, the police would concoct a statement to suit what they wanted.'

'But I signed it to save my own skin.'

'Nonsense!' she shouts, almost dropping the plates, but thankfully only some cutlery slides down and clatters to the floor. 'Damn! You make me so angry I could throw this lot at you. I can't forever keep telling you, you didn't kill Simon. It was the bloody SB and no one else. But if you must carry the burden of a false idea on your shoulders for the rest of your life, then so be it.' With that she stalks out to the kitchen.

# Chapter 30

(April 1983)

Five weeks later Moses is again waiting outside the Campbell lecture theatre. Richard has forgotten he was coming and, being blinkered by his gown, is walking past him when Moses speaks up,

'Good afternoon Doctor Atwell. Please forgive me for stopping you. You will remember I saw you last month – I'm Moses Ndlovu.'

Richard stops and looks around in a distracted manner. 'Oh yes. Yes. Um... Oh yes! You have come for your book.' Peering through the folds of his gown at Moses, Richard remembers Simon and thinks *this young man looks so much like his father*. 'I'm afraid the book is in my office. If you could wait a few minutes, I shall go and fetch it?'

'That is in order, Doctor. Will it be okay if I wait here?'

'Um... yes.' Richard pauses. 'Um, on second thoughts Simon, why not come with me?'

'Forgive me Doctor, my name is Moses. It was my father who was Simon.'

'Yes, um... of course. So do come along – it's this way.' Richard starts leading the way towards the main block, with Moses following a pace behind. After taking a few steps Richard turns to Moses and pauses for him to catch up. 'I think I owe you an apology, because last time when you were here, I didn't ask after your mother and your family. How is your mother and where is she now?' They walk on together as Moses answers.

'My mother is well. I will tell her that you enquired about her health. She is still living in Nongoma with her sisters and brothers. My older brother—'

Richard interrupts him pointing to the right and so loses control of the folds of his gown which falls over his face. He brushes the gown aside saying, 'We go down this corridor. But there is so much I want to know about you and your family. Why don't you come with me now to my home where we may talk and perhaps have a cup of tea and something to eat?'

Moses replies differentially:

'Thank you for asking me and it would be a great privilege for me to come to your home. Unfortunately, I must refuse your very kind invitation, because I have to return to the college this evening.'

'Oh – which college is that?'

'I think you will know it. It is the John Wesley College for Theological Education. You see, I too am studying to be a minister, like my father foretold.'

'I think your father would be pleased to know that.' They have now reached Doctor Atwell's office and, opening the door and shuffling about amongst the books and papers on his desk, Richard locates the book which he hands to Moses. 'I found it remarkably interesting and please thank your mother for allowing me to read it. I'm sorry you can't stay, but won't you come and visit me sometime when we can have time to talk?'

'That is kind of you Doctor. We sometimes have some spare time on a Saturday afternoon if that would be convenient for you?'

'Oh yes, yes, certainly. Here, let me give you my address.' He scrabbles around on the desk for a pen and piece of paper, hastily writes down his home address and hands it to Moses. 'There you are. Do you know that street?'

'Thank you very much. I will surely find it and shall greatly look forward to coming to visit you.' He turns to leave and bowing his head says, '*Sala kahle* Doctor.'

'Thank you. And *hamba kahle* Moses.'

Watching Moses walking down the corridor, Richard again feels that warmth inside himself that he felt in his friendship with Simon.

A few days later Richard is lecturing a first-year class on Aristotle. Towards the end of the lecture he pauses, caught up with a thought that has suddenly occurred to him. Some of the students look up, wondering why he has pulled up in his usual rambling. They see Richard scratching the few hairs on his head. One looks at his watch thinking that perhaps the lecture has ended.

Then, in an unusual departure, Richard, looking directly at the class and speaking with some animation says:

'Aristotle is one of the great philosophers, there is no question about that. But did you know, he believed that slaves lacked personality, unlike free people. Now does this ring any bells with you?'

There is silence. Richard never asks questions in his lectures. He gazes over the class. Many who were not paying attention suddenly sit up. Those taking notes have stopped writing. All look at the lecturer in amazement. The class do not know how to deal with this change that has come out of the blue.

Richard tries again:

'Come on,' he says with emphasis. 'Aristotle regarded slaves as being not fully human. You surely recognise some parallels in the twentieth century?'

By now the whole class is fully involved. One of them puts up a hand.

'Perhaps that is the way some white people regard blacks.'

Richard smiles.

'Yes, and I am sure you didn't intend it, but you spoke of white people whilst referring to black people as simply blacks. You see, there is an insidious tendency to depersonalize those who are different from us. There are many examples of this all over the world. It is something even this great philosopher did not recognise as far as slaves were concerned. He had been conditioned by the culture and tradition under which he lived to regard them as mere chattels and not fully human. So, you see, you must always bring a critical eye to bear on all so-called authoritative statements, be they from great philosophers or from the political authorities of the land. Perhaps you might like to do a little philosophizing yourselves and bring some examples of what we have been talking about to the next class. Thank you.' With that parting shot Richard walks from the room.

The astounded class remain in their places for a few moments. Then some make a note of the homework request while others are gathering up their books. One of them remarks:

'Well, I never! What's come over old Batty?'

Another grins:

'Perhaps he finally realises that this is the twentieth century. We may now start to learn something of use.'

Walking across the campus back to his office, Richard suddenly realises that he has forgotten to shield his head. He grabs the hem of his gown to hoist it up, but then stops. He feels the sun on his face and finds it to be rather pleasant. Shading his eyes, he squints in the direction of the sun. '*Sunny South Africa*,' he says to himself, and strides on with his head held high and his gown floating behind him.

# Chapter 31

(June 1983)

It is a miserable Saturday afternoon; a cold south-westerly wind is sending sprays of drizzle slashing across the window of Richard's study where he is not in the best of moods. He has been asked to write an article for *Acta Classica*. On the pad in front of him he has jotted down a few notes, but nothing seems to be gelling. He hears a knock on the back door and as Noelene is out at a church meeting, he knows he is going to have to answer it.

'Whoever can that be in this weather?' he mutters irritably as he gets up from his desk.

Opening the door, he is confronted by a young black man wrapped in a yellow plastic mac.

'Good afternoon, Doctor. You kindly said I might visit you at your home and I was wondering if this afternoon is convenient for you.'

The moment the young man starts speaking, Richard recognises Moses.

'Oh, yes; oh, do come in.' He ushers Moses into the kitchen. Memories come flooding back of how Simon would always come to the back door and, as Moses removes the cape shielding his head, Richard is again struck by how much he looks like his father.

'Thank you very much, Doctor.'

Richard responds:

'I always used to tell your father there was no need for him to come to the back door and I would be pleased if in future you knocked at the front door. But never mind that now. Do come through to the lounge.'

'Thank you, Doctor, but I am very wet – so if you don't mind, perhaps we can talk here for a little while.'

Richard notices that Moses has already shed some drops of water on the kitchen lino.

'No, no. If you take off your mac, I'll put it in the bathroom to dry and then we can go through to the lounge.'

Once seated, Richard has completely forgotten about the article he was struggling over and is asking about Florence and Amos. After that there is a long silence. Richard realises that Moses, unlike Simon, is very deferential, so he tries to draw him out:

'Please, tell me about your college and which theologians you are studying?'

This seems right down Moses' street and it soon becomes evident to Richard that his visitor is a keen theological student with academic ability.

'Oh, our hero at college is of course Dietrich Bonhoeffer, but we have been studying the work of James Cone and we also read Desmond Tutu's books. And of course, we do a lot of Bible study. You see we are working all the time to see what God is asking us to do in the places where we live. As you must know there is a lot of trouble with our people. The students also are arguing all the time. Some say they are for Buthelezi[19] and *Inkhata*, others are ANC. I try not to get into just one side.'

'Yes, I am vaguely aware that black people in this district have become quite polarised and that Buthelezi is regarded as a stooge of the white government.'

'Forgive me, Doctor, if I disagree. I am not for Buthelezi, but I can tell you, he is not a stooge.'

Richard is surprised at the vehemence and confidence with which Moses expresses a contrary point of view. He realises that whilst Moses appears to be in awe of the fact that Richard holds a doctorate and is a university lecturer, he will take issue with him. For the next hour their animated conversation goes to and fro and Richard finds that he is learning a great deal about the lives of young black people and their attitudes. He again recalls how, when he first met

---

[19] Buthelezi: A Zulu chief who founded the Inkathta Freedom Party opposed to the ANC and regarded by some black people as being used by the apartheid regime.

Simon, it was as though a whole new world was being opened to him, and now it was happening again. He feels exhilarated by their discussion and feels free to press Moses on what he meant by implying that he keeps out of the conflict.

'I'm sorry, Doctor. I didn't mean to give the impression—'

Richard gently interrupts:

'There is no need to keep addressing me as Doctor. I'll be really pleased if you call me Richard.'

'Thank you very much. If it is your wish, I shall address you as Richard. But I'm sure you understand that in our culture we are taught to show respect to those who are older and who have achieved positions of authority.'

'Yes, of course. But before I interrupted, you were saying...'

'Oh yes, I don't want to give you the idea that I keep away from trouble. Well, I do keep away from the wrong sort of trouble, drinking and smoking dagga and those sorts of things. What I mean is that I think it is my duty at this time to try to understand what is happening in our world and what God is calling us to do. I think it is too easy to jump into a camp and say, I am with Buthelezi or, I'm with ANC. In that way I think we can close our ears to the voice of God. So, I avoid their marches and demonstrations. Instead, what I am doing is quietly helping the families of those in jail or who have been killed. We collect clothes for the children and the college gets money that we take to their mothers for food. We do not ask if they are *Inkhata* or ANC. If there are people in trouble, we try to help them.'

'Wow, that sounds to me like you are deeply involved. Where then does the money come from?' Moses does not respond and looks at the floor. As a result, Richard assumes the funds are probably illegal and come from abroad via underground routes. So, he comments, 'It must be difficult for you to get money because the government has stopped money coming from overseas churches and organisations.'

Moses looks up and says:

'It is difficult, but God is good to us.' He adds, 'I think it has now stopped raining so I must return to the college.'

Richard has been so involved in their conversation he has forgotten to offer Moses any refreshment. He quickly rectifies his omission and after a quick cup of tea Moses takes his leave, with an invitation to come again whenever he is free.

# Chapter 32

(July 1983)

Moses takes up Richard's invitation and approximately each month on a Saturday afternoon he calls at the Atwells' home. Richard enjoys their discussions immensely, so much so that he has been acquiring and reading the new theological works that Moses refers to. He is particularly fascinated by the links Moses makes between theological theory and the events happening in black communities. Noelene has also enjoyed meeting Moses again and whilst she leaves the two men to talk, she has noticed the change in Richard and that Moses is like a tonic for him, infusing him with a liveliness she hasn't seen for a long time.

Then one Tuesday evening there is a surprise visit from Moses just three days after one of his Saturday visits.

Richard and Noelene are about to sit down to dinner and invite Moses to join them but, rather breathlessly, he says he can only stop for a few minutes. He explains:

'I am sorry I cannot accept your kind offer because I am writing an examination tomorrow, and I still need to go over some of my revision. I hope I am not delaying your dinner, but I have an urgent favour to ask of you. You told me last Saturday that in a couple of weeks' time you are going to Joburg for a conference and that you would not be here on that Saturday if I came to visit. I have told you before about the money we give to mothers whose husbands are detained. I did not tell you that the money comes from overseas and must be brought into the country secretly, usually through Botswana. Now a man will be bringing some money to Joburg, but because he is wanted by the South African police he will come with false papers and will go back to Botswana straight away. So, we are looking for somebody to bring the money from Joburg. This is a hard thing for me to ask you to do, so if you don't want to do it, I shall understand.'

Richard immediately feels he is back in that bakkie and is being involved in something dangerous. He hesitates; on the one hand he thinks he must decline, but on the other he would so much like to help Moses.

Noelene notices his hesitation and intervenes, saying to Richard:

'If you like I'll come with you so you won't be doing it all on your own, and while you are at the conference, I can do some shopping and meet up with my friend Rita in Hillbrow.'

Whether it is Noelene's support or something else, Richard doesn't know, but he suddenly realises he must do this thing.

'Ja, we'll do it,' and he takes Moses' hand in a firm handshake.

'That is truly kind of you. A lot of people will be helped by this money and surely God will bless you for it. I shall come again and tell you where you will pick up the money. It is all very secret, and I can tell you we are very careful so that the police don't find out.'

Once Moses has left, Richard and Noelene discuss the request. Richard is beginning to have second thoughts.

'Well, I agreed to that rather impulsively. Do you think it is going to be okay; we are really being rather rash?'

'Oh, come on,' says Noelene. 'Let's do something rash. In any case it is not all that rash. From what Moses has told us he keeps a low profile, and it's now a long time since you were under surveillance. Above all, this is something that is surely absolutely right and our Christian duty, so a slight risk is worth it. After all, the money is not going to buy weapons but to feed starving children and to help destitute families.'

'Yes, you are right. You know when he asked us, the image of the Good Samaritan came into my mind; and I thought if I said no, it would be like walking past on the other side.'

One evening a few days before Richard and Noelene are due to leave for Johannesburg, Moses calls again with their instructions.

'If you don't mind,' he explains, 'when you leave Joburg to come home, would you please take the Standerton road at Heidelberg. A little way down that road you will see people selling things at the side of the road. One of them will be selling pots. That is where you must go. There you must ask for Mrs Njenga. Here, I have written her name on this paper. You must tell Mrs Njenga that you were sent by Moses and then she will know you are the right person and will give the money to you.'

'Oh, this does sound exciting,' says Noelene. To lighten the seriousness of what they are doing she adds in a joking way, 'Shouldn't we have a password and perhaps Richard can wear a buttonhole and I my red hat by which Mrs Njenga will recognise us?'

However, Moses does not see it as a joke.

'No,' he answers emphatically. 'We have to be simple, not complicated.'

Richard asks nervously, 'Will the money be in a bag and do we have to count it to make sure it is all there?'

'I don't know what the money will be in, but it will all be there. We can trust these people one hundred per cent. That evening when you get home, I will be here at your house to receive the money.'

Ten days later Richard and Noelene are driving along Route 23 towards Standerton. Collecting the money has been very much on Richard's mind the whole time he has been at the conference. As a result, he has found it difficult to follow the various speakers and reports. Noelene, on the other hand, has enjoyed herself with her friend Rita and regards their tryst with Mrs Njenga as an adventure.

As they drive along, they are both watching out for the roadside stalls. After a few miles Richard says:

'Surely we should have come to them by now. Moses said it was only a short distance along this road and we have already covered several miles.'

'Yes, I was wondering about that, though the signposts show that we are on the right road. Oh, wait, isn't that it there?'

Richard slows down as the hessian shelters that house the various stalls at the side of the road come into view. He parks the car at the first stall which is selling beautiful highly-polished wooden giraffes, elephants and numerous other carvings. Several other cars are parked along the verge and groups of people, mostly tourists, are admiring the wares and some are making purchases. Richard and Noelene wander down the line of stalls past people selling jewellery, beadwork, embroidery, grass-woven mats and baskets and finally at the end of the line they arrive at a stall selling clay pots of all shapes and sizes and decorated in bright colours.

'Well, this must be it,' says Richard, glancing around to see if anyone is watching them. However, everyone seems to be interested in the various wares. Going up to a woman sitting on the grass next to the pots he asks rather tentatively:

'Is Mrs Njenga here?'

The lady jumps up shouting excitedly, '*Hau! Sawubona udokotela.*'

Involuntarily Richard hisses, 'Shoo, shoo, quiet,' but his protestations make no difference.

In a voice that is still too loud for Richard's liking, she nods her head affirmatively and pointing at her chest exclaims. 'I, Mrs Njenga,' and laughing she claps her hands with pleasure.

Noelene is standing by with a big smile, finding it all rather amusing.

Following his instructions Richard quickly says:

'Moses sent us here...'

'*Yebo, yebo,*' and with that she scuttles around to the back of the stall. In a moment she returns holding a large red pot with a narrow neck like a calabash. 'Reserved, *udokotela*,' she says, handing it to Richard.

He takes the jar, frowning, asking himself, *Is this the money*? He whispers to Noelene, 'I didn't expect it to be in a pot.' He notices the jar is sealed with a wooden stopper.

Just then some other customers approach.

In her loud voice Mrs Njenga holds out her hand and says to Richard, 'Fifteen rand.'

He is now even more surprised as he did not expect to have to pay to collect the money.

Noelene, however, reaches into her handbag and produces the required money. She hands it to Mrs Njenga who puts the notes in a tin box, fiddles around a bit and then hands Noelene all her money back saying emphatically:

'Change.' With that she turns to attend to her other customers.

Feeling a bit nonplussed at the simplicity of the handover and the way Mrs Njenga covered it up by pretending it was a normal purchase, Richard and Noelene stand there not sure what to do. Richard is carefully holding the jar as though it is worth millions which he thinks perhaps it is.

Noelene looks at a couple of other pots and then suggests, 'Well, I think we can go now.'

As they turn to wander back to their car Mrs Njenga calls after them:

'*Hamba kahle*,' and they wave back to her.

When they get to the car Richard suggests hiding the pot in the cavity where the spare wheel normally goes and to carry the spare wheel with their cases in the boot. Noelene, however, argues that in the unlikely event they are stopped by police, they are sure to look there, and a hidden pot will look suspicious, so it would be better if just left openly on the back seat.

'Remember,' she says, 'Moses wanted us to keep it simple.'

'But when we stop for lunch, I don't think it will be a good idea to just leave it in the car and it will be difficult taking it with us into a cafeteria.'

'Well, I'll stay in the car while you buy sandwiches for us which we can take to eat at a picnic site.'

When they do stop for their picnic Richard recognises the site as the same one where he stopped many years before with Simon and remembers his remarks about 'Whites Only' signs sprouting from the trees like apples. For Richard, this whole experience feels as though it is gradually undoing the hurt and guilt he suffered through Simon's murder and the trauma of being labelled a traitor and informer.

Later in the day they reach home without incident and Moses is there to meet them. Once inside the house they triumphantly hand the jar over to Moses.

Richard says, 'This is what Mrs Njenga gave us. We haven't opened it, so I trust the money is all inside.'

'Well let us have a look,' and Moses prises out the wooden bung.

Richard and Noelene peer in and are dismayed to see mealies in the jar.

Moses exclaims:

'Oh, Mrs Njenga is very clever. Noelene, have you got a bowl?' Once he has the bowl, he tips the jar over it and a scattering of corn pours out. Moses says, 'If you have any fowls you can feed this to them.' He then shows Noelene and Richard that underneath the layer of mealies are rolls of bank notes. He shakes one roll out.

Richard whistles in surprise as he realises the jar must contain many thousands of rands.

Moses remarks, 'The churches overseas are very generous to us. And you have also been courageous, and I must thank you for doing this brave thing. Many people are going to be grateful and I know God will bless you.'

Noelene replies, 'Oh, I think He has blessed us already through knowing you.'

Richard reaches over to hug Moses, with a profound feeling of gratitude that the burden he has carried for so long now feels that little bit lighter.

# Chapter 33

(Early October 1996)

Richard is strolling home from work. The jacarandas are in full bloom and where the blossoms have fallen on the pavement, they form a mauve carpet for him to walk on. It is not a long walk, but he is enjoying the warm sunshine and the perfume of the blossoms. He is feeling rather pleased with himself, having posted to the external examiner the completed examination papers he had to set. He remembers from his own student days the saying, that if you were not well prepared by jacaranda time, you would be in trouble in your exams. Enjoying the beauty of the jacarandas he also passes a bougainvillea hedge with its deep red flowers and reflects that this is in truth a rainbow country with a rainbow nation of people of many colours. He recalls how their friends Moses and his wife Leko came to watch the freeing of Nelson Mandela on the Atwells' television, and how they had cheered and celebrated that momentous event. This had been a turnaround in South African politics few could have foreseen. Three years later when the first free elections took place, Richard and Moses had had tremendous fun driving around in Richard's battered old Renault, ferrying ANC supporters to the polls to vote for the first time in their lives.

The result of the election had been that Nelson Mandela became the first black president of South Africa. Legal segregation was a thing of the past. People of all races could mix without fear. Black people could throw off the shackles that had held them in servitude under Apartheid. Schools were beginning to be integrated; a growing black middle class were taking up professional appointments and making their way in leadership positions.

As Richard strolls along he reflects that despite the speed at which some changes had happened, progress in the living standards of most black people had been painfully slow. The first flush of those heady days had now worn thin and there was still much to be done in sharing the wealth of the country. Apartheid had left a terrible legacy. He was only too aware of the growing tensions. Each time he visited Moses in the vast black shanty town where he was ministering, he was made aware that unemployment was high and poverty widespread and grim. The Truth and Reconciliation Commission set up under Bishop Tutu was trying to deal with the bitterness of the past, to lay a foundation for the country to move forward. This was a testing time. It leads Richard to recall the test he had faced the previous Sunday.

Ever since Moses received the call to the Methodist Church in the KwaThemba Township, he had been nagging Richard to come and preach at a Sunday service. Richard had resisted thinking it would be arrogant of him, a white man who lived in privileged circumstances, to preach to people living largely in poverty. Secondly, his Zulu is so basic that he would have had to preach in English with a translator, and in any case, he had not preached a sermon for some years. Moses had brushed all these excuses aside, insisting that God's Word was the same to the poor as to the rich and that most of his congregation understood English. Moses had continued cajoling him until he finally agreed, and the event had taken place the previous Sunday. Richard recalls how he spent hours writing and rewriting the sermon. He really wanted to get it right.

On the day he was terribly nervous, and, in any case, he and Noelene always felt apprehensive when visiting the township. Although Apartheid had been dismantled, this was a place few white people entered because of the constant news reports of murders and unrest. Moses was forever assuring them that reports of crime in the township were exaggerated, and that they would be okay. In fact, it had all gone remarkably well. They had received a tremendous welcome. Driving into the dusty yard of the church they had noticed that Moses was hastily assembling a group in the form of a guard of honour. These were the elders and deacons, all dressed in smart suits. Behind them were women in frocks of bright gay colours. Starting to move through the line Richard had extended a hand in greeting, but that was not enough. They were embraced by each person in turn.

Walking home now, Richard smiles to himself as he remembers how a very large elder had hugged him so tightly, that the frame of his reading glasses, which he carried in his breast pocket, had been bent and one of the lenses had popped out, rendering them useless. It had added to his anxiety because he had difficulty reading his sermon notes. However, the sermon was well received, and although unused to verbal reaction from the congregation, he soon warmed to the loud *Amens* and *Alleluias* that punctuated what he was saying. The only criticism he received was from an old grey-haired man who complained that the sermon was too short. For the rest of the service, he and Noelene soon got into the spirit of the enthusiastic worship with glorious singing accompanied by drums, clapping and worshippers swaying from side to side.

After the service they had been escorted to the community centre, where a lunch of chicken and rice awaited them. That was followed by more singing and dancing and then speeches thanking Richard and Noelene for their visit.

He is enjoying these delightful memories as he walks into his home. Entering the dining room, he sees a letter on the table in the familiar copperplate handwriting of Moses. His first thought is that it is a letter of thanks for their visit. He quickly tears open the envelope and is taken aback in reading that Moses and his family have been invited to a Truth and Reconciliation Hearing related to the death of Simon. In the letter, Moses asks Richard if it would be possible for him to be present as well. He writes that an ex-Sergeant Wilkinson, who was involved in the death of Simon, has made an application for amnesty. The words of the letter blur and Richard feels as though the blood has drained from his head. He grabs the back of a chair and, turning it, sits down heavily. At that moment Noelene comes into the room.

'What sort of day...?' Then, she sees the expression on Richard's face. 'Hey, what's the matter?'

He holds up the letter.

'You must read this. It is from Moses. That bastard Wilkinson killed Simon. He is now seeking amnesty through the TRC.'

Noelene reads the letter. She pulls up a chair, sits down next to Richard and takes his hand.

'Wilkinson was the man who interrogated you, wasn't he?'

'Yes, the swine.'

'Do you think it is the same man?'

'It must be.'

'Well, from what I've read of the TRC, they won't let him get away with anything. He will have to tell the truth and show real remorse and repentance if he is going to get amnesty.'

'You know, I have often imagined that he was the man who killed Simon. He was the sort of man who could do it. I suppose I got off lightly because I'm white.'

'So, are you going to go?'

'Well yes. I really want to. I think I owe it to Simon.' After a moment he hastily adds, 'and of course Florence and Moses as well. Yes, I'll have to be there...' He pauses for a moment. 'I'm just worried how I might react, seeing Wilkinson again. Moses and his family will be the ones who need support, and I don't want to break down or distract in any way from them.'

Noelene squeezes his hand.

'I guess it will be traumatic...' She pauses in thought, and then continues, 'But, you know, this time Wilkinson will be the man under questioning. He won't be in charge. He will be in the dock, not you. You will have to think of it like that. And as Bishop Tutu has said of the commission, it is also an opportunity for forgiveness and closure.'

'Good God, I don't know how I can forgive him.'

'Well, isn't it going to be even more difficult for Florence and her family? However hard, I think you will have to try to put your own feelings aside and, as you say, think of them.'

'Ja, you are right. I just don't know if I can do it.'

'Well, you're an older and stronger person now, you know. I think you will cope, and you may be surprised. Perhaps it will do you some good as well.'

# Chapter 34

(November 1996)

Three weeks later Richard is driving along the northern Natal coast towards Nongoma. Next to him in the car is Moses, with Florence and Amos in the back. It has been the day of the Truth and Reconciliation Commission's hearing. It is a day they will never forget. It has been a day of much crying. But now in the car there is silence. All four are bound up in their own thoughts.

In front, the road lies in a straight line until in the distance it disappears over a hill on the horizon. They are passing through sugar-cane fields and occasionally, on the right, there is a glimpse of the blue Indian Ocean. Shadows are lengthening as the sun nears its setting.

Richard feels drained of emotion, but images of the day keep flitting through his mind. The church hall, where the hearing had taken place, had been crowded and stiflingly hot. Now, at least, whilst it is still warm, the breeze through the car feels refreshing. There had not been many white people present at the hearing and so when he entered the hall, he remembers noticing a skinny bent-over grey-haired white man with a dirty-looking moustache drooping down on either side of his mouth, standing awkwardly near the front. Richard had thought the man was some sort of usher or the caretaker of the building. Two black police officers were standing near the man. Richard recalls his shocked surprise when the hearing commenced, and this decrepit looking man shuffled forward and identified himself as ex-Sergeant Theophilus Wilkinson. He spoke in a croaking voice as he described how he had believed that Simon was harbouring and encouraging Umkhonto fighters by having weapons secreted in the Manse or in the church. The operation, he had been told, was financed by a co-operative, run by the minister. All around Richard there were gasps and cries when Wilkinson described how he had tortured Simon in an attempt to get him to reveal the names of the Umkhonto operatives. Richard recalls being overwhelmed by all his old feelings of guilt, and for some minutes he did not take in what was being said, until he suddenly became aware that Wilkinson had mentioned his name. He was saying:

'We had thought we could get this Reverend on our side, because he was white, but when he wouldn't co-operate, we faked his evidence. We regarded Reverend Ndlovu as an extremely dangerous man and we had to stop him by any means.'

Even now, remembering those words, Richard feels anger welling up inside him, but as Wilkinson went on to express his remorse for what he had done, he also remembered how his feelings gradually changed. Wilkinson had said he wished he had never done these things and felt deeply ashamed over the pain and the deaths he had caused. He said things had changed. His grandchildren were now in a school with black children and he had seen them playing happily together. They were being taught by a black teacher. He had never believed that could happen. Now he could see how wrong he had been. He hoped to be granted amnesty, but even if it was denied, he had to confess to what he had done. He could not sleep at night without heavy medication, because every night when he tried to close his eyes, his mind would go back to the terrible things he had done. He could still clearly remember the faces of his victims and hear their cries as if it were only yesterday. Amongst them all, Simon stood out. He remembers him calling out Jesus' words; 'Father forgive them, for they know not what they do.' He said he never believed that someone could be as iron-willed as Simon. Only once did Richard see a glimpse of the Wilkinson he had experienced. That was when he told the hearing he was angry, because the men who had given him orders had not owned up to what they had done. But, he added, in no way did that excuse what he had done. Hearing this, Richard recalled reading in the paper that Major

Beukes had claimed he had never given any orders for anyone to be tortured, that he strongly disapproved of torture and that had he known subordinate officers under his command were indulging in this behaviour, he would have stopped it immediately. Subsequently charges against Beukes had been dropped on a legal technicality.

Richard remembers the touching scene after the hearing when Florence, on Moses' arm, went up to Wilkinson and with tears streaming down her face she took his hand and said:

'I can't hold this against you, because if I do, I can't go on. I wish you had never done these things, and I pray that God will have mercy on you.' With that she turned and was embraced in turn by Moses, Amos, and Richard, before others also came forward to embrace her. While that was happening, Richard recalls looking straight at Wilkinson whose sunken eyes looked blank and empty in his drawn face. Richard thought that it was like looking at the face of a corpse.

Driving along, the sun dips down behind them. Richard turns on the car headlights, and as he does so Moses begins reciting aloud the words of the *Nunc Dimitus* or Song of Simeon, which he now makes into the Song of Simon. He says the words slowly but with feeling.

'Lord, now lettest thou thy servant... Simon, our dear father, depart in peace, according to thy word: For our eyes have today, yes today, seen thy salvation, which thou hast prepared before the face of all people, yes Lord, all thy people. A light to lighten the Gentiles and the glory of thy people in this our beloved land. Amen.' Then as an afterthought he adds, '*Hamba kahle uBaba Simon, hamba kahle iAfrika.*'

There are some moments of silence, and then quietly Florence starts to sing:

'*Nkosi sikel' iAfrica*[20],' and it is picked up immediately by Moses and Amos and then by Richard as well. Although starting rather solemnly, their emotions take over and soon they are singing with gusto at the tops of their voices as the car speeds on along the highway, with strains of the anthem wafting out of the car windows into the beautiful South African countryside.

---

[20] Nkosi sikel' iAfrica: Zulu – God bless Africa. This anthem is now part of the official South African national anthem. Under apartheid it was sung as a freedom song.

# Acknowledgements

I wish to express my thanks to all those who have supported me as this novel has taken shape. I am especially indebted to Lord Peter Hain who read the manuscript offered helpful suggestions and wrote a cover endorsement. The Very Rev. Peter Judd also read the manuscript and he too offered a cover endorsement. Archbishop Walter Makhulu, Dr David Frampton and my nephew Warren Brown were all helpful with detail. Elaine Henderson, John Dean and Dr Nick Smith read the early draft, offered useful critique and with their encouragement I completed the work although none of the above should be blamed for anything I got wrong. The cover was devised by Nicholas Roberts who showed endless patience as we worked through the numerous drafts. My son Jonathan, with his media expertise has been helpful as I agonised over the title and has been a valuable consultant throughout. Finally my late wife, Frances, an avid reader, who commented that my writing was "quite good" and coming from her, that was praise indeed. To her memory I dedicate this book.

# The Author

Vernon Muller was born and grew up in apartheid South Africa where he worked as an Anglican priest. In 1976 he emigrated to England working as a hospital chaplain and psychotherapeutic counsellor. In retirement he wrote his first novel Mixed Blessing (2010). He has also written a number of short stories mostly about apartheid, children's stories and poetry.

Lightning Source UK Ltd.
Milton Keynes UK
UKHW010148121121
393819UK00002B/15